Hunters in the Dark

BY THE SAME AUTHOR

Ania Malina
Paris Dreambook
The Poisoned Embrace
American Normal
The Accidental Connoisseur
The Naked Tourist
Bangkok Days
The Wet and the Dry
The Forgiven
The Ballad of a Small Player

Hunters
in the Dark

LAWRENCE OSBORNE

VINTAGE

1 3 5 7 9 10 8 6 4 2

Vintage
20 Vauxhall Bridge Road,
London SW1V 2SA

Vintage is part of the Penguin Random House group of companies whose addresses
can be found at global.penguinrandomhouse.com.

First published in Vintage in 2016
First published in hardback by Hogarth in 2015

www.vintage-books.co.uk

A CIP catalogue record for this book is available from the British Library

ISBN 9781784700362

Typeset in Walbaum MT by Palimpsest Book Production Limited,
Falkirk, Stirlingshire

Printed and bound by Clays Ltd, St Ives plc

Penguin Random House is committed to a sustainable future for our business,
our readers and our planet. This book is made from Forest Stewardship Council®
certified paper.

To show you mercy is no gain, to destroy you is no loss.
— The Angkar

Karma

One

He came over the border as the lights were about to be dimmed, with the last of the migrants trailing their stringed boxes. With them came gamblers from the air-conditioned buses, returning short-time exiles tumbling out of minivans with microwaves and DVD units. The border forced them all into a defile in the rain. The gamblers complained about their summary treatment while opening plastic umbrellas provided by the tour company. It seemed a shame to them that the casinos on the other side could not manage it better. Their Bangkok shoes began to suffer in the coffee-coloured mud. Between the two posts the ground was already filled with pools and the dogs waited for the money. The hustlers and drivers were there, silently smoking and watching their prey. The officer ripped away his departure card in the Thai hut and his passport came back to him and he set off for the further side lit up by the arc lamps.

The drivers began to wave, to raise their arms and shout, but he could not hear what the words were. Carrying a single bag, he was quick on his feet. He had the aura of poverty about him, but still, he was white and therefore – in their eyes – affluent. He went under the dry eaves of the opposing nation and gave his passport anew to the men behind a shabby window. There were four windows and the men behind did not look very forgiving. They bore considerable weight in their eyes. In the bare concrete rooms, tables were set up with Thermos flasks and darkened TV sets. The new king high on the walls in his wise white uniform.

'Tourist,' he said, and they charged him a surplus two dollars for not having a photograph for the visa. He counted out his baht and pushed the filthy money across the table and they stuck a full-page green visa into a page of his passport and tossed it dismissively back at him. He had a month to roam their green and pleasant kingdom and he spent the first minute looking across at the neon lights of the casinos, the dusk and the men waving at him.

The pools opening up under the lamps had grown green as well and he walked gingerly around them with his shoulder bag and his straw hat growing soggy as the rain enveloped him.

'Sir, taxi,' the men were crying, already each one setting off towards a large run-down Japanese car. Forced to pick one at random, he chose a man with a Toyota and an umbrella and it was seven dollars into Pailin. Above them shone the red and blue lights of the Diamond Crown casino. But he was tired and not yet in the mood for a fling on the tables. He resolved to return the following night.

He sat in the back seat and drank from the bottle of iced tea he had bought at the border stalls. The verges were filmed red with sticky and wettened dust and in the dark were rolling green hills dotted with primeval-looking, isolate trees. Fields of mung and shaggy sugar cane. It was windy, the sky jagged with storm clouds and a peeping-Tom moon. The site of a disaster, or of a disaster about to happen. The earth dark with iron and cloying and musty to the nose. He was down to a hundred dollars so he asked the driver to take him to a cheap place for the night, he didn't care where. Turning his head for a moment, the driver told him there were only two or three choices in the town anyway and none of them were the Hilton. A half-hour later they were passing the traffic circles of the town, a few roadside bars with red Angkor beer signs. A small park with twelve golden horses prancing in a grit-filled wind.

The man took him to a place called the Hang Meas. It was on the main road to the border which was lined by one-storey shops. Pailin, to his eye, was clearly a place with three streets and little more. A town built on illegal gemstones and the undeparted Khmer Rouge. A dead and absurd sign on the hotel's facade read, as if contradicting its current lamentable state, *Le Manoir de Pailin*. The establishment's pink walls and the karaoke club on the ground floor gave a further dying look to it − he could tell that it was about to close. There were life-sized sculptures of deer on the roof gazing out to the Cardamom Mountains and white glass ball lamps on the balcony. A huge model cockerel stood in the car park and next to it a spirit house filled with kneeling figures with painted white hair and beards. The ancestors of that wind-swept place, secretly connected to the fields and the mountains which could be seen even in the night. The car left him by them and he waded into a decrepit lobby with his wet hat and his chills and the girls looked up with a subtle contempt.

He sat in a leather chair by some fish tanks while they photocopied his passport and stamped the forms, and he saw the entertainment hall next door to the lobby with a multitude of red pillars wrapped with ribbons and covered with mirrors. In there the karaoke was going on, Viet or Chinese businessmen singing badly. The girls were in clasped silk skirts playing them for a song. It was a Bee Gees number, 'How Deep Is Your Love'.

A girl ambled over and invited him to come with her to the room on the third floor. They went up the stairs and their scents came into awkward contact.

'Holiday?' she said, as if it was the sole English word she had.

'Business,' he said.

It was the word that usually ended all conversations.

'We closed next week,' she said sadly.

They came into the room and the same smell pervaded it. It's OK, he said, as if there was a choice in the matter. She showed him the workings of a few switches and left him alone. He turned on the A/C, stripped off and took a tepid bath with the lights on. One had to fear such a wonderland of roaches. He smoked his last three Thai cigarettes and considered if he had the gall or the energy to go out straight away and find a casino. There would be little else to do here anyway. The other foreigners who crossed the border – nearly all Thai – either went straight back into Thailand or carried on towards the capital a mere five hours away. They would have to think of a reason to stay in Pailin. He would have to think of a reason other than not having more than a hundred dollars. But it was a reason at least. He opened his bag and pulled out a cheap dress shirt and pressed it out with the iron in the cupboard. He could make himself half presentable after a shave and an oiling of the hair.

At nine thirty he went down to the lobby and asked them to call a taxi to the gates to drive him to one of the casinos back at Phum Psar Prum. He strolled out in his awkward shirt, his pockets filled with US dollars, and the car was summoned by the boys outside in their 'security' uniforms. He said 'casinos' to the car that pulled up, and when he added that he didn't know which one, there was a confusing consultation. In the end he was driven to the towering place he had seen an hour or two earlier, the Diamond Crown. It was a pointless forty minutes driving there and back again, but he didn't mind. Anything was better than karaoke or an empty room.

The Diamond loomed over the village around it. There was a forecourt garden of towering palms, and a blaze of neon across the facade in Latin and Khmer lettering. Outlines of playing cards and golden women. A KTV to the right, and a hotel of the same name. Inside, red carpets, sky-blue vaults with painted clouds. There were Chinese shrines; a tacky, run-down feel. The tables were green felt. The Khmer girls in their equivalent green waistcoats watched him slowly with a dim interest. In one corner two staff workers struggled with a large rolled carpet. It was a hot crowd, mostly Thais playing simple poker and baccarat and roulette. They looked like officer workers on a lost weekend. He walked around sizing it up and wondering if he had luck on his side that night, or ever for that matter. Finally he sat at a drunken table and played roulette for five-dollar bets against a ring of Thai middle managers downing the Sang Som and Yaa Dong and far gone in their daze. There was no time to calculate or think and later he thought to himself that was how he had won. It's how an outsider always wins. He pulled in two hundred, packed up and went outside to buy some Alain Delons. At the far end of the forecourt was an outdoor restaurant filled with half-dead gamblers and he sat there and smoked and saw that the moon had appeared again out of the fast-moving black storm clouds.

Fireflies now shone in groomed-looking frangipani trees nearby and he felt his skin moisten and harden at the same time. He had spent nearly all his cash and was due to go back to the homeland, but he had stuck his neck out for a few days across the border and suddenly it seemed to have paid off. It sometimes came up like that, a flash of good luck out of nowhere and the night – and the nights after – looked a little different. A little more and he'd be able to pay the fee to change the ticket home and linger on. You want to linger on sometimes, when there is nothing better awaiting. A teacher from England did not have any worlds at his feet. He did not have anything at his feet but doormats and cigarette butts and the plucked fins of cooked fish.

The Alain Delons were harsh but the face of the French actor was everywhere on the billboards. He smiled down above the streets on scaffolds, his face from around 1960 more youthful than the twenty-eight-year-old Englishman's. So time passed but not for Delon, not for the immortals.

He lit a second cigarette and smoked it down just as coolly and slowly. The waiters didn't even bother to give him a menu. There were no barangs here and he didn't fit the scheme. Yet he liked this new country a little better than the previous one. It had a different feel to it, a slower spin.

As a teacher he profited from a long summer holiday.

Two months were enough to slip away entirely from one's life, however complicated that life might be. But as it happened his life was not complicated at all. He lived alone at the edges of a town called Burgess Hill close to the Sussex Downs, in a damp cottage with a wooden lintel and horseshoes decorating the walls. He had not even redecorated it to his taste. He had done very little to personalise anything in his surroundings. He did not, in the end, raise much objection to his own passivity. It suited him.

Did it make him dull? He didn't mind. The dullness was only an impression made upon outsiders to whom he was, in turn, completely indifferent. He had gone through three years at the University of Sussex as inconspicuously as he could. Reading English and dallying with a few girlfriends. There had not been much more to it than that. A dream that passed quickly. He had chosen the university because it was close to his family, to his parents, and even to his grandparents who lived in a council house in Bevendean on the road from Brighton to Falmer. They were a family whose members never strayed far from each other. The elements of life remained stable. He could take a bus to the Bevendean estate every weekend and walk to his grandmother's gooseberry bushes. They made him trifle and he went for walks in the hills above the estate.

Outwardly, he remained stable as well. Even his haircut remained the same for years. Long at the back, with a parting to the right. At weekends, after visiting his family, he went to the rowdier pubs in Lewes and sat at the bars and talked to strangers. Then he left on his own and rode his motorbike back to his cottage. This invariable pattern was never broken by anything surprising. Naturally, he

9

reasoned, this was because he wanted it to be so. His unconscious wanted it, and therefore he wanted it. It was like a period of waiting, or a period of sleep from which he would suddenly wake up armed with a sword.

But every year there came the summer holidays and with his free two months he tried to engineer a few surprises. One year he went to the island of Hydra in Greece. Another summer saw him in Iceland. He went alone and came back alone, and he was mostly alone when he was there. Even in Hydra he was alone, walking the dust paths that ran around the island. Swimming alone, eating alone. Most importantly, sleeping alone. He couldn't say why he was alone; he was pretty in his way. But then again he was a dreamer and a loner. It was the way he was.

Iceland and Greece: the northern extreme of Europe and the southern. But he had found them to be remarkably similar. All he had come back with were photographs and a general irritability. There were times on Hydra, in particular, when he had felt more like rage. He never told anyone where he was going, not even his parents. He would say, 'I'm off to Greece,' and they would say, 'Oh, are you? Take care then.' But his rage was not obvious to himself. What was it directed against? Not the Greeks. Not the ruins of the house of Ghika looking over that beautiful sea. Something else. Sometimes he thought it was merely his own anxious, unsteady blue eyes staring back at him from a hotel bathroom mirror. Could you feel rage against that?

Places in Europe, he sensed, were now the same tourist mills. The same restaurants, the same nightclubs, the same hotels, the same sexual escapades. This summer, however, he had saved up for two years so that when July had come round he would have the money to sail off into a deeper, more distant, blue. He had never travelled very extensively when he was younger and resented that he had never explored much of the planet. And even now, the Far East was not that far. The flight to Bangkok had been less than six hundred pounds.

He went back inside the Diamond. He felt even cockier and surer now and sat at a different table, but one nevertheless swarmed by the same Thai managers with their throat-scorching herbal Yaa Dong. The game itself was still a mystery to him. He had never even played cards much, let alone roulette. His game was amateur chess. But now he felt the attraction of a larger risk, a more uncertain venture. He played for an hour, throwing down his bets blind and hoping for the best. There was a hilarity in it. And the voice in his head urging 'One more, one more' until he was running with the unfamiliar idea of playing and imperilling his small amount of capital. It was the kind of spontaneous risk that ordinarily he never took. He threw himself into it innocently. It turned out well. Who could understand it? Then, as if in a single moment, he had a thousand and the staff began to notice. The girls came over in their starched white blouses and bow ties and asked him if he would like a Black Label or a vodka neat or, you know, an orange juice or some fried ants. If it was a joke he didn't know and he took a Black Label and looked at the clock on the far-off wall and decided that he might as well keep on destroying the middle managers and padding his new nest.

He did so. It was the moon, of course. It was something in the atmosphere. Soon he had two grand and some change and that was a fair winning for the Diamond Crown. Before unease set in and decline came upon him he wrapped it up with two grand in dollar bills and collected the stash at the window without ceremony. The staff didn't seem especially put out or surprised. The Thais were often high rollers themselves and wasted extraordinary amounts of money in the border casinos. It was something they saw every week.

'You have a heart of gold,' the floor manager said as he escorted him out, and as he passed to the gates he saw Alain Delon smiling down from his scaffold and the moon full of juice rising above the one-storey shops and the road where the motodops waited. He could sense unlit roads rising up the hillside with dark bars and men with bottles in their hands. It was quicksand, all of it. He took the cash out of its envelope and squeezed it into one of his front pockets and took a farewell of the thugs in cheap suits who had come out to stare him down. They wanted to remember his face.

He took a motodop back into Pailin. The town was now almost asleep and in the Hang Meas restaurant he ordered a *pho* and a Lao beer and pork satay with cucumbers. The karaoke was still going strong and the grounds were alive with roaming Khmer girls in heels, the eyes finding him with ease and laying upon him a dallying charm. He drank on with the dark Lao beer all alone in that restaurant with the red lanterns stirring quietly as the wind picked up, the long tassels moving slowly back and forth like horse tails. Two thousand. It was something from the half-forgotten realm of sorcery. Years ago, he thought, you got an education for nothing and now here you are, boy, a rabbit shooting out of a hat, all set up with no future at all but with a stroke of luck that has served you right. It was a fine thing and no one saw it coming. Moreover, he resolved never to set foot in a casino ever again. He was not going to lose what he had won so flippantly. He was going to hold on to it and plant it for a while and, if possible, make it flower.

Two

Across the fields of grass came the winds that had no obstacle, the summer breezes that still tasted of the Downs and distant fuel. The heads of the tall grasses rippled and they made a green horizon that moved with this spirit, and he ran through the stalks on his bloodied feet until the wind forgot him and he was alone on the rise that culminated in the Stensons' barns. He woke just as he saw them. The room in which he found himself was bathed in early sun, the curtains flapping because he had left the windows open. The heat came upon him as if suddenly. He found his skin already drenched and acclimatised and the cocks crowed in the Khmer gardens across the road where sugar cane grew along the verge.

He got up and showered and dressed, his fingers shaking because he was not yet sure how real or unreal it was. The plants coated with dust and the skies already beginning to darken at the silver edges. Packing neatly he went down fully ready to move and asked the sleepy boys if they could find a car to take him on to Battambang.

'No can,' they said, sadly shaking their heads.

'Of course you can.'

'No can. It no can.'

'Just call a car — I'll pay one dollar.'

'No dollar, no car.'

It went on for some time.

It took fifteen minutes to organise the car and he went into the restaurant and ordered Nescafé and *pho* and another pack of Alain Delons with a glass of watermelon juice. He sat there by the window looking out at flame vines hanging above a pool of shade. The hotel now seemed to be ruinously empty but for cleaning staff and hordes of boys in pressed white shirts, and from afar came the vibrancy of the mountains that were nevertheless burned half black and the white glare of frangipani.

At this hour the stillness had returned and the quiet vitality of things. You thought of home, but with a distant sadness. He wondered where he would go. Battambang was just the next city along. He knew nothing about it, it was just a place to go. Drifting, and drifting consciously. One could drift for a long time and not mind and where life was cheap and unhurried it rarely mattered. He decided then to go and walk around Pailin since the car was not going to arrive for some time. He told this to the girls. They smiled and said nothing and he went out into the heat with a curious determination.

He walked up the main road, up and up until he was at a Victory Monument exactly like the one in Phnom Penh. From here a road led up to a temple on a small hill called Phnom Yat. It was announced by a gigantic Buddha statue which looked down on the town. A giant in a gold tunic, a clean pink skin, the immense hand raised in the mudra of *ayodha*. He climbed up the steep shaded path to the temple steps, with a line of blue demons pulling the naga serpent like a tug of war. And so into the walled plateau filled with life-sized figures brilliantly painted. Trees hung low among the pavilions and the broken green glass floors, and they tossed and hissed in a burning high wind. He passed a basin of black water with three stone human heads half buried in it. Next to it was a depiction of Buddhist Hell: white figures in black loincloths being tortured. A man having his tongue pulled out with a pair of pincers. The local Khmer Rouges must have known it well. Higher up, bodhisattvas, princesses playing long lutes (he didn't know, he had to guess). A figure of a corpse lying on the earth while vultures tore out his intestines. At the top he came into a little court with three-headed elephants and tall gold flag posts and here the tree-dotted plain appeared with the mountains around it. A polished gold-plated tapered pagoda with tinkling coin-like chimes around the top mast, a reminder that the temple had been built by Shan Burmese immigrants.

He sat on the wall and watched the shades of quick clouds speeding across the plain. There was no sound but the wind-tormented trees and the chimes of the pagoda. Why not here, then, he wondered – a place to linger? It was a place with its own solitude and austerity and he liked it. It seemed to have an idea about death and about suffering. He could feel it very clearly. He didn't know what it was and he didn't need to know. The monks half asleep in the shade, the shrill chimes and the scenes of Hell just below the mirror-bright gold spire. There was something that beckoned him deeper in.

He walked slowly back down the hill and went to the market alongside which the notorious brothels were supposed to lie. There was nothing there, and it was clear there would be nothing there later either. The former life of the town had moved on, it was taking a different shape. He returned to the hotel and asked the girls if his car was there yet. It was on its way. He sat in the lobby and drank a Sprite.

When the car finally rolled into the Hang Meas courtyard with its monumental gold cockerel he saw that it was the same man who had driven him from the border the day before. So it seemed that everyone knew everyone in this incestuous land. The Toyota was caked in dust the dark red of ground chilli powder.

It was now ten. Robert went out into the hot sun and they shook hands and he said 'Battambang' and they haggled and settled on a price.

'Where you hotel in Battambang?'

Robert shrugged because he had no idea. That too was settled. The driver knew the best place for seven dollars, and there was no luxury option in Battambang. The dollars were handed over and they had a coffee together outside. As they sat on plastic chairs without shade the sun made him dry and still and happy and the driver looked him over with a cool shrewdness. It was certain enough that wanderers like himself had passed this way before. They represented a living to some, to the drivers and guides especially. The driver asked Robert now if he needed a guide. Didn't everyone need a guide in Battambang? But the other shook his head and said that he was just passing through and had no thoughts of visiting things. He didn't even know there were things to visit. Oh yes, sir, there were things to visit. The temple of Wat Ek Phnom and the temple of Sampeau and others. There was an all-inclusive price and Mr Deth knew all the history.

'Your name is Deth?'

But the driver saw no joke in it, not at all.

'My name Deth. I know all facts and the temple.'

'So I'm going to Ek with Deth?'

'I very safe driver man. All hotel recommend Mr Deth.'

On the road with Mr Deth. He shaded his eyes and looked up at the deer on the roof of the Hang Meas. One couldn't say what they were for or what they meant. The deer of Buddha's park twenty-five centuries ago. Deth played Thai music on his radio and the windows were rolled down because it was not yet high heat and the fields offered a cooler wind.

They went through wide meadows filled with bales. The hay was already roasted dry and dark. By the road great acacias and cherry trees shadowed the pitted surface, robusta coffee bushes with umbrella forms. The sky was untouched by clouds. Kapoks with pagoda-shaped tops cooled the walls of polychrome temples. The land near Battambang was charred black. The fields smouldering as far as the eye could see, since the farmers had burned the topsoil, leaving ghostly papaya trees standing in the smoke. They churned the iron-red dust and children in the yards of stilted houses watched them go by and the strange demonic charred darkness of the hills began to disquiet him. Yet the dry season was ending. The trees on the plain were entirely solitary, gaunt in their apartness and they threw no shadow onto the chocolate earth. Through this paradoxical dark brightness the people moved with a vivid lethargy and calm. Bicycles floating, the women with poles slung across their shoulders and masked by their *krama*, glancing up without animus. It was a day of dust, and yet the rain would come later.

The first thing he saw in Battambang were faded billboards looming over the river advertising ABC beer.

That river was green and still, men asleep on the grass slopes on either side. Under that vast sky now puffed with plume-white rococo clouds they seemed becalmed. Deth stopped and they got out and stretched for a bit. They were on a boulevard laid out alongside the river, with new cement benches inscribed with the words *Diamond Cement*. There were cream-cake French facades on the far side of the road, old shophouses. There was a generator chugging on the riverbank, and a series of nets lying idle. A bridge baked in the sun and along the embankment lay a sprinkling of trash and glass sparkling amid the high grasses. The traffic circles with their whitewashed kerbs buzzed with a soft rotary motion of bikes, and the air was light and dry and saline with the near-invisible dust. He liked it at once. There was a dried-out fountain with sculptured nagas and a mosque singing somewhere up the river. He couldn't imagine leaving in a hurry, any more than he could imagine arriving in one.

At the Alpha Hotel, Robert went up to his cell-like room and had a cold shower. He had paid off Deth and they had parted amicably, though the Khmer was a little clingy as they did so. Did Monsieur want a driver for the following day? He had declined, but now he wondered if he had done the right thing. He heard arrogant French voices wafting up from the lobby. Arrogant merely because they assumed they were understood when they were not. He lay on the bed and smoked: the Delons, he decided after all, were raw and bad. There was a sign on the door which said, 'Do not to bring the explodes or the cars into the room.' After a short rest he went down to the bar, which was entered through a lobby filled with marble Buddhas and disturbingly exuberant fish tanks.

Little red lanterns swung in the wind from the open doors, as they had at the Hang Meas, and above there was a polished wood ceiling with Chinese paintings of birds. The place, he could sense, was about to be remodelled into something more modern. A year from now it would look completely different. He got a shot of Royal Stag and watched the French group of middle-aged women trying to order from a garbled menu.

'*C'est quoi*, dove on fire?' one of them asked the waitress.

'Chicken fire,' the girl said slowly.

'*Et* Salad bin Laden?'

When the day had cooled he walked down to the river along a straight road by a temple complex. Where it greeted the water there was a sign for *Electricité de Battambang* and a row of rather grand French government buildings each dedicated to different indispensable functions. 'Battambang Water Supply' announced by a grandiose sign of gold decoration, with the water tanks rising behind it, the 'Provincial Hall' like a viceroy's villa. Mansions with guardian lions and cannons at the gates, but with a slight suffocation, a feeling of termination and decay. A faded park with a statue of an ape rising from the long grass and a tricerotops dinosaur. A legless beggar on a skateboard followed him for a while on this road, saying nothing, just paddling indefatigably with his arms as they went under the tall trees that almost met in the middle and formed a very French vault.

There was a shimmering in the air: the eternal frangipanis. He walked for a few hundred yards until the skateboarder gave up, his arms exhausted, and the Englishman sat down on the bank among white flowers and tall lush grass blades and caught a little repose. The place was so quiet that he could lie there until the sky began to darken and the sound of the cicadas rose in the high grass as dusk approached.

Looking down the river it seemed almost rural, with only a girdered railway bridge in the distance. People had begun to walk under the trees at the top of the bank as if in a *passeggiata* and a longtail came puttering down the river. The Sangker was unusually high because of a downpour earlier in the week. He got up and walked as far as a long cable slung across the river, though submerged deep in the middle, and on the other side he saw huts on stilts and little boys throwing themselves nonchalantly into the water with fishing lines wrapped around their wrists. Stumps of archaic trees separated the drifts of trash. Further back were new hotels, the Ty King and the Classy. They seemed to have come out of nowhere, crystallisations of alien capital. The lights in front of the French palaces came on but the windows offered nothing but a kind of administrative torpor and as he made his way back to the Electricité de Battambang he wondered about the stern and splendid functionaries who must have once inhabited them.

It made him think of his own shabby clothes, his semi-poverty. He hated being poor as much as he hated how predictable he was. His blond hair always cut in the same way, thrown casually to the right of a parting all his life. The clothes that never varied because he hated thinking about them. His life never seemed to go into surplus, into wonderful excess. He never had a surplus, never had a truly fine pair of shoes or a shirt that wasn't strictly necessary. His girlfriends came and went too easily; acquired in fits of absent-mindedness and lost in the same way. It baffled him. But when he was lucid he realised that he was waiting for something different. Beyond his own life there was, without question, a parallel one that he might one day acquire. It was a fantasy that could not be defended.

Like his father, he had a fear of being in deficit and in need. It was a fear that came from nowhere, it had no real source. 'It's just my character,' he used to think. He never bought himself anything extraneous or luxurious. Just those cut-price tickets to Reykjavik and Athens. Yet he was never broke, never in trouble. He always looked ahead and made sure that he had those extra pounds under the bed just in case. He never jumped off cliffs with empty pockets.

But here such calculations didn't matter so much, and maybe that was why he had warmed to the country. Almost everybody was poorer than himself. He had arrived in Bangkok a month earlier not even knowing where he was going to stay and he had been able to live in that tangled city quite well for almost nothing: a flophouse in Ekkamai and salted fish grilled on the street with *kanom jeen* noodles and lettuce for ninety baht every night and nothing to do but walk around by himself and meet the occasional hippy girl at pavement eateries. He was sure, however, that it had been the happiest month of his life thus far. The happiest and also the vaguest: the two were connected.

After two weeks in Bangkok he moved down to an even seedier place, the Rex on Sukhumvit near Soi 38. His money began to run down. He had come there without any plan or vision, and a two-month summer holiday was always hard to fill satisfactorily. He called his parents and they sent him a little more money. 'What *are* you doing there?' his mother asked, sounding as if she were on another planet. 'It doesn't sound like a holiday to *us*, Bobby.' What did it sound like to them?

He was beginning to like the heat and the pace, the day-by-day gentle sinking into his own laziness. The other backpackers whom he met at the outside cafe in the passageway in Soi 39/1 – a place he went every day for lunch – told him about Laos and Cambodia. They portrayed Cambodia as a tough paradise where you could live even cheaper than you could in Bangkok. He learned all about the gambling buses that went to the border from Lumpini Park every morning at 5 a.m. and the $3 flophouses in Battambang where you could live 'like a fish'.

Some nights he went down to the dingy eatery on the ground floor of the Rex and sat among the lonely old white men and their solemn girls eating spring rolls and drinking Coke. Even this place was better than being at a loose end at the pub in Elmer, the Jack and the Beanstalk. Even the girls here were more beautiful than the ones in the Jack and the Beanstalk. He read novels that he bought in the second-hand shops and later at night, with a few baht, he went down to Nadimos, a Lebanese restaurant on Soi 24, and sat outside next to a fake temple wall and smoked a shisha pipe with a Lebanese coffee in a copper pot and daydreamed. The towers all around shining with lofts and gardens, the ridiculous lions of the Davis Hotel across the street and the fat Arabs with their enviable molls lounging with their shisha and looking remarkably well maintained. There was a life here that he had never imagined. Even Bangkok was not at all what he had expected. It was not the city of *Hangover II* or *The Beach*.

23

It purred with affluent leisure and women dressed to kill. It was a shop window with no glass. One could feel the sucking tide of Asian money flowing through it.

It was in those moments at Nadimos under the awnings when the evening rain fell, smoking his shisha, that he realised how much he hated where he came from. He was certainly beginning to realise that he didn't want to go back. Night by night the thought grew in immensity inside him until it no longer felt quite as incredible.

To begin with, there was no future for him in the little village of Elmer. It was like a posting on a colonial frontier, except that the frontier was merely East Sussex. Elmer had a green like most English villages. There were timbered pubs and gardens that petered out into cornfields, and paths with stiles and fields with stooks in summer. You could walk around it in three hours.

There was a railway station and an abattoir. It was sweet with old secrecies and it was home and would be for a long time. He hiked among the abandoned flint farmhouses above Bevendean when he dropped in on his grandparents. He had been going there all his life and it was like turning over stones that have been turned over already a hundred thousand times and yet what else was there to do but turn them over? He talked politics with his grandfather, an old trade unionist with a dark red china bust of Lenin on his front-room mantelpiece. Old Albert had once been a trombonist on a Cunard cruise ship and later a chauffeur for a famous professor at the University of Sussex. He was filled with quiet disdains. 'Those blummin' people,' he would say vaguely to his grandson, referring to the classes above him who were perhaps dying out as quickly as his own class. He complained bitterly about the trashy hip hop blasting from the house next door as he was quietly trying to practise Count Basie tunes on his trombone in the basement. 'Those blummin' people, they play their blummin' noise all night long at weekends. They've got no jobs.' The old man told him he should go and live in London. But Robert himself had never wanted to live there. He was not suited to a city like that. He had always wanted a quiet life with his books and a hint of woodland and sea out the window. Too quiet and withdrawn, his parents had decided. They ceased preaching to him about his ambitions. He didn't have any.

One had to have a future. But, as it happened, he didn't have one. The drawn-out economic crisis was gradually overwhelming the once eternal-seeming middle class and eroding it day by day. He was one of the eroded. His parents were barely middle class anyway. His father had been a customs official at Gatwick airport. Their money was in a converted council house. The only thing that Robert had in his name was the fact that he had always wanted to be a teacher. He went every day to his little provincial schoolroom and stood in front of a blackboard and drew diagrams illustrating the connections between great English writers and kept the kids awake with the occasional sharp word. But to what end? It was little more than ventriloquy. Every day there was a long walk home to a cottage with odorous carpets and a kitchen with a hot plate. An evening playing YouTube videos and old jazz and waiting for something to come on the TV. The sweet bird of youth, in his case, had nowhere to perch and had not taken flight to begin with. His youth was a wingless dodo. One could go on and on and that bird would still not sing. You waited for life to begin and yet for some reason it did not begin. It hesitated while you wondered about the risks. You stood in the wings of your own play, afraid to walk onto the boards and begin.

He had a sense, meanwhile, that the country's fortunes were not going to recover for a very long time, perhaps centuries. He was never going to be as comfortable as his father, or even his grandfather. The machine of progress had begun to go backwards, and like an Irish navvy a century ago he was better off emigrating. Only there was nowhere to emigrate to. Nowhere that would take him in and give him employment. The world which had once been wide and commodious with America on the horizon had gradually become small and anxious and walled-off. His parents didn't understand it, and nor in a way did he.

The embankment lamps came on. How had the day passed so quickly? The swallows were out. Along the roads came the bulbs of pushcarts. It must have been that most surprising thing, contentment, an onset of happiness. The happiness that never is.

The bridge was alive with motodops. The hive stirred and he felt as if his childhood had been returned to him. Only twenty-eight, and there was no reason ever to feel otherwise. So what a con his life had been up to then, burdening him with things that were not his, and how long it had taken him to find a place which disburdened him. But there it was. Now it was the first cool hour and the phone shops on the far side of that road and the clinics with their blue crosses – Clinic Nouvel! – were as alive as little bazaars. He got up and walked back the way he had come. In front of the guardian lions and the cannons was a pedestrian bridge, people lounging over the river. Below, blossoming cafes, outdoor tables, the thin, elegant young men in their clinging ironed shirts. A place called the River where the handsomer set gathered, the fans stirring a hundred paper napkins. The nights here were soft and aimless and endless. He walked back into the town centre. On the pavements, families drinking cans of winter-melon tea with straws. On the televisions, Khmer music and soap operas and the children transfixed. There were fairy lights strung across the streets and beggars hanging by the river wall moving towards him as if they knew already how soft and young his thoughts were. They came out of the darkness with toys and books about Pol Pot and the eternal words *one dolla*.

He moved through the twilight quietly until he was at the White Rose on Street 2, a place marked in all barang guidebooks. It was empty so he went to the first-floor balcony. He sat under painted lampshades and plastic vine leaves and ordered *lok-lok*, fried morning glory, a baguette and an Angkor beer. In the Lean Hoa Chinese School opposite, a mass of schoolgirls scattered in slow motion towards the gates: they looked up at him. There was always a curiosity in the eyes here. It had not yet been eradicated by familiarity or contempt. A few drops of rain fell and there was a flash of soundless lightning. By the time he had walked back to the hotel it had become a fine warm drizzle. A small group of drivers waited in the courtyard playing cards by torches attached to their heads. Robert hesitated before going up to his room; he wasn't quite ready for boredom. The sister hotel to the Alpha, divided from it merely by a flimsy wall, was the Omega; it was a riot of lecherous neon advertising the massive KTV next to it and a sauna in the lobby, whose denizens − in the absence of any clients − sat around on the sofas looking up at a TV. The Alpha and the Omega. But it was at the Alpha that he lingered. He soon found a kid called Ouksa who agreed to drive him around the next day for a few dollars. He had no plan but he wanted to visit a temple and say a prayer for his parents.

The 'kid' was in fact about the same age as himself, in square-tipped shoes and a knock-off Tommy Bahama camp shirt with a black and white Mojave tile pattern, and he said he often drove around the Chinese people staying at the Alpha or the Omega, but usually the Omega.

'I can start at six,' he said hopefully.

'I think nine is a better time,' Robert said. 'Come at nine.'

'Where we going?'

'We'll go to a temple. Do you know a temple?'

The kid held up four fingers.

'There's four temples?'

'Four I know.'

'Then we'll think about it tomorrow.'

Ouksa shook his head for some reason.

'I can take you winery.'

'I'll think about the winery too.'

'Think about it. You can drink wine.'

'Well,' Robert said irritably, 'I don't really want to drink wine in Cambodia. Who does that?'

'Many, many.'

Three

But in the morning the heavy rain had come at last and the river flickered with more forceful lightning. The drivers sat disconsolately in the Alpha lobby and drank Yaa Dong medicinal liquor and waited for the weather to break. Robert sat with them and bought Ouksa a few coffees and they talked about his girl and the abominable price of car parts. It was amusing enough. The boy seemed to have ironed himself into one long crease for his payday, his hair slicked and the Brut pungent on his cheeks. He had clean hands and girlish nails properly cared for. From time to time he glanced out at the rain and the lax banana fronds flapping in slow motion and his eyes rose in a silent disdain. He was training to be an engineer and he drove a taxi in his spare time.

His spare time, as it turned out, was quite ample. In Battambang the days were long and, as Robert now thought, gently *uphill*. Ouksa had a contract with a Chinese company that manufactured plumbing parts on the outskirts of town. He took the middle managers around and showed them a good time in the evening. He took them to Kirin, a club where the girls were all dressed like government officials. Did he know it? The

Chinese were very into that. They tipped him recklessly and with the proceeds he bought his girl silk dresses and Nokia phones. Such were the visitors from Harbin, flabbergasted in their short-sleeved shirts.

'The barangs, they stay in Angkor place. There were four barangs from Siem Reap yesterday but they left.'

'I think I saw them,' Robert said.

'They did not like. I took them to Kirin and they did not like. I am going to take you to temple Phnom Ba Nan. At the top it is many hippies.'

A great atomic cloud had formed, bright silver at the edges, and as it evolved upwards it grew darker. The thunder did not seem related to it. In the street the long puddles brightened for a moment then grew dim, and the electricity which rippled through the air drew the eye to the slow-motion mushroom cloud and its impending crisis.

Ouksa's face was smooth, open and yet impervious to camaraderie. His fake gold watch had a charm, his eyes were slow and accurate. They didn't miss a mote of dust.

'I gave you good discount,' he said sheepishly, and as if to reward this acknowledged fact Robert ordered more Nescafé and crêpes.

'If you are happy with service, maybe you will take it day after. Or are you go to Phnom Penh?'

'I don't know, I might.'

'Thirty dollar take you and come back.'

'Maybe I won't come back.'

'It OK, stay. I can take you Hotel de Paris!'

'You can take me everywhere, I guess.'

'*Au kun*, if you want it.'

After they had eaten the crêpes Robert sauntered to the bar and bought some cigarettes and a bottle of Stag for the road. When he returned to the table, Ouksa asked him where his wife was.

'Not got one, as it happens.'

'You such a good-looking man, I don't believe.'

'No one wants to marry a schoolteacher. There's no money. You understand that, I'm sure.'

'Sure, no money girls run away. Same here.'

He sniffed glumly at the window for some reason.

'Where do you live, Robert?'

'In England. You know England?'

Ouksa made a knowing nod. 'Of course I know it. Man United.'

'More or less, yeah, that's about it.'

'So you come here for better living.'

'More or less, you could say.'

'Long way you come. You have girl here?'

'No girl yet.'

Ouksa grew a little bolder.

'But you at White Rose last night!'

'Word gets around, I see.'

'Rainy season – no barangs. So you are news.'

'I see, I'm news, am I?'

'Yes, sir. Everybody see you.'

'Well, I'll be damned.'

'Next time I take you to Kirin Club.'

'That's OK, Ouksa. We can leave the girls to the Chinese.'

'Aw, they prefer you, Mr Robert.'

'But do I prefer them, Mr Ouksa?'

'You never try Khmer girl? Very sad. We can go to Savuth Club. Girls are dressed to be farmers, all in black. Very kink.'

The rain cleared and they went out to the car and

turned on the air conditioning and waited for a while, then set off through the puddles and mud towards Phnom Ba Nan.

The roads had turned to chaos and they pulled in at the winery after all, a place called Chan Thay Chhoeung. They could wait a while and let it dry out. There was a kind of rose garden with tables for drinkers and a reception with bottles of Chardonnay and Shiraz. They sat in the garden under a shade and played cards with Ouksa's battered pack. Then, after an hour, the clouds parted and a moist, heavy sunshine came down. The road improved and Ouksa put on his sunglasses and said, 'It hot again.'

The ruins of Ba Nan lay at the top of a steep hill which had to be climbed on foot. The site was deserted after the rain, and it was probably deserted most of the time anyway. Even the hawkers had scattered. They parked under the monkeypods. Ouksa waited for him at the foot and Robert set out to climb the two or three hundred steps to the top, watching him as he went. A barang guarded by nagas, slow-footed among the hungry. It made him smile. It was torture for nothing, for very little. And sure enough halfway up Robert stopped and rested. He was young but he was out of shape. Soft and sweet, like some kind of fruit that has ripened too early. So Ouksa thought, and after all he was the same age.

Halfway up the hill, the forest was quiet. A monk sat just above him with crazed eyes, motionless under a parasol. At the bottom of the steps the beggar mites had reappeared with their matted hair, but looking up at him they were thinking that he was not really worth the bother of a climb. So he went on alone, suddenly dark at heart, the mosquitoes stinging his neck, and he came above the flat canopy and into a magnified light and a forest horizon that had no gaps, seamless as a flat layer of algae resting upon water.

Ba Nan was strewn all across the hilltop. Its tea-dark blocks scattered into piles which no one had disturbed for a thousand years. He walked through it knowing that he must be alone, since no one had come up with him. The heat made him dizzy. Tall dark pink flowers grew up among the stones. Sprawling prickly-pear trees stood between the prasats and on every one of their paddle-shaped cladodes spells and graffiti had been carved, the letters turned white with hardened sap. Yet there were blue signs which read *No Touching and Writing*. So the spells were written on the cactus blades.

He took pictures. Trees rose over the ruins, tossing and hissing like the trees at the temple in Pailin. But these were far older. Dark clouds loomed over them, sparkling with menace. The apsaras slowly fading away, the lintels carved and faded. Inside one of the claustrophobic prasats a huge but beautiful carved female foot, severed and orphaned forever. At the edge of the platform, then, he looked down at the silvery haze of the fields and the tall sugar palms and soon he heard voices and looking up he saw two soft-drinks hawkers picking their way like herons across the stones towards a barang standing alone at the far edge of the complex and smoking a cigarette. He was aware that the man must have been watching him all along, but there he stood in elegant summer whites, dark blond and incongruous and indifferent all the same. Robert heard the pedlars cry *choum reap* and the man took the cigarette out of his mouth and said something to them in Khmer. They turned away and the solitude of the two foreign men was resumed, the man in whites simply returning to his contemplation of something on the distant horizon.

One might be surprised to meet another Westerner in the ruins of Ba Nan, and he was sure this one was a fellow English speaker. But the surprise was not curiosity, it was just the elegance of the whites and the manner and their dainty anachronism.

He turned and walked back to the top of the steps. The monk was still sitting there under his broken parasol but he now saw that a small shrine lay to one side of the steps and that a lone incense stick burned there. Another monk had appeared and reclined there, shaded by a piece of tin on a stick. Black butterflies, stirred by the sun, began to swing lazily across the steps, circling their heads, and from the undergrowth came the susurration of revived cicadas. In the shrine behind him, a fortune-teller was reading texts to a small cluster of women and children. Suddenly they all laughed. The plain now shone far below and he felt for a moment an unsteadiness in his calves. He reached out and held himself firm against a huge carved jamb. The drinks sellers were talking behind him and he turned to see them putting up a plastic umbrella and come towards him. In that moment he came to a decision, but it was unclear what it was going to mean – it was a decision about the plane ticket and the plan to drive back to Bangkok the following Wednesday. In the space of a few minutes that plan had dissolved and he knew that he would be staying on a little, now that he could afford it – a week, a few weeks, however long his winnings would last here. He would explain it to his parents by phone if he had to. One could always come up with an excuse about travel delays or minor illnesses. He could say that he had the runs and was laid up in bed for a few days. Many such things would sound entirely plausible. He began to descend the steps, followed by two young girls who had suddenly appeared waving paddles made of pieces of cardboard torn from commercial boxes. They came towards him and when they were a step from him they began waving the paddles as fans to cool him. They followed him down, fanning his back and giggling. It would cost him 2,000 riels. Soon he saw Ouksa waiting patiently at the foot of the steps in all his starched composure with his hair parted laboriously to one side and his dramatic scent. One didn't know what to make of him. The way his eyes lifted slowly to find the man who was paying him, and to whom he was only partially obsequious.

'How was it?' he said as Robert came down into the clearing where the car stood and the children swarmed around him crying *one dolla, one dolla.*

'It was a hell of a place. There was a white guy up there too.'

'Oh? I not see that one.'

'He was doing was I was doing, I guess.'

It was noon and the heat made him fumble inside his own mind. He paid the two fanners a dollar and they cocked their heads with pleasure. He wondered about lunch. He wanted to invite Ouksa and make him feel more at ease. The flies tormented him, but they could not be discouraged.

'Why don't we go and eat somewhere?'

'Why not. We can go to Wat Ek Phnom and buy some things.'

'I'd say I owed you lunch.'

They drove back into Battambang, shadowing the river promenades again. They went past the Masjid Dhiya

mosque, and then northwards out of town towards Wat
Ek Phnom. The temple lay next to a pond filled with
bursting water lilies. It was clear that these temples
were all part of a known tourist circuit through which
a privately rented car was bound to pass with the driver
peddling cultural information. Ouksa, however, did not
provide it. He sensed that this white man was as empty
as himself and it suited him fine.

They had bought some chicken skewers and Cokes
on the way and they walked to the edge of the pond
and sat. The new part of the temple was a riot of
gold leaf and dubious taste; the ancient prasat rose
from shattered piles of blocks. They sat and ate and
there was somehow nothing to say for a long time. A
monumental chalk-white Buddha sat among the weeds
on an unfinished brick pedestal, his hands raised in a
mudra. Water-lily flowers opened in motionless heat
on the surface of the water. Ouksa lay down, taking a
small liberty with his young and easy-going employer,
and they listened to a plane droning in the far distance
and gardeners in straw hats raked the edges of the
flower beds.

'Still,' he said eventually, 'you are not really on
normal holiday. You are doing some pass time, no? It
must be nice to have money. *Ort mean loy*. I have no
money yet.'

'I usually don't have any.'

'Ah, but you have.'

'I got a little saved up for my holiday. But I'll be going
back soon.'

'How do you like this Ek?'

'It's quite a place.'

'It's haunted, did you know? The Ap is here.'

'Ghosts?'

'Like a lady ghost. She hunts all about at night. Can eat the dead water buffalo, you know, and eat children. A head that flies about – just the head. Ah.'

'And she is here in the temple?'

'Baht. So someone said. It may not be true. I never came here at night to see. I wonder you have Ap in your home?'

'England. We might, but I stay home at night.'

'Home?'

'Yeah, I stay at home.'

'Ah, Robert, you are not home now. If the Ap sees you she will hunt maybe. Believe it?'

'No.'

'You don't know . . .'

Ouksa smiled at him; his eyes had their inborn mischief and he folded his hands on his chest. Robert had no idea if the Ap was a genuine folk belief or if Ouksa was just inventing it to spook him. The latter seemed more probable.

'I'll bear it in mind,' Robert said.

He didn't succeed in being as dry as he had intended.

They walked through the ruins in the crushing heat but in the interlocked shade of trees. A swarm of half-naked children followed them, brushing against their legs, their hands outstretched, the eyes mock-pleading. The shrines were filled with coloured metal flowers. There were plastic tablecloths and bowls of incense sticks embedded in ash. A sign pinned to a ficus tree: *Give earth a chance.* They stood for a few minutes under a prasat tower open to the sky, the blocks arranged in concentric squares that tapered upwards. The children had hung back. Ouksa seemed to be holding his breath.

An uncharacteristic patch of sweat had appeared on his temple and his mouth had tensed. They came out into the open again and insects deafened them, and Ouksa shot a sharp word at the beseeching mites and caused them to scatter sulkily into the woods. The two men walked on. There was a fragment of ancient wall half buried in the trees, strangled by ficus roots, and they dawdled here for a while chatting desultorily about the remainder of the day. Would Robert like to see a curious monastery by a river outside town? It was a place that barangs did not go to see because there was no one specific attraction there. It was just a place where the monks would talk to them. The prime minister, Hun Sen, was building a bridge there, a special project that was a marvel to see. Though the words he actually used were 'a big special thing'.

Robert was half-hearted. He was already thinking of going back to the Alpha and getting a nap in his chilled room with the blinds down. Darkness and sleep and a swig of Sang Som from the minibar. Another day of life. They walked to the car in the sun's glare and he saw the brilliance diminishing at the sky's edges and the mood of rain returning yet again. The weather was in see-saw mode. Why not? he thought. A day existed to be filled with bright activities and labours.

'Let's go to the river and the bridge,' he said wearily. 'Can we get a beer on the way?'

'Of course, mistah.'

Four

They drove past old Khmer Rouge field guns rusting in paddies, the shell of a tank lopsided at the edge of a ditch. Thunder rolled in from afar, incongruous in that silver light, and the dried dust began to rise up again, shivering around the kapoks. They came to the river where Hun Sen was building his bridge and there a construction crew of several dozens spilled down the dark ochre banks with hods and sandbags. They went into the water where some of them bathed in their *krama*. The bridge was half completed. Ouksa parked above it among cement mixers and walked across a narrow footbridge to the monastery on the far side.

The river curved here and a mournful chanting echoed down it, a funeral service of some kind with the whiff of incense, while on the cliff opposite the dormitories of the bhikkus could be seen by the lines of saffron robes drying on lines along the walls. Silk cotton trees towered above these walls and cast down an almost impenetrable shade, within which a few cows moved, stirring their bells. They stopped halfway across the bridge and took in its jagged silhouette and the girls washing clothes on the mud isles dotted like stepping stones across the river.

They went into the monastery and the shade of the silk cotton trees and as they wandered around the ramshackle dorms they heard the rustling of hundreds of bats hanging in the higher branches.

'Are you fraid of bats, Robert? I want to show you something very nice. Come here a little and we stand underneath them.'

They were between the monks' houses and the boys were watching them from the walls and Robert felt a quiet dread go through him. Ouksa raised his hands and then clapped as loudly as he could and a moment later the mass of somnambulant bats stirred and rose as a single body.

It crackled and hissed as it lifted itself clear of the treetops and whirled around in a circle while the air rushed down and touched their faces. It was a little party trick but it made Robert put his hands over his ears and the monks had their laugh. They walked back down to the river.

The older monks had not come out to talk to them and the rain was clearly on the move. Ouksa said he knew a place a little further up the river where they could relax if the downpour arrived. They drove there in fifteen minutes. It was a shack on the water, an NGO bar by the look of it, with the usual Bob Marley paraphernalia and one-dollar Tigers. They went out onto the empty deck and sat on the moth-eaten sofas and poured ice cubes into their beer glasses. In some breathless way the day had passed more quickly than they had realised. The waters here were faster and dyes from the construction site upriver swirled past. They felt rather good sitting there with Bob Marley and Smashing Pumpkins on the system. The rain was just beginning.

'I hear you went to the casino two night ago.'

'You heard that?'

'*Baht.* I know all the guys there. I take the Chinese to Caesar. They love Caesar.'

'Well, I did.'

'Win or lose?'

'Lose.'

'Lose a lot?'

'Not very much.'

'Win nothing?'

'Nothing.'

He could feel that the part-time driver did not believe him. It was not easy to say why.

Robert made him drink more, and they waited for the rain to abate and the dusk to settle in. At six the drying-out began and the clouds parted; the ironwood trees still dripped as they made their way back out to the car and the edge of a moon had appeared low in the sky. The road was wet and the car slid a little as it made its way parallel to the river before coming to a crossroads and the edge of wide fields, where Ouksa turned by a corner shop garish with rod lights and they began to cross the fields towards the town.

A sudden dusk had come. The road dipped slightly by a second crossroads and they paused while the engine turned and they could hear the insects purring wildly in the fields. A headlight was coming across the opposite field at high speed but they could not see the surface of this other road. The sugar cane was high here on all sides and tall banana trees lined the road. The moon now flashed between their leaves. It was because the road curved sharply that they did not see the other beam of light for a few seconds. It came round the bend at a leisurely pace and they saw that it was a motorbike and on it was the white man that Robert had seen at the temple earlier in the day.

He recognised him at once and when the bike slowed the barang looked up and saw them and drew to a halt at the side of the sugar cane.

'It's the guy I saw earlier,' Robert said to Ouksa, and he felt a desire to get out of the car and make himself known.

Ouksa said nothing, but the sudden frown was telling.

'I'll say hello,' Robert said.

He was out on the road and the quietness came down upon him now that the motors had been turned off and he saw that the barang was handsome and only slightly older than himself and dressed in his sharp summer linens and dark blue suede drivers.

'Are you lost?' the man said, laughing and showing all the openness in the world.

'Half lost, maybe,' Robert said.

'Englishman?' the American said.

'Can't deny it.'

'I thought so. A Brit on a country road – I thought you might need some help.'

Robert turned towards the car and the face of Ouksa peering through the windscreen.

'I don't know about help. I suppose he knows the road.'

'Depends where you're going.'

'Back to Battambang, I guess.'

The bike rider shook his hand.

'I'm Simon Beaucamp.'

'Robert Grieve.'

'England then? That's a long way to come. Or go.'

'Yes, it is.'

'Me, I live here.'

The voice was aristocratic New England, slightly clipped. Money, ease and familiarity with out-of-the-way things.

'In Battambang?'

'Down by the river. I have a place there.'

He made a motion to the fields, to the high trees.

They were as if alone in the sweet darkness, the two barangs, and mutually amused at the coincidence.

'Well, I just thought you might need some help. You travelling?'

'Yeah, passing through.'

'Come down to the river and have a drink if you like. There's a bar called Angkor Town down there.'

'That's a good idea – I'll ask the driver if he doesn't mind.'

'He won't turn down a drink.'

Robert walked back to the car.

'What say we go with my new friend here and have a drink down by the river? He says there's a bar called Angkor Town. You know it?'

'Yes, sir.'

But Ouksa was pale and he kept his eyes upon the motorbike gleaming at the far side of the road.

'You look a little worried,' Robert said. 'It's just a drink and you can join us.'

Ouksa shook his head emphatically. 'Not with him.'

'What's wrong with him? He's just a barang like me.'

'No, sir.'

'Why not?' Robert said irritably.

'He has a bad feeling about him. It's clear.'

'Clear to who?'

'Clear to me. Don't go with him.'

'Nonsense.'

But Robert himself now had a small doubt. Should he listen to the more knowing Khmer? But his pride kicked in and he decided to go for bravura. There was also his sense that Ouksa's emphatic warning was itself a con. He didn't know who to believe and who to trust and so he went with the benefit of the doubt he was inclined to offer a fellow Anglo.

'Anyway,' he said with a kind of counter-emphasis, 'I'm paying, aren't I? It's my call.'

'I don care you pay.'

'Come on, Ouksa. It's just a damn drink down by the river. There's no harm in it. We'll drive back to the hotel after. I'll pay you more.'

'How more?'

'OK, twenty dollars more. Plus drinks.'

Seeing that he had little choice the Khmer relented.

'I won take him in the car,' he said, however.

'All right. He'll just lead us down there.'

Robert went back to the stranger.

'I talked him into it. He seems a bit spooked for some reason.'

'Oh? Well, I've been known to have that effect.'

'Never mind him, we'll follow you down to the river. I hope we aren't putting you out.'

'Not at all.'

Beaucamp went back to his bike and mounted it, and the smile had not left his mouth.

'Just follow me,' he called out.

Robert nodded and walked back to the car and got in the back. The night suddenly felt a little hotter and he rolled down the window despite the air conditioning. There was a scent of burning rubber coming from somewhere and of singed hay. The Milky Way had appeared and yet there was still a cloying rain in the air, a claustrophobia of monsoon.

'We'll go for a drink at this Angkor Town and it'll be OK,' he said to Ouksa. 'It won't take more than an hour or so.'

The driver said nothing, merely caught his eyes in the mirror. He was not happy about it but he would not say why. There was something tough and unspeakable in the air.

Perhaps he didn't like being out in the fields at night. One never knew. He didn't trust what he found on those roads where ghosts roamed. They set off anyway and they followed the tail light of the bike. Soon they were passing through more of the lifeless fields and the lines of tall sugar palms that made the sky seem even larger than it was and the wind rushed against his face. He had noticed that at night a ghostly music floated across those same fields, a music of *roneat*, bamboo xylophones, and *pai au*, flutes, as if being played by men wandering through the fields blind. Of course, the farmers had radios. Within ten minutes the river had come into view, mostly dark but with a few lights strung along it. It was the outskirts of town, the same road that led straight to the French buildings on Street 1. He didn't know where exactly but he didn't care, it was just the same river and a river was a welcome thing in that flat, disorientating land. The suffocation lifted and one felt, paradoxically, the intimate immensity of the land again. The air changed and a voice inside Robert said 'Yes' and he licked his lips and he saw the houses on stilts on the far side and felt glad to be down by the water at last. The road had many small houses with gardens on the water and a temple called Wat Kor.

Angkor Town was the only bar on this stretch, a large red Angkor beer sign — as always — hung above its gates. A narrow courtyard led down to the deck over the river. It was a Khmer place through and through, almost boisterous but never quite reaching that critical point. Red tables and red plastic chairs, jungle foliage right at the elbows of drinkers on the deck. Rows of small Angkor flags hung from the rafters and posters for Freshy orange juice. There were longtails hauled up into the reeds, red blossoms arching down to the water.

Beaucamp waited for them, with the bike tilted in the courtyard, and when they came up he pointed at the red sign above the roof and for some reason made a face.

They went out onto the deck.

The waters glided past like black oil, momentarily lit by fusty lamps with their colour of honeycombs. On the far bank the massive trees looked like the columns of some destroyed Babylonian palace which even centuries of violent rain could not wear down.

'This is my spot,' Beaucamp said, the place where he passed his evenings reading novels. 'It's a fine spot, too.'

The barman did not move from the bar, but called out Simon's name and waved a pair of ice tongs. Then he came over with a bottle of Royal Stag and a bucket of hacked ice and they laid out their tumblers and filled them with the ice. Ouksa finally relaxed a little and the smell of the opened bottle chased off his superstitious timidity. When the glasses clacked some of the fear seemed to go out of his eyes and he swigged back the Royal Stag with a relish that was clearly customary. The suave American spoke fluent Khmer to him, a language he seemed to speak as easily as he did English. It must have taken years to master. He said his house was a little way upriver, a place he had built himself after buying the land from a policeman.

'So you're passing through our little town,' he said to Robert. 'Not that many people come through here. You came over the border at Pailin?'

'I took a taxi from Bangkok.'

'It's a cheap way to come. I like that trip myself. See the casinos?'

'I played.'

'That's what my friend said.'

Robert cocked his head, and he felt a small disbelief.

'Everyone seems to know —'

'It's a small world up here. A barang wins two grand at the Diamond, everyone knows. That's the way it is.'

Beaucamp crossed his legs and laughed.

'Like our Ouksa knew too, I'm sure. Yeah, everyone knows those things.'

'I got lucky for a night.'

'Everyone gets lucky for a night. You're not here for the casinos though.'

'As a matter of fact, no. I'm not here *for* anything,'

'When I first came here years ago I didn't know why I came either. Then I ended up never going back. Don't ask me why. You could get a house back then for about ten grand, which is what I paid to build it. Got real teak from the Cardamom Mountains too. Can't get that now.'

'Like you say, it's a sweet spot. I can see that.'

'It is and it isn't. It's a tough spot too. I like it. Not everyone likes it. Seems like you're undecided.'

'I don't know,' Robert said, 'I only just got here.'

'So you did. How do you like our Indian whisky? It's better than the Thai one, I think.'

'It's great.'

'You can drink it all day and not get a headache. One day I'll give you some Golden Muscle wine. The local stuff. It's made from deer antlers.'

Simon switched to Khmer.

'Did you give him a fair price, brother?'

'Sure I did,' Ouksa said. 'Same price as everyone else.'

'Every other barang you mean.'

Ouksa shrugged. 'Every other barang, sure.'

'Why don't you drive back to the hotel and get his stuff and bring it back here? I've decided to ask him to stay tonight with me. Can you do that?'

'Sure.'

'Don't forget anything in the room. It's paid in advance, I think.'

Ouksa put down his drink and Simon explained to Robert in English.

'At your place?' Robert said.

'Why not? The Alpha is a fleapit. It used to be called the Teo and it was a fleapit then too. You'll like my place much better, believe me. We can play chess. Do you like chess?'

Robert shrugged. 'I do, sometimes.'

'Splendid. Then we can play chess.' Simon's eyes began to shine with mocking humour. Did he really enjoy these sorts of games? 'I haven't played in months. I can't find anyone here to play against. You'd be doing me an enormous favour actually.'

But the favour was also the other way around.

Within a few minutes, in fact, Robert had begun to feel curiously attracted to Simon. It was not a sexual attraction, but it was certainly physical. The American's body was relaxed and affable and confident. His elegance was simple, unaffected. It suggested a man who didn't care what judgements he was subjected to because they couldn't possibly be all that bad. And usually they would be flattering. It was Robert who was confused and a little blinded, and both of them knew it. Simon had acquired a fluent familiarity with his surroundings. He obviously spoke the language perfectly, and it was not by any means an easy language. At first Robert had wondered if Simon was gay and the purpose of the game all too easy to understand. But gradually his instinct told him that this was not the case; he might be bisexual, but either way the game was not sexual. It was about something else. Perhaps Simon was bored on his luscious river and he needed something, or someone, to manipulate.

Ouksa finished off his drink and stood up.

'Drive straight back here,' Simon said in Khmer. 'I don't want to go looking for you.'

'No, sir.'

'Is it all right for him to go alone?' Robert asked.

'Sure it is. Everyone knows everyone here. He won't do anything amiss. He knows I'd find him.'

When Ouksa had gone and the car had begun its short trip up to the Alpha, Simon filled his glass again and put fresh ice into it.

'All the same, Robert, you should be a little careful moving around with that kind of money. It could be tempting for some people. Not for this one. But others. Two grand is a fortune here.'

They watched the slow river for a while. Someone holding a lantern at the end of a stick moved along the opposite bank, the light flickering behind reeds and trees, and you could tell that it was swollen by the rains. Near the reeds the water rustled against debris and the edge of moon lit the smooth, unctuous surface as it constantly shifted. All along its length the frogs sang at full throttle, a sinuous chorus that seemed to possess a relaxed relentlessness, and it served to calm slightly jangled nerves, the apprehension that for Robert always came with night. He let go of his glass finally and sank back against the pliant plastic chair. His skin was dry; his eyes felt keen and lucid. He wasn't nervous at all, but he was not at his ease either. It was surprisingly easy to linger between these two states of mind.

'It's a damn warm night again,' Simon said. 'But it'll get hotter tomorrow. Does it bother you?'

'I'm getting used to it.'

'It's cool by the river. It's why I live here, of course. On the river, I mean.'

Robert said he loved rivers too.

'It's a British and American thing,' Simon said.

'Is it?'

What did that mean? Robert wondered.

Simon took out a cigar box, opened it and took one out. He left it open and asked 'Smoke? They're bergamot cheroots I get in Burma.'

'All right. It's been a while since I had a cheroot.'

'Why's that? Don't have them in England?'

'We have a few. I just don't smoke them.'

'Is that right, hombre? Well, we got more here than that. These are fine enough. Not Cuban, but they'll do. Of course they're not cigars.'

Simon smiled, lit up both cheroots and closed the box. Soon the smoke had enveloped the table and the river breeze did not remove it. There was something manly and satisfying about it. The scent of bergamot, like a pot of brewed Earl Grey tea.

Simon continued his questions, about which he was quite casual and slow, as if it was just the normal pace of his curiosity. A barang who did not talk with another barang all that frequently. One had to wonder if he was lonely up here on the river of Battambang. He didn't seem lonely or even put out. There was something, to the contrary, smoothly oiled and implacable about him. As if he was used to questions and answers.

'Moving on soon?' he asked Robert.

'I guess I should be. Though honestly I hadn't thought about it.'

'Where to?'

Robert shrugged. 'Phnom Penh – maybe.'

'It's an underrated city. Lots of girls there.'

'It's all right, I'm not going for the girls.'

'You don't have to be prickly with me about things like that. Visitors like you are always much more moral and decent in word than they are in deed. It's OK. Everyone's the same.'

'I hadn't really thought about it.'

'Oh, sure you thought about it. Everyone thinks about it.'

'Even if I thought about it I wouldn't do it.'

Simon smiled. 'You young barangs are so earnest. Wait till you're forty.'

'Are you forty?'

'Damn near close. I'm trying to find a way to avoid getting there.'

'Well, good luck with that.'

'I wouldn't leave it to luck. Maybe I'll just change names.'

'Anyone can do that.'

'So,' Simon drawled, not looking up, 'are you going to take a bus tomorrow?'

'Maybe.'

'You can take a boat down there too. I have a boat I use myself. I can call the guy down for you. He'll be here any time you like.'

'Is that the best way to go?'

'Sure it is. Relax, take the sun on the deck. And all that.'

'All right then. Maybe I will.'

'You do say *maybe* a lot, Robert. Life is not *maybe*.'

'All right, I will take the boat.'

'That's better.

'Do you have business there?'

'I'm on holiday.'

'Ah yes. Holidays. I forgot about them.'

They smiled. Simon eyed him carefully over the edge of his glass.

'I say we have three chess games. Best of three. All right with you?'

'I'll do my best.'

'That's the spirit. You know, Robert, you seem like a sport. When I saw you at the temple earlier I thought, *he's a sport*, you can tell from his body language. Well, that's what I say. You can tell a man's a sport from his body language. And from his shoes of course. I gave you a pass on the shoes. But overall I think I was right. You wouldn't believe many of the people who come through here. Pure Flintstones. I don't look down at them but it's how I feel. One can't help it. It's like they come here to die and they aren't sports about it either. They do it as if they're too lazy to do it properly. In fact *a lot* of them do.

They throw themselves in the river. Three or four bodies wash up every week, barangs down on their luck and tanked up with Yaa Baa. It's a cottage industry for the crematoria at the monasteries. I never can figure out who pays for the funerals.'

Simon looked out across the waters, momentarily distracted, and picked a shred of tobacco from his lips.

'Well, I pay for some of them if you want to know. I have the money. I don't care. It seems a damned shame to let some kid go uncremated because no one came in to claim the body.'

'Then you are a sport too.'

'It's nice of you to say. I think of myself as the guardian of this part of the river. I watch over it, you see.'

They mixed the Royal Stag with soda now and made it very cold.

'You're lucky you can live like this,' Robert said. 'You must have a business here.'

'I had the money when I moved here.'

That's luck, Robert thought. The lucky have great timing.

'Back in the days when the dollar was high,' Simon went on, swirling his ice. 'Back when we were rich. It's a rather different story now, isn't it?'

'I'll say.'

'But you came into a bit of cash.'

'I didn't think I'd win it in a casino.'

'It's a sign. The Khmers believe in signs. Every sign means something. When my housekeeper told me about it I laughed and I thought, there's a sign if I've ever heard of one.'

'Your housekeeper?'

'News travels on *gossamer* wings. She told me and we agreed it was a real sign.'

53

'Of what?'

'Who knows – one never knows. That we would meet tonight? That we would play chess? You have to think in the Khmer way.'

They were laughing and Simon was thinking how much more elegant Robert would look with a proper pair of shoes. He was a good-looking boy all the same, a boy with swing and lilt and charm. The English farmlands in his cream complexion and open skies in the eyes. It was a charm that survived all changes in locale, one felt it quickly and it was not something one could walk back from. But his English solidity let him down. He was still harnessed to another way of life, you could see the cowed look in his eyes.

Robert, for his part, had begun to give in to this charm offensive even as his mind kept returning to that grisly image of bodies floating down the river. He congratulated himself on ignoring Ouksa's advice. Simon, he reasoned, was not understandable to a Khmer boy with no experience of the wider world. He was an oddity even in the Western context. To Robert, in those slightly giddy moments, he suggested a man of another age, an anachronism that was appealing for all the affectation it implied. There was a subtle menace about him, but it never quite broke into open view.

Robert pushed a hand through his loose, foppish blond hair and the moths buzzed around his head. The car was returning and Ouksa was driving it with paranoid slowness as the tyres slipped in the wet gravel. Simon smoked his cigar down and they waited for Ouksa to come back into the bar with his sheepish look and his acute suspicion. When he had done so they all rose and went to the car in a jovial mood and the owner emerged and told them not to worry about the bill. They came out into a faint moonlight and the glimmer of open sky and the bushes seemed alive with moths. They followed Simon's tail light as he turned left from the bar and followed the river-hugging road past the last small villas and family houses and into the sombre, purring open countryside and its dark palm-shaped silhouettes.

Here there was a network of unsurfaced roads that had no lights. Beaucamp's house seemed to be the very last one of all, and was half a mile from the nearest neighbour, its back garden sloping right down to the river where there was a small private jetty. It was surrounded by a low grey wall and had two grey gateposts and a rusting iron gate. The garden was startlingly lush and wildly overgrown, with black ceramic amphorae standing about in the uncut grass and a hammock between two cotton trees. It was a simple concrete villa raised above the ground in the Khmer-village style by posts. But he had turned this ground-floor area into a kind of veranda which projected out to the water's edge and was filled with sofas and carpets and low coffee tables. It was an original arrangement, artfully dishevelled in the way that a superb dresser will be. The ceiling had four propeller fans and there was a drinks cabinet in one corner nicely protected from the elements.

Ouksa carried his bag to the door and Simon told him gently in Khmer that his duties for the day were at an end and he could leave.

'He looks relieved,' Simon said to Robert with a merry eye. 'Can't wait to be rid of us.'

But Robert walked Ouksa back to the car.

'This bad man,' Ouksa said in a low voice. 'Dun you stay here.'

'He's just a little odd – don't worry. He's American – I understand him. I'll be fine.'

He slipped Ouksa the extra twenty dollars.

'Thank you. This man not what he look.'

The thought had gone through Robert's mind several times by now but it had not been enough to deter him. He was not sure why. It was an open question whether it was the very thing that he was attracted to.

When Ouksa had driven off, the two white men sat on the veranda with gin and tonics. The open rafters of the house seemed immense in the night shadows, the moths spinning around the wooden beams. It looked like a house which Simon had built himself since it was so much better-looking than the houses he had seen up till then. Simon put on some music from the house above them. He took out his ornate Moroccan chessboard, with its pieces carved from argun wood and hand-painted, and they set it up on the coffee table between them. He said he had bought it long ago in Essaouria on the Atlantic coast and it had a 'spirit' that helped his game. He laid out the pieces and they flipped for black and white and Robert got black. He kicked off his sandals and the alcohol swelled within him and he absorbed the humid smell of datura coming in from the forest. The *roneat* music was faintly chiming out in the pitch-black fields, a wailing of fiddles as well. Simon made the first move and soon he was winning easily. He was the kind of player who had all his moves prepared in his head long before he touched a single pawn.

Five

Slowly, the whole sky visible above the bend in the river began to empty of clouds. It filled with a soft light that gradually made the sugar palms on the far bank more distinct and the piles of the jetty sharp and clear. The sweetness of this ripening night sky made Robert not care what time it had become. Birds sang in the forest, looping sing-song calls like those of macaws, and a million falling waterdrops merged together into a single sound. It was strange how trees kept dripping long after the rain had stopped. A country like a water wheel, like a mass of wind chimes.

The second game had begun but it was slower in pace than the first one. More cheroots, lit with a certain ceremony.

There were feet on the steps, a pair of bare ankles appeared. They paused and Simon engaged his eye and smiled and put a finger against his lips. The girlfriend came down in a bathrobe, a slender Khmer yawning, and when she was at the bottom of the steps she turned and looked at them and said nothing, just walked over to the drinks cabinet and poured herself a tonic water.

'Sothea,' Simon said, 'this is our new friend Robert all

the way from England. He's a little deaf so you'll have to speak up.'

She was dark and long-haired and oiled, and she looked from one man to the other and back again and said nothing at all. Simon said to her in Khmer, 'You can go back to sleep if you want. We're playing chess.'

'I can see what you're doing,' she said.

She came over with her feet faintly oiled and smiled for Robert and he saw that her hair was wet. Her long fingers grasped the glass of tonic water with an awkward uncertainty, as if she were already resigned to the idea of dropping it and watching it smash.

'Sues'day,' she said, and nothing more.

'Are you hungry?' Simon said to Robert. 'We can eat satay if you want.'

'Maybe a little.'

She went back up the stairs and soon there was a smell of cooking and they played the second game while the frogs seemed to come closer in the undergrowth. The moon became very still. The girl returned with a plate of pork satay on sticks and a little dipping sauce. She sat at the edge of Simon's chair and watched his hands move his pieces back and forth. One could see the easy familiarity, the sexual tenderness between them. Simon began to dominate the board just as he had before and yet he seemed reluctant to win the game too quickly. He wanted to know about Robert.

'You don't seem like a schoolteacher.'

'What do they seem like?'

'Oh, I don't know. I only know American ones. They seem – depressed. It's sort of a dead-end career, isn't it?'

'I don't know if I'd say that.'

'Well, obviously you wouldn't. But that doesn't make it untrue.'

'It doesn't make it true either.'

Robert talked about his last two years. There was something false about it, a slight artificiality in his voice as he complained about his town and his job and his solitude.

'Do you believe in ghosts?' Simon said suddenly.

'Not at all.'

'You're going to have a difficult time in this country then. You cannot be here and not believe in ghosts. Say, Sothea honey – do you believe in ghosts?'

Gravely, she stared at him and her mouth opened.

'See? They all believe in ghosts. Ghosts are more real to them than you and I are. That means ghosts are more important to them than we are. I like that view of the world myself. It seems serious.'

'Does she really believe in them?'

'It's categorical. I'm a Yale man myself. Highly reasonable. But don't hold it against me, because she doesn't. And I believe in ghosts just as much as she does. I've come around to the idea. I prefer the idea. It goes against everything I was raised with.'

'I'll drink to that.'

'Let's drink to ghosts –'

The girl got up brusquely and walked out into the garden, where her hair shone and her cool distaste was removed from them. It was a disreputable thing to make a toast to but Robert had the sense that Simon had done it on purpose.

'There are many ghosts along the river, hombre. Quite a few. I don't see them but she does. She has a knack of seeing them. I used to say, oh it's a Khmer thing, and it was a bit patronising, but now I wonder. I wonder if she's just got a flair for it. A nose.'

Along that river a longtail now moved, a lamp hung from its rear end, the motor purring quietly. They got a little drunk. The girl went back upstairs and Robert lost the game and they sat for a while under the careering moths and the oil lamp hung on a black wire.

'I suppose you'll leave tomorrow,' Simon said. 'My boatman can drop you off in the city and just tip him a twenty if that's all right.'

'I'm grateful — it seems cheap.'

'It's not cheap at all. But if you think it is, that's great. I might even come with you, though I think we have things to do up here tomorrow. Meanwhile, I have a bit of red opium left over from last night. Shall we smoke it and be hippies?'

'Let's.'

As they lit the pipe Robert felt ants crawling across his naked feet, things crawling between his toes, and he didn't mind. The air had suddenly become deliciously cool and the heat and bustle of the day had receded even mentally. So this was what it was like here. The days pinned you down in stress, sweat and misery and then the nights came along to rescue you and set you back on your feet. Nights were the key to survival, the way out of the stultifying labyrinths of the days. Without the nights humans would shrivel up like cockroaches and die. Simon won the game and they began another, and as they did so they puffed at the pipe which Simon had prepared with delicate dexterity. It tasted sweet, like stewed plums, and the smoke passed easily into Robert's lungs and out again into the air.

'It's tasty,' was all he could say. 'I've never —'

'It's hard to get these days. It became an unfashionable

addiction at some point. I can't imagine why. It's so mild and pleasant.'

'It's like something for children.'

'In a way, yes . . .'

Robert began thinking about the boat the next day.

'Maybe I should go early,' he said. 'That's what everyone recommends here, isn't it? Get up early and avoid the heat.'

'Generally that's what we do. Shall I call him now?'

Simon made the call and spoke in Khmer.

'Six all right for you?' he called over to Robert.

Robert nodded and so it was decided. He would probably have an opium-and-beer hangover but it didn't matter.

'Where does the boat go exactly?'

Simon put down the phone and extracted his pleasure from the pipe which he held with three fingers as if an ancient Chinese man had shown him how to do it properly.

'Where you want. We usually go down to a small town a few miles out of the city and taxi in from there. The piers in Phnom Penh can get way too busy with all the tourist boats.'

'I'll do that then.'

'You'll be there for lunch. Do you eat lunch, Robert?'

'I can't remember. I can't —'

'I know a place you could go. Right on the river.'

'Yes, on the river.'

Robert felt light-headed. The lights along the far side of the river had begun to seem more spread out and their reflections in the water shimmered more violently. The outlines of the trees had grown more imposing in some way.

'I'll write it down for you,' Simon went on. 'You can go there and eat fish amok. Very nice.'

Simon rose and walked over to the paraffin lamp hanging from the rafters and lowered the flame. He half turned and glanced down at the stoned visitor who had stretched out his legs and sidled onto the entire length of the sofa he was seated on. The music had stopped and it was just the insects now, the sound of the fields. The pipe lay in the centre of the table on a dish that seemed to serve that specific purpose, its wisp of smoke perfectly vertical. A life of casual idleness was expressed in that single upright line of smoke and it was a life which, looking at it, Robert suddenly wanted for himself, even though he was repelled by its uselessness. It couldn't be that hard to attain. He thought: I am in some kind of fairy tale and nothing can be that hard to attain. All I have to do is wish for it on a star. Simon came back to his own sofa, fell into it and restocked the pipe so the smoking of it could go on. He lit it up again and passed it at once to his guest. The conversation between them had now run dry, but without awkwardness. Like a stream that peters out at its appointed place and time, without drama. It no longer mattered. It is always the way when conversation no longer matters. It dies its natural death with a quiet submission to fate. Robert felt himself falling backwards into the rough fabric of the sofa while the ants ate his feet alive. He thought to reach down and scratch the skin or crush the ants but when he raised his hand to do so he found that he could not.

'You can sleep down here,' Simon said at last, and his words came to Robert like something whispered at the far end of a long tunnel.

Robert rolled slowly onto his back and his mind let go

of the unfinished chess game and the ants. He stared up at the one of the shiny black fans. The mosquitoes were audible, their beating wings as loud as rotary blades. Out in the darkened rows of sugar cane the rabbits nibbled at the edge of the covering shadow, their eyes shining for a moment as they turned and listened to birds of prey. He placed a hand over his eyes and felt his mouth go dry. He remembered the bats which Ouksa had roused earlier that day, their wings beating just like the insects now. What world, then, did they inhabit?

Six

He came over the Downs in the tall grass and the flint walls of the old barn stood high on the crest almost with a view of the sea through a gap in the hills. There were large holes in the walls filled to bursting with stinging nettles and through these a small boy could step. Inside it was gloom and fragrance but he always hesitated because he was alone. Around the barn the grass quivered and rippled and there were momentary patterns upon its silvery surface. He reached out and ran his hand along the rough flints and he drifted through the cornflowers at the bottom of the walls. Why always here, under this same apex sun which made the shadows stand still only a millimetre from the forms that cast them? The terror of the cows standing in their isolate shadows too all over the hillsides, in gleaming rivers of half-dried mud. Look up at the sun and you wake at once, always the same.

He did so then and he saw the blueness of a morning sky, almost the same as the sky of England and childhood. It, and not his eyes, seemed to blink. Then, almost at the same moment, he heard water and sensed it close by. The lapping of lake waves, weak but ploddingly insistent. The horizon tilted, then righted itself: he was on a boat.

It must have been the boat that Simon had called for him. Though his head still hummed from the night before he got onto his elbow and forced his eyes to work again. He was on the deck of a small shabby fishing boat with a motor at its rear end and above him in a ramshackle cockpit a man stood at the wheel smoking a half-crushed cigar. He was naked but for a pair of shorts and dark blue tattoos ran all down his back.

Robert was lying on a mattress, like that of a sunbed, and the early-morning sun had burned his nose a little. Water, he thought. I need a bloody drink. He got up with difficulty and steadied himself and made his way forward to the cockpit. The man turned without surprise and motioned to a Thermos lying in the shade. It was hot coffee with sugar and milk.

'Good morning,' Robert said as loudly as he could.

A godsend, the coffee.

The man grinned and made a playful salute with one hand. Robert unscrewed the Thermos's cap and fell gratefully into the coffee. He sipped it cautiously at first then took larger mouthfuls.

Instantly, he revived. They were on a vast toffee-coloured lake. Across it a saline wind swept, warm and menacing, and far off on the horizons he could see systems of nets laid low against the water. There was no land to be seen, they had left it far behind.

He sat half in the sun and gulped down the whole Thermos. It was only gradually that he became aware that he was wearing clean clothes and that they were not his. He looked down and spread his hands over his warm lap. He was wearing off-white linens, freshly laundered. He felt in the pockets and there was a hundred-dollar bill. The shirt was a soft dark cream linen with heavy buttons.

He got up and turned once as if looking at himself in a mirror. Incredible. Espadrilles too.

He called out to the pilot.

'Where is Simon?'

The man waved a silent hand but didn't turn again.

All right, Robert thought, he doesn't speak a word of English. That's to be expected, I suppose.

He took out the dollar bill and looked it over. Then he thought about his backpack. It was nowhere to be seen on the deck.

'So that's it,' he said aloud.

Exhilaration came upon him, and then a back-pedalling panic.

He leaned against the boat's side and let his senses clear and soon he saw low shimmers of green on the leftward horizon. It's a small country, he thought, and no one is more than four hundred miles from anyone else. For some reason he didn't yet care about the backpack and yet he knew instinctively that it was not on the boat and that there was no use looking for it. There was no point asking the pilot about it and there was no point asking him to take him back to the house by the river. He did not even know where the house was or where the jetty was or what the river was called. He would never be able to find it, and the pilot would never take him anyway even if he understood.

He lumbered to the rear of the boat and looked down into the toffee waters being churned by the motor. A five-mile swim in any direction. He shaded his eyes and saw that the shimmers of jungle on the horizon were in any case coming closer. But there was no way of calculating how long he had been on board this boat, or for how many hours they had been ploughing through this featureless wasteland. It could have been for several hours. It could, for that matter, have been for half the night. There was no way of knowing. Nor was there any way of knowing if a gentlemanly favour had been done him, or the reverse – one barang gentleman to another.

Towards noon, to judge by the position of the sun (he had no watch, he discovered) the boat began to near land – the same low forest and waterlogged banks of reeds and flat grass – and soon he saw people walking along a road, bicycles flashing in the sun.

The pilot turned to him and said something, the name of a place perhaps, Prek Pnov, and he stood up and walked to the bows which would touch land. There were long shelving banks of dirty wet grass and reeds, and above them a scrim of slum shacks made of tin. There were a few children with mechanical toy birds and fishing rods standing at the tip of a line of planks that led up from the water's edge into the shanty. It was not quite the city but over the slum and the river soared a modern bridge which suggested its presence. The thick dust of the country roads hung above Prek Pnov, the dust which dries in an hour and then rises to envelop the head, and through it he could see the gold tints of a ramshackle wat covered with wooden scaffolding and high sad trees caked with cement powder.

When the boat came to, Robert stepped onto the planks and looked down at the mysterious pilot who seemed unconcerned. This was not a stop that any commercial boat would use; it must have been a secretive place that Simon used to get ashore while going about his equally secretive business.

'Where's Simon?' Robert asked again, but now more clearly and forcefully. 'Where's my bag?'

The pilot smiled with a vast charm.

He had already unmoored the boat again and the craft was moving away from the path of planks as suddenly as it had arrived. As it did so the children closed in on Robert and began to pester him. *One dolla, one dolla.*

'Oh, OK then,' Robert called after the pilot, 'you dump me here and then you just leave like that? Just like that? What am I supposed to do now?'

The pilot waved cheerfully. Nothing to be said or expressed, just the fact and the consequences that sprang from it.

'Come back,' Robert shouted after him, waving too, but not in the same friendly way. 'Come back right now!'

He knew already that no such thing could happen. The men in the cluster of longtails below him stared at him and slowly their ironic smiles gained traction in Robert's mind and he desisted. 'Damn and fuck it,' he muttered and brushed past the children and began to climb the precarious gangplank through slopes of colourless plastic trash. The planks snaked through shacks on stilts, up into the shadow and heat of a single alley that wound its way through the slum.

He was just at a loss, and aboard the boat he had not been able to think anything through. He moved as an automaton until he was clear of the river and he thought wildly, in great leaps: go back up the river by car and find the house again or press on and see what happened. But there was no sense in going back, he knew there was nothing behind him and, far more importantly, he didn't want to go back. Secretly, he was thrilled. From now on he could tell himself that he was a victim of circumstance.

He laughed and the people out on the alley sitting around with their lunch saw it and laughed along immediately. It was the Khmer way. Their surprise was not melodramatic. It came out in that subdued collective laughing. He was in an alley filled with little shops and two-storey houses where the balconies were crowded with makeshift altars of bowls of fruit and decorative piles of beer cans. Great round earthenware urns stood outside the doors. As he turned and decided to walk to the right, his head narrowly missed a line of tiny fish impaled on a wooden pin that dangled from an awning rod. The children burst into laughter. He ducked and laughed along and moved awkwardly towards the cheap gold chedi of the temple which he could see over the roofs.

The wat looked like a half-abandoned construction site. But there were gold guardian lions erect and snarling in the sun and chedi which had been restored. The naga heads on the stairs had been repainted gold and green and there were smaller lions posted on the roofs. He walked in, seeing nobody and now no longer followed by the children, passing venerable trees whose shade covered a ground of rubble and grass.

He came out onto the road, and he could sense at once that it was the main route into the city. In fact it was the Battambang highway. Chaotic traffic pressed through it, a medley of motorbikes in swarms. The sun beat down on tangled cables and pink bricks and forlorn flag posts.

He walked along the dust bordering the tarmac until he came to a small shop with a curious sign for a thing called 'Alexand' brandy with a black head of a Greek warrior. He stepped into its shade and felt the sweat and burn on his skin. He cashed in the hundred-dollar bill for an Angkor beer. As he stood by the road, tuk-tuks and motodops began to stop. In his nice linens he appeared a profitable target but he soon beat the motodops down to five dollars for the run into town. Since he had no baggage they assumed he lived there. No, he said, I'll go to a hotel, you know one? The motodops were not as wise to the hotels as the tuk-tuks but they knew a few flophouses.

It was a choice, according to them, between the Sakura and the Paris. Both had girls. The Sakura was cheaper but the Paris had a nice location on Kampuchea Krom Boulevard and a restaurant on the ground floor. It was a difference of about five dollars. He chose the Paris.

They drove in through the heat of the day. The rain, the driver said, would not come in until the late afternoon that day. The suburbs, meanwhile, lay in a sullen calm and he went over in his mind the dozens of theories he had established as to what had happened. The most likely, to his taste, was that Simon had helped him on his way and would send on his things as soon as he sent word where he was staying. There must have been a reason that he had held onto the backpack, a reason that was not injurious, but, as it happened, no such reason came easily to mind.

Seven

On the outskirts of central Phnom Penh the light dimmed and clouds began to mass and they crawled through a river of traffic towards a thing called the Japanese Friendship Bridge. It was two o'clock. He could see already that it was a small, low-lying city with the great river pouring through it. They went past Chinese factories and loading bays, the metal boxes covered with Chinese characters, an office for Brunty's cider, mounds of rose bricks, the shapes of metal silos and the gleam of the pale green-tinted river below. They passed under the bridge, the tarmac shattered as if by mortars. The afternoon hysteria of car horns and the cafes along the streets filling up with anxious men in white shirts. A city with pools of slow life from another age. The trees along the roads then, the echoes of provincial France, a disappeared France of green shutters and dark yellow walls. The long pale grey walls of the French Embassy topped with rings of barbed wire and a riverine boulevard swirling with dust and violent wind.

The river curved slowly, dividing the city they were on from a further shore where half-constructed buildings rose up out of a slightly silver haze. New hotels, towers of dreary metal. They turned inland at a street market of some kind and passed alongside a baked city park, the frangipanis creamy in the sun. The driver glanced at his fare in the vibrating mirror. He looked like a young man about town, a rake down for the weekend. In fact, he looked vaguely familiar. But why did he have no money, so little that he had to stay at the miserable and ill-reputed Paris Hotel? But maybe he wanted a hotel with girls for the weekend. That must be it. But then, where had he seen his face before? Or something about the way he dressed. Most barangs dressed like beggars. This one dressed as if to hide the fact that he was a beggar. If he waited outside the Paris Hotel for a few days he might get another ride out of him. He might need something illegal like a passport.

Robert was not thinking about such things at all. He was watching the rotary swirls of girls on motorbikes, the back riders side-saddle and helmetless. People massed on the pavements under the shade of mango trees. The great heat slowing down even facial muscles. He was not as dismayed as he had expected to be. The city was, one could see, young and upbeat and fierce, and yet its traffic had a slow, almost choreographed motion to it. They sped leftwards into a large boulevard, wide and French – Norodom – and he could see old European villas and mansions set behind walls topped with broken glass and a dark monument at its distant end like a gloomy relic of Angkor. A quiet motor seemed to organise the city. The bikes whizzing in both directions simultaneously never quite collided. The tuk-tuks snaking their way through this chaos never quite came to grief. Almost, but not.

The driver had got lost and he circled back up to another boulevard – Monivong – and turned right into it until they came to Kampuchea Krom at a right angle to it. It had a sombre, commercial feel. After the second junction, they came to the Paris. The hotel's name was written over a curved entrance in English, Chinese and Khmer, and around its pale orange columns lounged a handful of cynical-looking drivers. There was a KTV with red Chinese lanterns across the street and a shop with a sign that read *Sony, Make Believe.*

He had no bags, he was free and light as he came into the colourless and empty lobby with 'international' clocks on the wall and the cool glance of two young receptionists.

They barely looked up, in any case.

The lobby had white leather sofas and a coppery bas-relief of Angkor Wat and a soft-drinks fridge with the word Vinamilk. Sashed boudoir curtains made it feel like something other than a hotel.

'Passport,' one of them said impassively.

And suddenly he remembered his passport. Which is to say that he no longer had it.

'It's at my other hotel,' he said quickly, not missing a beat.

'What hotel?'

'The Sakura. I can get it later.'

The two Khmer girls looked at each other doubtfully.

But it was a barang, a barang was not really a risk, and they didn't really care either way. Cash is cash.

One of them looked up at the clocks for some reason. The red letters below them spelled out the names of cities they would never see: Sydney, New York and of course Paris. The time in Paris would never be of any use to anyone staying at the Paris.

'All right,' one of them said, 'you can bring it later.'

'I will, yes.'

'But then you got to pay upfront now.'

'All right – two nights please.'

It was thankfully cheap.

'No bags?'

'I'll get them later.'

He paid the cash and one of the girls took him up to the fifth floor. As they passed by the lift he saw the photocopies of passport pages of wanted criminals taped to the wall next to it. Heng, Sarquen, Cambodian: eyes like pumice. Men on the run like himself, their images of little interest to guests of the Paris who probably had enough secrets of their own. The girl glanced at him. Her attitude quickly relaxed even though the lift was broken. The futility of the building's internal heat seemed to make her more amiable. It was the way here, the surface coolness quickly broke down.

'Holiday?'

'Business.'

'Ah,' and her face fell a little.

The Paris was a claustrophobic place, with half-lit corridors, a mama-san on every floor, and girls from the massage parlour sat around doing their day's make-up and coiffure. They looked up for a moment as he passed and the brushes and eyeliners came to a moment's standstill. So it was a single man's place and they kept track of the resident denizens. The room itself was the usual cheap affair in the tropics but there was a working fridge and air conditioning and a TV with a Japanese channel. The wooden ceiling was so polished that it looked like a floor. *No gambling in the HOTEL room* on the back of the door.

The receptionist gave him the key and left him there. He locked the door behind him and went to the window and looked down into Kampuchea Krom. Tired and stoic trees withered up in the last hour of sun before the rain hit the city. The traffic went by in a curious silence. Behind a blue grille on a rooftop a woman sat combing out her wet hair. He sat on the bed in a state of vast emptiness and relief and took off the clothes that were not his and looked at the back of the collar and the inside of the linen trousers. Were they not Simon's clothes, pretty obviously? They did not quite fit and Simon had been wearing the same kind of thing. The labels were of a tailor in Phnom Penh, a place called Vong. They were Simon's clothes all right, they even smelled of a stranger. The gesture was strange and murky and he could not think it through even now. There was the money, and this was merely a better way of getting rid of him than killing him.

He lay back on the stiff bed and smiled at the thought of Simon and his slender girl trying to kill him. Obviously this was better. And they would not have had the nerve to kill him. No normal person ever had the nerve. And yet it was also possible that Simon had given him a backhanded gift in the light of their conversation the previous night. He had read Robert quite cannily, and he had surely sensed that the Englishman would not protest too much. He would not come back looking for his things, not even for his passport. It was an incredible game, sending him off naked into the world like that, but he had intuited that Robert would survive and make the best of it. People lost their passports all the time, it was never the end of the world. He would not, Simon had guessed, even go to the British Embassy in a hurry and make a declaration, and if he did they would just give him a new one. It was difficult to see what difference it would make. But alternatively, he could go find himself a false one. They were easy to procure from the city's army of forgers. And in fact he was thinking about it already. He was thinking how he would step, lightly, into someone else's life.

But what life had Simon led here? Exhausted, he lay naked on the bed and turned on the TV set and watched a programme about outer space that was all in Khmer. He could tell that it was about some tiny distant blue planet which had just been discovered a few months earlier, a place where it rained shards of glass all day long and where the nights lasted barely thirty minutes. He dozed. The sounds of the hotel drifted down into his consciousness. The girls shuffling in nighties and hot pants from floor to floor, the Khmer pop music, the men coughing on their way out and flinging the spit in the back of their throats. The daily thunder rolled in with a generous laziness and the trees shimmered with lightning, spreading a subtle panic through the street below. He was easily refreshed. When he was up, he felt confident again and he shaved with the hotel plastic razor and put his expensive clothes back on after a cold shower. The air conditioner barely kept the grit-filled heat at bay but he no longer felt hot. He thought he would go out and find an Internet cafe and maybe something to eat as well. It was going to rain then, but rain never hurt a man.

He went down by the stairs, landing by landing. In the street the rain came down in terrible sheets, the drivers outside cowering at the edge of the lobby. There was a soft surprise in their faces.

He found a motodop and told the driver to take him to an Internet cafe. They set off through the downpour and he let go of any remaining apprehension about staying dry. They drove down Kampuchea Krom until they crossed Monivong, and then they had reached a street called Pasteur, passing clubs with names like Shanghai and Flamingoes and bars stirring into nocturnal life with a laziness that gave them a natural and inevitable force.

In the thunderous rain the neon had a frosted, childish quality. They passed the Sorya Mall, a ground-floor open space filled with bars and sofas, and at the end there was Street 136 and the Internet cafe where the driver let him off. He dashed inside, soaked through, and sat at a terminal by the window for half a dollar.

He had wanted to just check his emails but now he was not sure if he should. To open his account would perhaps expose his whereabouts to someone who might be looking for it. He didn't know who would be looking for it as yet, but eventually – surely – his on-off girlfriend Yula would be anxious and maybe his parents as well. Incredibly, he hadn't thought of them. It might be a decisive thing, to use his Gmail password now. Decisive, that is, down the line. He therefore hesitated before signing in.

His hand hovered over the keyboard and gradually it relaxed and retreated. It had to be thought over, and now he was not sure that he wanted to go back to anything. He only worried about his mother, even though there were other things to worry about, a thousand loose ends left in a chaos of abandoned responsibility.

He often thought, in this respect, how un-English he really was, because breaking away from home was not proving to be as difficult as he might have once anticipated. On the contrary. It was proving easy and harmless, at least to himself. Because his own motive was becoming clearer to him, he assumed that it would become clearer to everyone in his life as well. It was not the case, and he realised that. But he hoped it would be soon. If he could walk out of the door and not come back, others would eventually understand why. There was no point, then, explaining himself to a chorus of puzzled resentment. If they couldn't understand, nothing could make them understand. Most people appreciated where they were born and grew up. They grumbled, but they liked it, could not live without it. He was not like that, he now understood. There was nothing about his birthplace or his life there that he enjoyed or would defend to the death. There was nothing he enjoyed in that way of life. It was claustrophobic and petty, and the police watched everything you did and thought. It was a way of life that justified itself as being the pinnacle of freedom, but it had not come up with an alternative reason for existing once the freedom had been sucked out of it. There wasn't even sex or sun. There was health care, so that although life was expensive at least death was free. A society premised on free death.

It was then that he opened the Gmail account and quickly went through his messages. Surprisingly, almost no one apart from his parents had sent him anything. It was as he had suspected. He felt a bitter contempt for himself for even hoping that it might have been otherwise. The two messages from his parents, moreover, were simple enough.

> Bobby, we know you are on the road and it's awfully hard to send message sometimes, but *still* we are here, you know, not six feet under. You might pop us a message once in a while just to let us know that you aren't either!

The second seemed a little more anxious.

Bobby, are you all right? We don't know how we feel about you being in the land of Pol Pot. I mean, really. Awful things happen there, we've heard. We hope you are being careful at least. Send word, all right?

And impulsively he did.

Everything OK. Don't worry. Having a marvellous time in the land of Pol Pot. Would I be a monster if I decided to stay here a year and not come back to that awful job? Would you be furious if I did that? I met a girl. You know the story. But everything's dandy! It couldn't be better.
    Bobby.

It was fake, but it was not entirely so. The gist was true.

He imagined his father turning to his mother with a sly wink.

'So, he's got a girl out there. I told you so.'

It was then that he decided to 'go invisible'. He felt that he could cut off contact with them for a while without arousing their fears. How long that would turn out to be he couldn't imagine. It might be weeks, or even months. He knew how they thought — once they had received word from him that he was thriving in foreign parts they would tend to let it go for a while. He would send them a curt word later on, when he knew what he was going to do. He didn't know himself at that moment, and so there was little point trying to explain it to them.

Out in the rain there was a street almost in rubble. Wide, sultry, open to vice. Short-term hotels with little white neon signs were still open and freelance girls trawled the flooded pavements in pressed white shirts and black hair combs. He went onto some sites where people posted services ads and personals and looked through the Language Tuition section.

It was free to register and put up an ad, but in the Language Tuition Sought section there were quite a few people asking for English lessons at about $10 an hour. He scribbled down the phone numbers of six or seven and went out into the rain again and walked down 63 for a while until he came to a shop selling cheap phones and SIM cards. He got a ten-dollar one and a one-dollar SIM and fixed his new number up inside the shop so that it worked before he made his way out.

Now he didn't want to waste any money so he made his way back to the Paris — he was wet anyway and the humidity would never let him dry out — and on the way a Viet girl followed him slowly on a kind of damaged Vespa and called out 'Why not, why not?' until giving up and turning away. On Kampuchea Krom the pavements had emptied, the trees poured with warm water. When he arrived back at the lobby a man asleep at the reception desk raised his head and looked up with an aimless eye at the barang. Two girls ahead of him on the stairs turned and asked him what room he was staying in. They smelled like Ivory soap and turmeric. He said he only spoke Romanian. Then, when he was back on his granite bed, he remembered that he had meant to eat and had forgotten. He lay down and felt slightly feverish and decided to leave the curtains open because the lightning flickering through the window would, against its usual proclivity, help him sleep and forget everything. And so it did.

Eight

The following day he got up early and went down to the restaurant on the ground floor of the hotel. Its doors were opened to the street and the sticky tables attracted flies. He ate some Dried Sand Gobi in Soya Bean Sauce and some Kai Lan in Oyster Sauce and after them some weak tea. The day had risen in a new spirit, with a low, aggressive sun and a dry, acid dust that came onto the tongue and the eyelashes. It was strange how at this time of year the city did not remain either wet or dry for long. The men there ate silently reading newspapers with tin pots of Vietnamese coffee, the glasses beneath the metal filters lightened with condensed milk, and when he had tired of the tea he got the same coffee for himself and counted everything out carefully dollar-wise. He would have to survive on very little until he got a pupil or two. He sugar-loaded the coffee, which had a nutty, almost chocolate taste, and drank it down as slowly as he could. Soon the discomfort of the night and the bad sleep dispelled and he came back to life and set to work calling the numbers which he had culled from the Language Tuition section.

None of them answered. Perhaps it was too early in

the morning. He paid and strode out into the sunshine and walked slowly down Monivong until he reached the Victory Monument. The sky had lost all its monsoon darkness and looked forward to a dry and bright spell. It seemed like a city of twenty-year-olds in which only the old possessed the shabbiness he had expected, as if they had emerged suddenly from a distant age of terror. He went ambling down Neak Banh Teuk Park towards the Samdech Chuon Nath statue, an old man with large ears seated cross-legged surrounded by nagas and lions. Robert paid it no attention. He pressed on along Hun Sen Park and past the massive Nagaworld casino and a fairground on the left called Dream Land, the Ferris wheel temporarily stilled, waiting for night, but the street vendors already there with their barrows of tiny steamed snails topped with artful crests of red chillies. He went inside Nagaworld for a few minutes to cool off and sat inside a kind of Chinese pavilion with plastic willows and painted blue-sky ceiling and stone waterfalls. He came out dried of sweat and circled round past the Landmark Hotel until he came alongside the Himawara Hotel where the gold leaf of the palace was suddenly visible and the saline river could be felt in the nose.

There was a restaurant next to it, with tables set out above the river, empty at that hour. He sat there and ordered an omelette with cucumbers and pork and a fermented fish called *tray prama*. He made his calls again as he was drinking the next round of Chinese tea and this time a woman picked up. She was Khmer and spoke little English.

She said, 'Dr Sar coming back at eleven.'

He said it was for the English lessons.

'He will call you back, Mr . . . '

A name, he didn't have a name yet. He had not even been asked to give one at the hotel, or maybe he had signed his usual signature, he couldn't remember.

'Mr Beauchamp,' he said quickly.

He pronounced the 'p'.

She repeated it and he said 'Yes'.

'Mr Beauchamp, Dr Sar will call you before lunch.'

So he was a doctor.

'All right, I'll wait for his call.'

'Aw khun!'

He thought of continuing with the calls but his superstitious side was strong and he thought he might jinx this one and he didn't want to jinx a doctor. A doctor might pay well enough, and he loathed the thought that he might have to break silence and call his parents for money. That was unthinkable. He went back out into the street and walked down alongside the river until he was by the Cambodiana Hotel and then the wide, milky water itself with the construction cranes shining on the far side as if sprinkled with silver dust.

Although the day was typical of those that follow a night of rain – the earth patted down and compact, the insects somehow uninterested in humans – the sky showed the first anxieties of the struggles that would return by nightfall. In the centre of the blue void a great atomic cloud had formed, blindingly bright at the edges, and as it evolved upwards it grew darker and yet more brilliant at the edges.

The tension in the air did not at first seem related to it, but soon one began to know better. In the street the long puddles brightened for a moment then grew dim, and the electricity which rippled through the air drew the eye upwards to the slow-motion mushroom cloud and its impending crisis, which would not arrive for hours, maybe not even till the next day. Along the Tongle Sap the frangipanis and star trees were held in a total stillness, like things carved out of wax, and under them old ladies performed their t'ai chi to music boxes. The beauty of automata, the beauty of wax and stillness and sky-tensions. For the first time in twelve hours his clothes began to dry and become crisp again and the sun burned into his shoulder blades. He crossed the road and went into one of the spread-out cafe terraces with cane chairs that line the tourist stretch of Sisowath Quay. It was La Croisette. As he settled into one of the cane chairs the phone rang and a male voice said his new name with a gravelly amusement, as if he had heard it before but as if it didn't matter. The doctor introduced himself in a slightly struggling but distinctly American-inflected English.

'I was glad to get your call, Mr Beauchamp,' the doctor said. 'My wife and I have been looking for an English tutor. Could we maybe meet up for lunch in an hour? Where are you?'

Robert looked across the road and said, 'At the river.'

'The river? Whereabouts?'

'Near a place called the Wagon Wheel.'

'All right. Why don't you meet me at Le Royal Hotel at twelve?'

'I could do that.'

'Are you English?' the doctor asked.

'I am. Is it a problem?'

'Good, I thought you were. We wanted someone English.'

'Well, I am English.'

'We can have lunch at the Royal restaurant. I suppose you know it. The table will be under my name, Dr Sar. They know me.'

'All right.'

'I'll see you there. I think my wife wanted to meet you too but she can't come to lunch.'

'Next time then. I'll see you there, Dr Sar.'

'Twelve. If I am late, please do have a drink on me.'

'I'll do that.'

The man said, 'Au revoir!'

Dr Sar. It was such a resounding name. To kill the next two hours Robert went to the National Museum and wandered through the galleries of Angkorian art. The place was hot and almost empty and finally he came to a huge statue of Vishnu from the obscure temple of Phnom Da in Takeo province in the south. He sat down on the floor in the lotus position.

The god's hands clutched a flame, an antelope skin and a flask, and on either side of him stood two smaller figures of Rama and Balarama. Carved from a single block of sandstone, only five of his eight hands were still attached to surviving arms but all of them were carved with finesse, the individual nails carefully grooved. Like a young pharoah, the god wore a tall cylindrical hat and a folded loincloth, his physique slender and lifelike, with wide shoulders and a little bulging belly. The surface had turned a dark green from the unhappy centuries.

Robert, however, found himself thinking not about unhappiness but its opposite. Vishnu, destroyer of worlds, might have something to do with happiness but he didn't know what it was. The missing hands seemed to be the clue. They must exist somewhere even now, relics mounted in distant American or Chinese homes or buried in dusty museums on the far side of the world. Timeless. Where, though, did these oval faces, aquiline noses and almond-shaped eyes come from? Even the tear ducts, the pupils and canthi of the eyes were perfectly carved. The figure of Balarama, the elder brother of Krishna, which stood to the right of Vishnu, was arresting. His left eye had been obliterated but his gentle smile was still intact, as was the symbolic swing-plough he carried. His figure was boyish, tilted at the hips. Rama, meanwhile, held a tall bow and gazed down at Robert with a haughty gentility. As an avatar of Vishnu, he was associated with knowledge and eternity. He also partook of the enigma of happiness.

Robert walked to Le Royal after getting directions from the museum staff. It was a stiff walk, but he had an hour to waste anyway, and as he made his way through Street 102 he saw a lovely shaded colonial-looking apartment block called Colonial Mansions with a pool shining behind glass doors. If his fortunes improved he made a resolution to look in and see how much it would cost to live there. At Le Royal, on the far side of the park behind this building, the staff had stepped out onto the gravel driveway and were peering up at the sky as if something unpleasant had just happened or was about to happen. In his decent clothes he passed through them with a mere nod and a smile, and he felt a sudden pleasure at this automatic respect, which he had never enjoyed from anyone before. He had a different step now, a more confident stride. It had come to him quite suddenly. The grand hotel was gearing up for lunch and in the lobby the upscale barang types and the businessmen from Seoul and Shanghai were there in their dark suits. He slipped in among them and a few of the women looked up and checked him out with a quiet appreciation. He saw it, he felt it, and it made him smile. He was aware of himself looking quite glamorous, burnished by sun and idleness and a youth much less latent. Blending in, he passed through them with a quicksilver pleasure.

A long corridor to the left of the lobby led to the Royal restaurant, and the table was waiting in a still-empty room. It stood next to a door-sized bevelled mirror with a view of a pool. The staff looked him over without any trace of snobbery and he took the table and ordered a Singapore Sling and a tall glass of iced water. He did it without missing a beat. It was curious how naturally it came to him. Maybe Simon had been right — he was a good sport. Now stilled and appeased in some way, he stretched out his legs under the table and looked around. The walls were covered with French colonial lithographs, scenes of moonlit picnics and elephant rides, images with titles like *Pique-Nique sur le Bassac* and *Elephants au bord du Tonle Sap*. There were old photographs of dance troupes in traditional costumes, like child-women with painted white faces, *Des danseuses du roi se préparant à la danse*. It was a world within a world, and the world to which it had once belonged had entirely disappeared. The foreign correspondents had all lived here during the war in 1975. Even now there was something not quite right about it. The boys in bow ties and awkward waistcoats, the chandeliers moving slightly in the subtle gusts from the air conditioners. The ceiling's painted panels. Yet it was not a decor he felt out of place in now. He thought, with a quiet astonishment, that this would not have been true only a week earlier. It was like stepping into a grand house to which, although it appeared unfamiliar at first, he had been subconsciously accustomed all his life. From beyond the walls the koel birds could be heard in the towering trees arranged around the two colonial pools. High above which, on the room balconies, were little signs that read 'Please do not feed the monkeys'. It was the life of the rich, the tropical rich, and all one had to do was look the part and not hiccup.

Robert felt sweat spreading slowly all along his shoulders, his hand was unsteady on the stem of the water glass.

'Keep it steady,' he told himself. 'No passing out here. No scenes.'

The doctor, as it transpired, was late — he was a busy man — and Robert was alone until 12.20, sipping down his Sling and getting quietly tipsy on a stomach that now felt empty. The dining room filled and the music was turned up. Until, as if announcing Dr Sar, the doors finally swung open and the man himself walked in, a small and hairless head of about sixty-five with a body wrapped up in a white suit. He carried a briefcase and a strange-looking paper parasol which he had folded. One could imagine him stepping into the sun and suddenly unfolding it to protect his pale Chinese skin. The eyes were fast. He spotted Robert at once and came over rocking slightly from side to side on bowed legs. Yet the face was actually quite young, almost wrinkleless, and one didn't see at first the incredibly fine wire spectacles that lay across the bridge of his nose.

'You are Beauchamp, then?'

There was a laugh and a handshake and down went the briefcase into the arms of a waiter.

'Welcome, Dr Sar,' the boys intoned, bowing.

'They know me here,' Sar added unnecessarily.

It seemed that he sometimes took wealthy clients here to break bad news to them and, by Buddha, it was better than doing it at the clinic.

He looked over the foreigner with a careful attention to detail. The boy's clothes didn't quite fit, and there was a dogged rigour in his eyes. So he had come to put on a show for the doctor. He needed the money.

'The truth is,' Sar said almost at once, as the salmon carpaccio was brought in and a bottle of Perrier was broken open as if it was champagne, 'that my wife and I are looking for a language tutor for our daughter. She's twenty-five. She just came back from a year of medical practice in Paris. A place called the Hôpital Dieu. Do you know Paris, Mr Beauchamp?'

The eyes twinkled and Robert decided that lying was better than not.

'I do, yes.'

'Mrs Sar and I are terrible French snobs, I am afraid. Even though I applied myself much more to English. Not that I speak well or anything —'

Robert's protests were waved away.

'No, no, I know how badly I speak. But anyway. My daughter has never learned it properly, since like us she is French-mad. But now she finds that her sorry English is stopping her progress here. The tyranny of English reached us a long time ago, I am afraid to say. I am against it myself — but what can one do against a whole age? At least at the Royal we have Tournedos Rossini for lunch.'

'Ah.'

'Have you ever had them? Of course not, you are too young. You've been raised and brainwashed by *doctors*. You are all vegetarians now, or worse. Let me take you back in time then. Tournedos Rossini. Steak with foie gras riding on its back. I am a doctor eating such things. My wife does not know. Shall we have two orders of that? And no salads, please!'

'No salads,' Robert said, and they seemed to instantly agree on something — but it was not the undesirability of salads.

A waiter brought to the table what looked like a cologne bottle, with a label that read *Huile d'Olive*. He set it down.

'So I put out an ad,' Sar went on, his hands relaxing on the surface of the tablecloth. 'I thought there must be a fair number of nice educated young foreign men in a city like this — and one of them might be the right person to teach my daughter perfect English. Between you and me, however, we want — how can I say it? — a gentleman. We are not going to hire someone in cargo shorts and flip-flops who wants a few months bumming around Cambodia.'

'I understand.'

'I interviewed a few fellows. They showed up in shorts.'

'I'm sorry to hear it.'

The doctor expelled a heavy sigh tinged with a kind of macabre hidden humour.

'This is the way it is these days. Well, I won't have it in my house. Do you wear shorts, Mr Beauchamp?'

'Never.'

'Not even at the beach?'

'I never go to the beach.'

'Excellent answer, by Buddha.' The doctor finally laughed. 'I think that merits a glass of Sancerre, don't you?'

'I do.'

The doctor's hand rose and the ordering of the Sancerre

consisted of two quick motions of his index finger but no click. A whole world of sly provincial wealth was expressed in that gesture, an authority whose true root was obscure to an outsider.

'They know me here. They know what I drink.'

He's easy, Robert thought, and he relaxed. The doctor looked like he would give him some work. He just had to be a gentleman.

'Naturally,' Sar was continuing, 'we need to know a little about you. 'My daughter has been rather ill lately so she is staying at home with us. Nervous exhaustion, I think.'

'Was she working here?'

'Not yet. She is looking. Her time in Paris didn't do her much good. I don't know what she got so exhausted from – I have scratched my head over it for weeks. My wife says – but she always has a theory. It's easy to have a theory, isn't it?'

'It is, yes.'

'I say there's no point having a theory. Just give me an explanation and a plan of action. I thought working on her English would do her the world of good. The social scene here –'

He pulled a face which, unexpectedly, made his face much handsomer. The wine arrived and they made a silent toast, but the doctor had not let go of his train of thought.

' – I mean, for kids of good family. The high-society kids. Well, it's appalling. They can do what they want. Sophal hangs out with the sons of air-force generals and suchlike. The children of the rich. I can't seem to talk any sense into her. They do a lot of drugs and do what they want and no one will touch them. The boys are utterly worthless. They can kill any homeless person they want and nothing will happen. It's difficult to explain to you, you being a foreigner. I can't stand the thought of her ending up with one of them. I thought if she got her English up to speed . . . '

The doctor emitted his second sigh and the Tournedos Rossini arrived, the foie gras laid carefully on their surfaces. It was *service au guéridon*, the steaks prepared table-side.

'Then her chances for happiness will increase?' Robert said to himself.

'Wrong wine for steak,' Sar laughed, 'but I don't care. Do you care, Mr Beauchamp?'

'I don't care, no.'

'Then we don't care. If we don't care, no one does!'

'It's delicious wine – thank you.'

'Thank you for coming to a job interview at such short notice. Bon appétit. Now tell me about you. What brought you to Phnom Penh?'

On his long walk over from the National Museum Robert had prepared his story. He thought it best to be at least half truthful. The issue was whether he should own up to being a teacher; it had its pros and cons.

In the end he decided against it. English teachers were two a dozen in this city and in most cities like it. They formed a kind of sub-society all over the Far East, a loose confederation of dubious individuals with their own social niche and their severe reputation for being mangy and broke, though somewhat successful with the girls. Several of his friends at college had gone on to pursue that way of life in places where the koel birds sing and nothing more was ever heard of them. The tropical English teacher in his cargo shorts and flip-flops and his bad haircuts, saving his pennies by eating local every night and scouring his adopted city for sexual scraps and titbits: easy to find here and free for the young. No money, yet still plenty of honey. But that was not his niche and he intended to stay as far away from it as he could. The clothes he had unexpectedly inherited, strangely enough, had nudged him into other ideas. It seemed absurd, in fact, to *step down* from them. He didn't really want to go this route at all, it was just that he couldn't think of any other way to make some quick cash. It was ironic, given that it was the only skill which he actually possessed. The doctor, meanwhile, seemed to sense — or rather wanted to believe — that this artfully dishevelled youth was more than he appeared.

'The truth is,' Robert said, 'I'm just travelling around Asia for a few months. I know it's a horrible cliché — but there we are. I was working at a bank in London and got absolutely fed up with it.'

'A bank, you say?'

'Just a company that audits banks, actually. Terribly boring.'

'I see. What was the company called?'

'Deloitte.'

'Well, all you young people seem to be travelling these days. Sophal says she wants to travel as well. Travel where? I ask her. She has no idea. Anywhere as long as it's travel. I can't really understand it myself, but then I am not twenty-five any more. What is the point of travel just to travel? How old are you, if I may ask?'

'Twenty-eight.'

'A fine age, a fine age. A fine age for a man if you ask me.'

A fine age for anyone, Robert might have replied.

'At twenty eight,' Sar added, 'you can do whatever you want. Or you can nowadays. When I was twenty-eight it was rather a different matter. When I was thirty I was in the countryside being whipped.'

This seemed like an unpleasant topic so Robert steered the conversation away from it. He talked on about himself. Outside, the light visible through the windows dimmed a shade and Robert knew that the sunny part of the day was already over. He talked about England, life in London — tedium, monotony, grey skies, high taxes, the usual things that people living far away always like to hear about, as if they simultaneously both damaged and solidified the sterling image of Albion. He began to talk about his parents, but then stopped, thinking that he was overstepping the mark.

'No, no,' Sar objected, 'do go on.'

'My father worked in a bank as well and my mother wrote plays for the radio. They live in East Grinstead.'

'East Grinstead?'

A thin smile came to the old man's lips. He always seemed to know more than he immediately let on.

'Are they aware that you are running around the world?'

'They disapprove, if that's what you mean.'

'I would disapprove too if I were them.'

Robert decided to find this amusing.

'It's only for a short while. I wanted to see the world a bit.'

'Where are you living, by the way?'

'I found a place called Colonial Mansions. It's just round the corner.'

'I know it well. The American Embassy sets up many of its employees there. It's not terribly cheap, is it?'

Robert shrugged.

'It's all right. It's cheaper than East Grinstead.'

'Maybe you should come round for dinner at our house and meet everyone. Would you do that?'

'Certainly.'

'Not tonight, Sophal is out doing music. What about tomorrow then?'

'All right.'

Robert's voice wavered and he sensed some tensions coming to him from afar, like something clammy and malevolent carried over a body of still water.

'I'll have my wife ask the cook to make something Khmer. Do you like Khmer food?'

'Of course.'

'Some barangs won't eat it. They survive on steaks and milkshakes.'

Robert shook his head. 'I find that hard to believe. It's so delicious.'

'I'm glad you think so. You seem like you've been here a long time.'

'A few weeks. But it feels like a few days.'

'A few weeks already. You don't sound too sure.'

'Maybe I've lost track of time.'

Robert smiled but the doctor did not return the gesture.

He said, instead, 'That's what happens when you come here when you're young and you're not Khmer. It makes the time fly by. Everyone says so and I believe it.'

From the shadowed corners of the room the boys in the bow ties watched them with a wary aloofness that found its only expression in the permanently upturned corners of their mouths. There was a fixity about them, a muted beauty which made them, strangely, unapproachable. They stood there watching the Englishman in his odd clothes listening to the old Khmer doctor, whom they knew for his kindness and dottiness, and they reminded Robert of the children he taught in Elmer and who sometimes walked home with him across the railway bridge to his cottage at the edge of the woods. Their eyes moved as slowly as marbles rolling on a gradient which the eye could not detect and they spoke reluctantly only when they were spoken to, but there was thought and a subtle malice in their stoniness and gravity. It was a form of respect that does not shrink from quietly judging. The children were always curious about him and he was sure that they felt sorry for him: he was a forlorn figure to them. They could smell his loneliness and mediocrity, and in a perverse way it drew them to him. The doctor, for his part, could sense the same thing but it didn't draw him to Robert. It made him aware that there was an opportunity here.

'Maybe you'll stay a while, now that you are here,' he said affably. Their plates were covered with mustard-seeded blood. 'Do you not have a girlfriend back home – or something like that?'

'Not really, no.'

'That's a shame. Maybe you are living in the wrong place. It's always wise to live in the right place.'

'I guess it is at that.'

'What does your father say?'

'My father?'

'What does he say about you not having a girlfriend?'

'He doesn't say anything about it.'

'Does he not, indeed? Does he not?'

'Not at all.'

'That is rather strange. Maybe he is under the impression – '

'I'm an obscenity?'

The doctor roared with laughter and raised his fork.

Obscenity? Robert thought wildly. What did his father think he was? The doctor's insinuation was strange, but it was a provocation to sound him out about his sexuality. It was better to ignore it.

'Well, never mind, Robert. You are in our land now. You don't have to pretend to be anything you are not.'

'Pretend?'

'You know what I mean. You can let your hair down here.'

Again, the index finger was raised.

'Garçon, let's have some crème brûlées, by Buddha. Why not? Does anyone have anything against it? We'll grow fat for a day then deflate to normal size.'

The doctor now receded an inch or two from the edge of the table and took off his glasses and then wiped them with his starched napkin. He apologised for using the phrase 'by Buddha' which was entirely inappropriate and heretical, but he had taken to using it in the old days and he had stuck with it because he found it amusing. He discouraged his guest from doing the same.

'Tomorrow night, when you come – here's my card with the address – I'll give you crème brûlées again, it's our favourite dessert at home. I hope you won't be bored. We are rather quiet people who enjoy our evenings in our garden. We rarely go out or throw dinner parties.'

They drank green tea with the crème brûlées and Robert asked if Sophal would know why he was there when he came.

'We'll talk to her this afternoon. She's not terribly enthusiastic about English lessons, I'll admit, but she'll go along with it because it pleases her mother and she doesn't

97

have to do it fanatically. We are thinking something like an hour every day or so. Would you be able to do that?'

'An hour every day?'

'Well, I know it's a bit bold of me to suggest every day, but we'd be very grateful. It's honestly what she needs to do in order to improve.'

'I suppose I could.'

'You sound a bit doubtful. I understand. I'll be willing to make it worth your while. If you could do two hours, even more so.'

'Two hours?'

'Of course, I don't know how much time you have —'

'I have time,' Robert said. He held himself back from adding 'A lot of time'. How easy it was! They finished up their meal and walked through the Royal corridors to the Elephant Bar on the far side of the lobby, which was more crowded than the restaurant. There was a pool table there, the arches were painted with images of elephants and there was a case of fine cigars with a thermometer and little boxed posters of Jalisco and Gaulois.

They went to the bar and ordered Cosmopolitan Flights and the doctor paid again. One of the three shots that made up the Cosmopolitan was with black pepper; another with orange. The glasses were expertly iced and the little silver elephants around them seemed to be keeping an eye on Robert's hands. He noticed how short and curiously shaped the doctor was. Like a bowling pin. From where did his inexhaustible good humour come? But it was a humour that was like light playing on the surface of oily water. Peer into it and all you saw was rainbow oil and reflections that moved constantly.

The doctor sipped his over-coloured drink and his lips were sugared.

'It was pure luck, Robert, that you answered my ad. But do you really believe in luck?'

'I can't decide.'

'It seems like an impossible idea, doesn't it?'

'I've never experienced enormous good luck, to be honest. Just once or twice.'

'We all get lucky one time in our lives. And usually four or five times. I've had a stroke or two in the past. I should have been dead by now.'

Some pretty barang girls looked over at Robert with a detached curiosity. Here the whites always looked each other over at a distance, suddenly aware of something deep within them that never needed to come into expression.

'I am probably more superstitious than you,' Sar said. 'It's said that we are a superstitious people. But I think superstition is a biological trait in human beings.'

'Like being honest then.'

'Yes, and like murder. Murder seems to be really universal, doesn't it?'

Robert laughed, though keeping his voice down.

'You could say that, yeah.'

'I do say it. Surely your literature studies have proved that to you.'

'I see your point. But I try not to think about murder if I can help it.'

'Neither do I. I do think about superstition, however. I'm not convinced, in short, that all superstition is superstitious.'

'I'm only superstitious about ladders,' Robert said. 'I'll never walk under one.'

'You might get hit by a pot of paint.'

Sar was now carefully measuring the English boy.

His tone, the way he paced his sentences. He was not as obvious as he had at first appeared. There were thin, layered depths to him. There was something about him that was affected and forced. His accounts of himself were not quite true. But they were not sufficiently false for the doctor to dismiss him out of hand. He was playing a role, but Sar felt tolerant towards those who played a role. He had had to play many roles himself during the terrible years. It was survival, and the roles a man assumed in order to survive did not seem to him a capital offence. Robert (or Simon to him) had level and transparent eyes that gave the lie to some of the less trustworthy things coming out of his mouth. Should one trust the eyes then? His father had always told him that the eyes never lie.

He disguised his thoughts, however.

'Now let's drink to making Sophal speak perfect English in a matter of weeks.'

'Maybe she should meet me first,' Robert said.

'She'll like you well enough. I do.'

It was a promising start, and when they went out into the now-thunderous afternoon the doctor called a tuk-tuk for him, paid the driver upfront and said that they would expect him the following evening at eight.

'Don't bring anything, Simon. Just yourself.'

'I will and I won't.'

'The girls will be thrilled to meet you.'

Maybe they would be. The doctor had his own car and Robert rode in the tuk-tuk as far as the Paris then went up to his room and slept for an hour. The city was now sweltering and sunless but his mood was up. He had a good feeling about his prospects which only a few hours ago had seemed as dark and uncertain as could be. His luck had turned. Luck always turned. He slept as if drunk. Thunder in the afternoon. Rain swept in while he was unconscious, beating down the dust and the people slipping under the trees. At six in the evening the electricity went off in all the streets around Kampuchea Krom and the roads overflowed with caramel water. He opened his eyes and felt happy. A drifter always knows when he has drifted far enough from the system to feel the thrill of surviving against the odds. The flood when it came would see him float like one of those little paper boats that even children know how to make.

Nine

The deluge lasted all night and through the following day. It was hardly worth getting up and he spent most of the day in bed reading the *Herald Tribune* and drinking from a bottle of Royal Stag which he had bought on the street for a few dollars. He lay there naked with his clothes hung on wires to keep them clean and uncreased. The city, meanwhile, sank into a pre-modern gloom hour by hour, fragile and beautiful as it seemed to diminish into a lacework of newly created canals. When he went down to the lobby to buy some fried rice at the restaurant he saw the girls sitting glumly on the stairs with their iPhones, texting and chatting with nothing to do. The rooms were stifling. Yet the street was fresh with a menacing wind. The tuk-tuks still raced along them like boats, spewing dirty water on either side and the drivers laughing it off.

He took one, eventually. Robert leaned over and handed the driver Dr Sar's business card with the address printed on it, a numbered street off Norodom Boulevard, and the driver handed it back to him with a nod. Water roared against their doors as they set off in entirely the wrong direction, eventually coming to the Wat Phnom which was marooned in a virtual lake. The American Embassy was high and dry to one side and at the unsubmerged street corners people stood in plastic capes stoically waiting for Noah's flood to recede. They went past the self-generating lights of the Sunway Hotel and then crossed the little bridge by Street 106. Here by long park lawns and trees the sudden darkness was even stranger. On the bridge a few people also stood under beaten-down umbrellas paralysed by the sudden disappearance of light and the pools emerging within the lawns behind the Phsa Reatrey market. The power had still not come back on by the time they reached Norodom.

The usual illumination of that immense French street had been knocked out and the usual crowds had scattered with the downpour. They went down what was now a half-empty boulevard plunged in gloom, with restored villas and ruins alike behind high walls and sugar palms. The gardens suddenly more magnificent than the houses they served. They splashed through the corners where the traffic hesitated in the dark and careered to miss collisions. The people standing there had taken off their shoes and carried them in one hand. It was as if they didn't know what to do now with a lightless night. Tramp through it and hope for fun, soldier on and pray that nothing went wrong before first light? What did one do here when the lights went off and the streets became like this – hushed and ancient and the trees suddenly remarkable?

They crossed the traffic circle of the Monument. On its far side, Norodom continued. The streets became quieter, perceptibly more refined. At the corner of Street 334 they turned but only for a moment: the house occupied the entire corner. Behind cypresses and palms a dark yellow European house rose up with trims of white stucco. There was an ironwork gate with an electric bell, but none of the lights were on and it was hard to see anything clearly. The potential absurdity of the situation was suddenly obvious to Robert. It was possible that they had not been able to call him. He got out nevertheless and paid the driver and the man simply parked the tuk-tuk there on 334 and said he would wait for him. It was a narrow street darkened by spreading trees. Outside the villas of the affluent stood sentry boxes with all-night guards. The wall of the adjoining property a dark and somehow menacing red.

'There's no need to wait,' Robert said.

'No, I wait.'

'I don't want you to wait.'

'But I will wait. I wait here.' *What will you do if I do not wait?* his face said.

It was true.

Robert turned, walked up to the gate on Norodom and rang the bell, the cascade of water slithering down his back. He could see a loggia of some kind with potted palms, a lone chain lamp suspended above it. The garden hissed with cicadas. To his surprise the door opened and a maid stood there holding a candle in a glass cage in one hand. She was old but subtly elegant in that small circle of light and behind her he could see the shadowed, unlit house with candles flickering inside it.

'The power is off,' she said sweetly, 'but the doctor and his family are waiting for you inside. It's going to be a *candlelit* dinner.'

She led him up a brick path under takien trees and the closer they got to the house the brighter the candlelit windows seemed. As the door opened he heard music, a piano being played quite well, and the doctor's quick, rippling, girlish laughter. The Sars were sitting in their front room, among their Khmer antiques. At the far end of the room the piano was being played by their daughter. *Kinderszenen*, he was sure.

He tensed and then made a resolve to be suave and calm. To be Simon, in effect. The room was lit with dozens of tea-light candles and there was a table set for four with painted terracotta dishes and a decanter of red wine that looked as if it had stewed badly in the oppressive heat. The windows were open in the hope of catching wet breezes, but the air inside the room had come to a numbing standstill and he felt his hands burst with perspiration. The doctor got up and a tall, thin woman next to him did the same and as they rose together the alarming difference in height between them made itself known.

'Simon, so here you are! Allow me to introduce –'

The wife was younger, much younger. She had a peering, inquisitive face, half Chinese maybe, the eyes full of hope.

'My husband has been talking about you non-stop. Now the power is out.'

'Sit down, please,' the doctor cried. 'Sophal!'

They sat and the girl at the piano rotated on the stool, hesitated and then got up and walked over to the coffee table and the fabric sofas.

Mrs Sar asked Robert if he would like a glass of brandy.

'It's the best warm drink, isn't it?'

He accepted and the girl, small and willowy, alighted like some human-shaped moth on the padded arm of the sofa on which her parents sat.

'This is our daughter,' the doctor said. 'She knows all about why you are here.'

The family laughed, as if among themselves.

And in a moment the soft eyes of the girl were upon him, made even darker by the lack of electric light, made quietly bolder by this artificial privacy of candlelight. Her hair was immensely wavy for some reason and it reached down to her waist, its volume exaggerated by shadows. The hands folded on her lap, the feet unshod and loose in her own home. She had an effortless confidence in the hearth of her father. He couldn't see any trace of the illness to which her father had referred, her hands rested perfectly still, the eyes were also as still as magnetic needles pointing north. She was dressed in cut-off jeans and a white T-shirt with the image of a Burmese pop star — Chit Snow Oo.

'Did you get a tuk-tuk here in the rain?' she asked in perfect English.

'I managed all right. I think the guy is waiting outside for me.'

'Shall we tell the maid to get rid of him?' the doctor asked, obviously amused.

'No, keep him,' his wife objected. 'It's going to rain all night and we'll never find someone else.'

'So be it,' from the doctor. 'Now, shall we have some home-made prawn crackers?'

Sophal turned to Robert more fully, perhaps as a matter of politeness. Robert had the sense, already, that she was playing a game with her father.

'Daddy says you are living in Colonial Mansions. Are you?'

'Yes, I took a small unit.'

'I think they changed the name to Central Mansions. New owners from Hong Kong. I have some friends in there, maybe you know them. Mary O'Neil at the Embassy?'

'No, I haven't met anyone yet.'

She smiled archly. 'Oh, you're too busy, just like her. Maybe you'll run into her.'

'I might, yes.'

'I love the pools there.'

'You know it then?'

'I know it very well. I sometimes go in pretending to be a guest and use the pools. No one's ever stopped me.'

Her English was indeed quite perfect — it was too awkward to bring the matter up, but how was he going to improve it?

It was baffling.

'I wonder how much you're paying,' she went on. 'The city is getting so expensive for barangs. Do you find it expensive?'

'It's all right for me.'

'They say it's more expensive than Bangkok now. For the real luxury.'

'It's Asia rising,' the doctor said with firm jollity. 'The Chinese are pouring their money in here. Not that we're rich yet. But they are.'

'People say,' the daughter continued, 'that barangs are also pouring into Asia looking for jobs these days. Do you think that's true?'

'I don't know,' Robert said. 'It might be.'

The maid now brought in dishes and set them on the dining table.

'One can see the way the wind is blowing,' her father said. 'For our generation it's a remarkable thing to witness. All we knew was poverty.'

'It's true,' said Mrs Sar.

'Everyone in the army's rich,' the girl laughed.

Robert upended the brandy glass. He would go along

with this. There was money in it. The house was obviously an old French mansion. Teak floorboards from the old days, high windows and airy rooms. The doctor had filled it with antiques. With the rain sliding in sheets down the windows and with the candlelight it was cave-like and yet charming. The small family seemed almost lost inside it, like dolls in a doll's house, but the doctor had put his medical certificates on display on a mantelpiece and the two servants were not deferential.

Before long, the doctor rose and they rose with him and they went to sit at the table where a French dinner had been laid out.

'Chicken Dijon!' he said mysteriously.

The doctor chattered with his anecdotes of the Khmer Rouge years, during which time, as a very young doctor, he had been posted to a small town near the Thai border.

'They asked us to do terrible things, Simon, but you would hardly believe me if I told you what they were. It was like life on a different planet.'

'You've been to the genocide museums?' his wife asked.

Robert shrugged, and he said that he hadn't wanted to go since everyone did.

'But they're our biggest tourist attractions,' Sophal said. 'Don't you find that cheerful and exotic?'

'That's why I didn't go. It's so tiresome, all that.'

'I quite agree,' the doctor said. 'It was all right for twenty years and then, suddenly, one gets tired of being an atrocity circus. You should go once, however. I am sure Sophal will take you if you want to.'

'Daddy, that's a terrible idea.'

'You can discuss it between yourselves. Meanwhile, do you like our Chicken Dijon? Don't look so surprised. It's a dish I invented myself. It has a secret ingredient –

entirely French, you see, but for a single component from the *Cambodian forest.*'

'He's always inventing dishes,' Mrs Sar put in. 'I can't stop him. If it's disgusting please don't eat it. We have plenty of bread.'

It was strange-tasting but Robert soldiered on, mumbling a few compliments to its inventor. Sophal, however, wanted to know about him. He had expected this all along and had prepared his speech carefully in advance. His invention now flowed thicker and faster than the one he had offered to Dr Sar the previous day. He depicted his new imaginary parents, a disgruntled stockbroker father and a mother who wrote radio plays, giving them appearances that roughly matched the real ones but also giving them backgrounds that were vaguely upper class. He borrowed traits from his real parents to keep it realistic and then went off into elaborate riffs which he knew were really inventions based on what he thought Simon's parents were like. But how strange it was that he should even have a conception of what Simon's parents were like. He described detestable garden parties and weekends in Istanbul and clubs in London that he had no idea about. He said that his father was a member of White's, because he had read about White's in a novel and it sounded appropriate. On it rolled, musical and rushed.

'White's?' the doctor exclaimed to his wife. 'He says there's a club called White's.'

'Is there a Black's?' she asked innocently.

Soon he realised that as he talked he was holding his knife in his right hand with a clenched fist. He quietly put it down and told a silly joke.

'Your father,' Sophal said, 'is he one of those typical English guys?'

'He used to wear a bowler hat on the train, if that's what you mean.'

'I love that idea,' she laughed.

'What school did you go to?' the doctor suddenly asked.

Robert didn't have to think, he simply plucked from memory the name of a random village in Sussex.

'Chalvington,' he said. 'It's a small school – no one's ever heard of it.'

He had made the calculated risk that Sar would not look it up online later that night.

'Did you board there?'

'No, I lived at home. My mother said she'd never allow me to board.'

Chalvington with Ripe – it was where Malcolm Lowry died of alcoholism.

The doctor listened patiently and something told Robert that he didn't believe it. He didn't believe Robert, but he also didn't care.

When the chicken was finished they went back to the sofas and the maid brought the candles over. The doctor said that it was an unusually long power outage and that normally they only lasted two or three hours at most. Yet they did seem to be getting worse. It was the rain that triggered them. The city flooded easily and the generators went out. In his youth, however, they had got used to doing without electricity. He and his wife didn't mind it, they liked the return of heat, starlight and nature. They secretly preferred it. One would have thought, however, that with the advances of technology and the huge increase in the country's wealth – well, it was exasperating. He told Robert that he ran an exclusive private clinic for patients with psychological problems. Such problems were on the rise these days and doctors were at a loss to know why. The recent protests in the capital against Hun Sen had contributed, perhaps; dozens of people had been shot dead. There was a curious ripple effect from such things.

The maid then brought in coffee and some rice-ball desserts not unlike the Thai *boua loy* Robert had eaten in Bangkok. Sophal next to him on the sofa with her legs crossed and their arms rubbed against each other as they used their spoons. It felt like centuries since he had felt anyone close to him. He could smell the rose talc under her T-shirt now turning faintly sour with the heat. Her father suggested they set up a time for an inaugural lesson and she said, 'Well, I can come to Colonial Mansions the day after tomorrow if you like.'

'How about it?' the doctor said.

'If you like,' Robert replied, but now he had to think fast. 'On the other hand,' he suggested, 'we could just meet in town. You can take me somewhere.'

'All right,' she said slowly. 'I can take you somewhere.'

The doctor and his wife exchanged a clearly delighted look.

'You two will figure it out,' Dr Sar said with finality. 'What about a Vietnamese lunch?'

'I'll come and pick you up at the Mansions,' Sophal decided. 'We can just stay in the lobby there if it's convenient.'

'I'm not sure what I'm going to teach you,' Robert said. 'Your English seems perfect as it is.'

'I need to practise – don't we all?'

'If you say so.'

'She gets her future tenses mixed up,' the wife said. 'And her past tenses too.'

Robert put down his dish, looked at his watch and said,

'Maybe I'd better be going. That driver has been waiting outside for two hours.'

'So he has,' the doctor said, and put his dish down as well. 'Sophal, give Simon your phone number and you two are all set.'

The girl, in fact, walked him down to the outer gate in the rain. She seemed nonchalant about the lessons and said that all she wanted was some fun conversation, which her family was prepared to pay for. She saw no reason to pass it up.

'By the way,' she said, 'my father said to give you this. He didn't want to give it to you himself. He's quite shy about things like this.'

It was an envelope, and it obviously contained money in cash, and she pushed it gently into his hand and shook her head as if to say, 'Don't worry about it, it's normal – he likes you.'

He took it and there was no awkwardness at all.

'He needn't have,' he muttered and quietly gauged the amount inside.

'Tomorrow I can't,' she said as the gate came open, and they saw the driver sprawled inside his tuk-tuk, his bare feet balanced on the metal rail. 'The day after, Colonial Mansions. About two is OK, isn't it?'

'Yeah, that's fine with me.'

'Goodbye then, Mr Beauchamp. I forgot to tell you what a weird name that is – but I've heard it before somewhere. I can't remember where.'

'It's not a common name.'

'Is it an American name too?'

'I don't know. Maybe it is.'

She shook his hand, and there was a subtle mockery in her look.

He said, 'Bonne nuit,' and went down to the tuk-tuk, whose driver had stirred. She waited by the gate and the driver peered out and then looked up at the rain. He saw that the electricity had not come back on.

'It's going to be dark night,' Sophal called down to him. 'I'd go straight home if I were you, Mr Beauchamp.'

'I'll do that.'

'Bonne nuit yourself.'

And as the tuk-tuk pulled away she smiled and the gate closed and the driver shot him a knowing look. Robert asked him to drive to Street 102 and he slumped into the back seat and held the rails tight. The evening had been a success, but he couldn't really say why that success had happened.

They went down Norodom again and the lights came back on. He opened the envelope and looked inside, feeling slightly guilty that he had taken the unexpected gift without more of a protest. It was five hundred dollars which he had done nothing to earn and which the doctor had given him as an encouragement. Or else as some obscure gesture which could not be reciprocated. Five hundred. It was the windfall that changed the situation. It made no sense at all but, as he now thought, the lucky have great timing and he knew that he wouldn't think about it again.

He pocketed the bills and threw away the envelope. At Colonial Mansions, which was his destination, he found the boys scooping up the water that now formed a moat around the buildings and the night manager standing in a black suit with an opened umbrella. Robert jumped over the moat and went into the ice-cold lobby where the air conditioning seemed to have been on the whole time.

The manager came to the reception desk with him and Robert asked him if he had any units he could rent him starting from the following day.

It took a while to find a smaller unit on the first floor that Robert could rent by the day or by the week, as he pleased. It was furnished and it was discounted because it had an obscured view and little natural light.

'All right,' Robert said, and laid down a hundred to hold it. 'I'll take it from tomorrow afternoon. Does it have a table?'

'A table, four chairs and a sofa. And a king-sized bed.'

'Kitchen stuff?'

'All equipped. It's a one-bed apartment.'

It was perfect.

Robert thought for a moment about whether he should see it first but then he let it go: if it was unacceptable he didn't much care.

The manager gave him a receipt then took him around the ground floor to show him the facilities. There were two wings to the property, one with the handsome old pool and one with a sleek new pool. Both were lit from below and the rain puckered their surfaces.

'Most of our guests are long-term residents,' the manager said. 'They work at the Embassy next door or with the Korean construction company up on the boulevard. It's very quiet.'

'I was looking for a quiet place. I'm having good luck today.'

'We are getting more Chinese now.' The manager lowered his voice. 'They like to swim late at night.'

At the centre of the old pool was a woman's head patiently making its way along its length, beaten by the rain but calm-looking, the hair trussed up above it. A strangely nightmarish sight, with the goggles and the rhythmically gasping mouth.

Robert stood just out of range of the rain dripping from the eaves and looked up at the balconies stacked on top of each other with their foliage and waxy flowers. The French windows darkened and yet open here and there, the resumed glare of the city glowing against low-hanging clouds. Every step of the way things had been laid out for him, from the very moment he stepped across the border. It was neither good luck nor bad, just luck in itself. Phnom Penh was a city that encouraged such things. He could see the tight discretion which had come over the manager's inscrutable face as they turned and walked back into the lobby, upon whose walls old photographs of colonial Indochina made an unnecessary case for a difficult romanticism. Robert told him that he would be around after lunch the following day.

'You can try it for a week and see if you like it,' the manager said gallantly.

'I don't think I won't like it.'

He went back out onto Street 102 and he saw at once glimmers of welding torches high up within the skeleton of the half-built skyscraper rising on the far side of the street. The Hangul characters burned into the plastic sheets that covered the building, undulating slightly as the elements tormented them. So they didn't stop work even for a storm or a blackout. They found a way to keep slaving for their masters.

The same driver was waiting for Robert and the tuk-tuk wheeled around in the great scummy pool that still divided the hotel from the rest of the street. Seeing which, the staff had a low laugh as they lay on the hoods of the cars parked under the trees. It was not a difficult laugh to understand. There was a magisterial tolerance and indifference in it, as well as centuries of clandestine observation. As Robert clambered into the tuk-tuk, moreover, the driver turned with exactly the same laugh and said, with an iron evenness, 'Boum boum, mistah?'

Ten

He arrived back there earlier than he had predicted and on that now dry street swarms of dragonflies played around the clumps of weeds and the still-damp datura. Like the day itself, the hotel seemed completely different. The ground-floor restaurant was serving its bistro lunch and the old pool was filled with paunchy white people who appeared to be on some kind of antagonistic holiday. His room was not yet ready and he sat by the pool windows and ordered a steak and fries with a glass of Coke and kept his shades on because he had slept badly and his eyes were fragile.

The men out in the pool all had shaved heads, the concentration camp look, with tattoos hard-edged on painfully white skin. The girls were immensely fat and arrogant and loud, and carrying much the same tattoos though on different parts of their bodies. They disported themselves through those blue waves like elephant seals, and the Asians coolly dressed at the restaurant in their pressed white shirts and cufflinks looked at them with a kind of despairing amazement and a quiet certainty that the economic decline of these beasts was somehow legible in the obscure codes of their tattoos and the weight of their belly fat. They were no longer the lean aggressors and masters of yesteryear. Robert felt the same way.

He ate his steak slowly then ordered a tarte tatin and a double espresso since he no longer had to worry about money, at least for a few days. The day manager then came to his table and said that his room was now ready, and left the key politely on the table. She asked him if he had any luggage and he shook his head and said something about having his things brought on from somewhere else. She nodded and wished him a pleasant stay then turned as she was about to move off and asked him how long he was going to stay. He said he hadn't decided but at least a week. Afterwards he would see. It was all that needed to be said.

While he enjoyed his coffee, he called a few more of the numbers he had taken from the Language Tuition site and set up some more private lessons as best he could. There was a Khmer lawyer who offered him a few hours a week and a female musician who needed English to write songs. It didn't seem that difficult to make a few bucks doing this sort of thing and he calculated that with five or six clients combined with the generous Dr Sar he could do quite well for himself.

All it needed was time and patience and application. He already knew how to teach, it was second nature to him. It was a city where people didn't ask many questions, certainly not as many as Dr Sar had asked.

He would not need to repeat his performance of the previous evening. He could sense that it was like a giant wall of coral through which thousands of mutually ignorant fish swarmed night and day going about their secrets and evasions. There was no surveillance here, very little police presence and almost no puritanical curiosity or disapproval. The Khmers, thankfully, didn't seem to be driven by a tormenting and malicious need to know everything about their curious visitors, the barangs whom they found faintly ridiculous but undeniably lucrative. The core occidental principles of nosiness and constant outrage were not their thing. They simply went about their lives without mentally harassing everything and everyone around them. They lived in their coral and tormented each other in different ways, no doubt, but their history had at least taught them the terror of destroying privacy and individuality. With Westerners, it was going in exactly the opposite direction. In the body language of the human seals, with its lack of discretion and tact, you could see the retreat of privacy and the individual. It was curious.

He went up to his room unnoticed. On the landings he paused and glanced down the tiled corridors at the rows of doors and the garden tables on the balconies where the more discreet Chinese girls liked to sunbathe with their books. It was like a hotel where people spent their whole lives instead of a few days. The unit was right under the roof and there was a smell of disuse about it. He went in, turned on the A/C and the single fan and waited for the two rooms to cool down. It was obvious no one had occupied it in weeks. Why then had he waited for it to be readied? While the place cooled he wandered up to the roof. There was a jacuzzi there and a small ornamental garden. It looked over a good portion of the city, including the nearby fortified American Embassy. The scraps of park burning in the afternoon heat with their piles of scattered refuse, the radio towers and the Hangul characters of the skyscraper where the welders were still hard at work. A single white girl lay on a sunbed under the little frangipanis, her face covered and oblivious to his presence. It was a genial hideout for him. He went back to his room, locked the door and unpacked a bag of groceries which he had bought earlier in the morning at the Sorya Mall.

Cartons of lychee juice, shampoo, soap, paper towels and both razors and a pair of scissors. He had also bought some cheap local hair dye in a dark blond colour. He showered and then dried off and began to cut his hair carefully with the scissors. He cut his fringe straight and then shortened the hair around his ears. He mixed the two elements of the dye in the washbasin and applied the emulsion with a toothbrush to the top of his hair, making streaks which he toned down by rubbing them at once with a towel. He went back into the shower, washed off and waited for the hair to dry. It came out a dull blond-brown which was what he wanted. A gradual, barely noticeable change. Then he clipped his eyebrows.

He looked again at the label on the back of the shirt Simon had given him and he saw, as before, that it was a place called Vong with the street number. Street 200. It should be easy to find.

At five he left the Mansions and walked across Kossamak and the Freedom Park towards the street market at the far end. He walked in the direction of the river and then turned south onto the Quay. He had decided to spend thirty dollars on two new shirts and when he was abreast of the hustle-bustle streets behind the river he turned into 130 and wandered aimlessly until he was on Street 19. Here he caught a motodop and told him to go to Street 200. It was a quiet street with little to recommend it. There was a row of cream-coloured shophouses with metal grilles and above them balconies with plants. He quickly spotted the sign for Vong that he was looking for. It was next to another tailor called Beary. He had not stopped to think why he was going to the place where Simon had gone. It was more a dark curiosity than a rational move. He went in, and a Viet man of about seventy rose from a newspaper, a glass of tea and a pipe. There was, of course, no recognition in his eyes but neither was there any surprise. Robert simply said, 'Are you Vong?' and the man said that he was. There were Vietnamese calendars all over the walls and a blood-red Buddha in the corner with electric candles. Bales of cloth stood in the shadows with coloured pins stuck into them.

'A friend recommended you to me,' Robert said, and he closed the door behind him.

The old man was in a collarless Viet shirt with a tape measure draped around his neck. A bamboo cloche hat hung on the wall behind him and there were paper chits all over the counter, seemingly in disorder. Vong asked him who his friend was.

'An American – I met him here.'

'I have a lot of Americans I make shirts for.'

'Well, I'd like a replica of this one – can you do it by tomorrow?'

Vong touched his mouth with his thumb and there was a sly irony in the air.

He said, 'If you leave it here.'

'Well, I can't leave it here.'

'All right, I will measure you up now.'

'Can you make it from linen like this one?'

'I got it.'

'If you measure me up can you do it by tomorrow?'

'I can do by 3 p.m.'

'Make it twelve and I'll give you two bucks extra.'

'You're in a hurry.'

'Yeah, I'm in a hurry.'

'What's the hurry?'

'What does it matter to you?'

'A man in a hurry —'

'I lost my other shirts,' Robert blurted out.

'Lost them?'

'Yeah, I lost them. A drinking party.'

Vong laughed. 'You jumped in the river?'

'Yeah, I jumped in the river. Can you do it?'

The tailor said he could and stepped out from behind the counter with the tape already extended.

'All right, good,' Robert said, and he felt, suddenly, the sweat pouring down his face and into his neck.

He held out his arms and Vong measured him.

'You're not NGO,' the affable Vong bantered. 'NGO don't jump in the river and lose their shirts.'

'Sure they do.'

'But you're not NGO. I wonder who your friend was. I might remember him.'

'His name was Simon. Tall and blond.'

Vong continued measuring, a pin between his lips. When he removed it, he said, 'Don't remember that one.'

'Never mind, I was just curious.'

'I make a hundred shirts a week.'

When the measurements were done they looked over the available linens. Robert picked out a pale green and a sand colour. They came with mother-of-pearl buttons and trimmings. He went for soft collars and three buttons on the cuffs to make them look a little dressier.

The tailor stepped back and looked at the shirt he was wearing.

'One of mine,' he said immediately.

'I didn't say it was one of yours.'

'I know my own shirts when I see them.'

'It was a gift.'

'From your friend?'

Robert realised now that he had made a mistake.

'Never mind. Shall I pay you upfront?'

'That's the way usually.'

Out came the thirty dollars.

'Thank you,' Vong said. 'What about trousers?'

'I'm all right for trousers.'

'Your trousers look a bit beaten in. But they're mine too.'

'Excuse me?'

'They're my trousers too. No way I wouldn't recognise my own trousers.'

Robert looked down helplessly at the trousers, which were indeed looking a bit beaten in.

'Maybe they are,' he stammered.

'Lose those too?'

'It's a long story.'

'You seem to like Mr Vong's clothes!'

The tailor wasn't really curious, he was more amused, and that kind of amusement could be brushed aside if Robert held his nerve and laughed along.

'But I like them so much I decided to get some more.'

'Good, good! So how about some trousers?'

Blackmail, then, Robert thought.

'All right, I'll get one pair. Just like these.'

Vong measured him again and they picked out the very same material.

'They'll look nice,' he said affably. 'Twenty-five for you.'

It was more than Robert had wanted to spend but he had to let it go. His irritation burst out, however.

'Have those ready tomorrow as well. You may as well.'

'Yes, sir.'

Vong rolled up his tape.

Robert paid the extra twenty-five and Vong wrote him out a ticket for the three items.

'You want to have many Vong clothes,' he said. 'Don't be one of those barangs who look like homeless people.'

'I'll try.'

'Everything will be ready tomorrow at noon. Is your friend Simon in town?'

They were at the door now and Vong had opened it and his body had moved into a small bow.

'I don't know — why do you ask?'

'So you can tell him to come by and get some more shirts, of course.'

'I'll tell him if I run into him.'

And then Robert's curiosity returned and he asked Vong once again if he remembered the tall, blond American's face.

'Not at all,' the tailor said. 'But I might remember it by tomorrow. I might.'

'I hope you do,' Robert said.

His voice was dry and slightly hostile but he couldn't help it. He felt victimised and he wanted to know where his predator was.

That night he went to Street 136 and ate on the outdoor terrace of a place called Okuncha. Salmon tartare salad and a cold Angkor. Sitting there he looked up at the first-floor balcony of a place called Candy Bar opposite, and the girls under the propeller fans looked down at him and smiled and cocked their heads like spaniels. What an easy life it was. Just moments randomly pieced together. Then he walked over to the Sorya and played pool by himself among the open-air bars. The rain swept in at about nine. For a long time he sat brooding close to the street and the puddles and the drunks with umbrellas and the white college boys dumbfounded by the easy sex and the way the middle-aged men didn't move on their perches for hours. The bars were playing Psy that night and girls danced around the tables with quiet, spinning motions that were footsure and elegant and distant. He thought about Vong. It had clearly been a mistake to get involved with him and he cursed himself for his stupidity. Tailors are always shrewd. They are observers of men. Robert had bought some postcards in the supermarket and now he wrote one to his parents and one to Yula. He wrote that he was having a good time and that nothing was out of the ordinary. The phrases were trite and typical of the things he wrote home. It might be the last thing he wrote to them in a long time, and he wondered if he could rise above the clichés he had scribbled. But the less dramatic he was, the less they would feel suspicious or become alarmed. His parents would shrug and criticise his irresponsibility, but Yula was the tricky one. She would pore over every word for hidden meanings. She was already suspicious, he could sense it even from a distance of five thousand miles. They had no commitment to each other now, but she would be hurt by his silence.

He wondered if he should send either postcard after all. He finished them anyway, then put them in his pocket and thought it over. Perhaps not, then. Disappearance ought to be an event that is thought through carefully. One ought to take it seriously. It couldn't be undone flippantly, and in any case he didn't want to undo it. Surely she had known how miserable he had been when she knew him. It wasn't her fault, but then it wasn't his either, and in his mind it was only a temporary situation. He might be gone for a year, or two, or three, and then he would see.

He lit a bitter Alain Delon and got a one-dollar rum and Coke. Things disappeared in any case for different reasons. One day, not long ago, he had given to his class of thirteen-year-olds a copy of the famous daguerreotype of the Boulevard du Temple in Paris taken in the year 1839. He asked them to write an essay on the theme 'Why is the street in this photograph empty?' It was the kind of thing they relished. But none of them got the right answer. The street was not empty because in those days there were very few vehicles and very few people and very few pigeons. Paris in 1839 was not empty. One could clearly see the awnings of busy shops and cafe. It was just that the exposure time had been about ten minutes, and thus nothing moving within that window of time had left a trace for the ages. There was just the ghostly silhouette of an unknown man having his boots polished by another man, at the corner of the cobbled Boulevard du Temple. It took more than ten minutes to shine a pair of boots in those days and he told them that he often wondered who that man was — the Frenchman with the thin, manly leg raised upon a shoe polisher's stool.

Eleven

Sophal arrived early for her lesson, while Robert was still at Vong collecting his clothes. She went into the busy lunchtime restaurant and sat at a table and ordered a coffee and then asked the boys to go up and alert Mr Beauchamp. 'He's out,' they said at once, and she nodded quietly and resigned herself to a salad. She was early, it was true, but it was still a little odd. She looked out at the brilliant pool and the dark-skinned boys with nets skimming its surface. Her mind soon emptied and grew out of its irritation. She had spent the morning being interviewed at a clinic and she felt she had done well, but in the end it was of no interest. There was a futility about trying for such things. In the back of her mind she had a growing sense that her efforts were going to yield nothing down the line. Even in the last few weeks the future – the feeling of the future – had become foreshortened. It had narrowed and dimmed, just a little but enough to make her anxious. A suffocation had come upon her. What if she had no future at all?

She had been in Paris for a year and now Phnom Penh felt alien and small. Just as once there had seemed no way out if it, now there seemed no way into it. Even her command of Khmer had weakened a little — it was strange how that happened, as if the brain could handle two languages at a time, but never three. All her friends had what they called 'language partners', those fairly well-to-do foreigners who liked to spend a few hours a week with a pretty girl pretending to hone their English skills. It was usually their fathers who went out and found them — it was more seemly that way. She thought of herself as too old for these kinds of childish games, but sometimes there was nothing for it, one had to play by the local rules. Why care too much?

She impaled the cherry tomatoes lazily on her fork and wondered about Simon Beauchamp. He was good-looking all right. Young and nicely aloof and undesperate. He had been quite a surprise when he appeared the other night since, she idly supposed, she had been expecting a goofy desperado in shorts and flip-flops. When he walked in in his nice linens and his clean-shaven cheeks she had been pleasantly surprised. So what was he doing in Phnom Penh? she had wondered even as she was turning away from the piano and getting a good look at him. He was not an English teacher, for one thing. And nor was his name Simon: she felt it in her bones.

His eyes were spacious and pretty and you could open their doors and enter on light feet. A man of wide-open portals, but what was he expecting? A man didn't float around a foreign city for no reason whatsoever, not at the age of twenty-eight. A Khmer boy would never do that unless he was working at a large company in Germany or the United States. Yet there was no aura of leisure about Mr Beauchamp. He was far from being a pathless wanderer. He bustled and bristled and his eyes were quiet and malicious.

He was a bit Heathcliff, wasn't he?

She smiled and wondered if she should have a drink. Her hands were itching to do it, to rise and click the fingers and say 'Drink!'

But she waited. There might be someone there she knew, but there wasn't. She continued thinking about Simon. She was a little tired of men, in reality, because one could only go through the process a given number of times and suddenly one came to the realisation that the repetitions were not only dull but toxic. And her parents were so desperate for her to get married and worse. She was almost twenty-six and, to their eyes, the danger zone was approaching.

For her part, she felt no such thing. All she felt was fatalistic curiosity and a desire to return to the outside world. Maybe even London, given how affluent his family seemed to be. It was a sin to think like that – and stupid, too – but it crossed her mind anyway as she finished her salad and ordered a gin and tonic out of boredom. It came with a sprig of mint and a pile of ice.

Her father would be shocked but she drank them quite a lot these days. They went down well in the hour before lunch, the black hour before consciousness arose. She had given up rising early like her parents. Now, with nothing to do but study and wait, she could get up when she wanted and go to bed when she wanted. It was contemptible but she wasn't yet twenty-six and she had her excuses. Everyone knew the future would be different.

Meanwhile, as she was sipping her freezing gin and tonic, Robert was watching Vong folding his clothes and looking at the clock on the wall. He would be back just in time.

'Now I think about it,' the tailor was saying with his back turned to him, 'I remember your friend Mr Simon. He came in six months ago to get some shirts. My assistant said he was the most dashing man in Phnom Penh. I don't know why I forgot him. He is an antiques dealer, isn't he?'

'I never ask him about his work,' Robert said.

'I think he said he was an antiques dealer. I might have his card somewhere. These ones will fit you better than the ones you are wearing. It's always a problem wearing another man's clothes.'

'It certainly is. Did Mr Simon say where he was living these days?'

'Not a word. You'd know that better than me. I just remember his shoes – he was wearing a remarkable pair of shoes.'

'Oh?'

'I thought he must be a man of taste.'

Vong turned with the package neatly tied up and handed it to him. There was nothing more to say between them and Robert let the awkward conversation die where it was. He went out hurriedly and rode back to Colonial Mansions on a motodop.

When he came through the lobby he immediately saw Sophal sitting alone by the window and it was too late to go up and change into his new clothes. It was too bad but he had to make the best of it. He came up to her table and she was sucking on a straw inserted into a gigantic gin and tonic and her eyes had gone askew. But he was not late at all. He apologised anyway and held up the tailor's bag and sat down opposite her and asked her if that was indeed a gin and tonic.

'It's the real thing,' she said.

'Then I'll have one too.'

When it came he touched her glass with his and they agreed that their English lesson had got off to a flying start, by Buddha.

'I don't expect you to give me an English lesson,' she said. 'I've been speaking it since I was five. I thought – I thought I'd show you around the city a bit since my father is paying you anyway. So who cares. He's not going to know.'

'You know, I used to be a teacher,' Robert said slowly. 'It wouldn't be any sweat for me. I know how to do it.'

'Yes, but it's a bore anyway. I just thought – I don't know, I thought you might be interesting. In some way.'

'Interesting?'

'A foreigner is always interesting. Even if he isn't.'

'But I'm not interesting.'

'It's not for you to say though. Were you really a teacher?'

'Yes.'

'Really?'

'Why?'

'You don't seem like a teacher.'

She ate the mint sprig and looked at him calmly.

He said, 'It's not the first time someone has said that. I think I have teacher written all over me.'

'No, you don't. You look like something else. I don't know what. A cattle rustler.'

'Oh?' He laughed, but she didn't.

'Something like that,' she said. 'Something slippery.'

'I'm not slippery,' he snorted. 'I wish I were.'

'You're slippery enough. My father doesn't think so though.'

'Your father is a good judge of character.'

'He's anything but that. But I look out for him. Shall we go for lunch somewhere else? I have a feeling someone I know is going to walk in and I don't want them to.'

'You said you'd show me around.'

'Let's go to Street 136 and eat some *pho*. Then I'll take you somewhere else.'

'Let's.'

'It'll be stinking hot.'

'I don't mind.'

Robert was pleased to be out of Colonial Mansions. He made to pay for her salad and drink but she had already settled up. He left his bag at the reception and they went out into the cloying heat and took one of the tuk-tuks that were always loitering along 102. They sat side by side and rattled without words into the maze of streets which shone in a dour, metallic sunlight. Sophal now assumed a cool, tensile posture as if she were in public and this required a different composure. She looked straight ahead with her neck poised and upright and her eyes did not stray to either side. High above the city, however, the same-looking atomic cloud that seemed to appear there every day was moving with its silent fatalism towards the sky's apex where the sun monopolised all the light. Its edges were frilled like the coat of some unimaginable sea creature. There the mass of cloud turned suddenly brilliant and hysterical. It's moving, he thought idly, watching from under the tuk-tuk's shade, moving like a predator towards our light.

They came to 136 and 13 and a place called the Cafe de Coral. It was a Viet place with cheap outdoor tables opposite a Smile supermarket. The little area had an alarming concentration of dentists, with molar-shaped signs dangling above the mayhem with happy faces painted on them. They sat outside just at the edge of the fans' refreshment and ordered iced water. When it came she loosened up and took off her straw-brimmed hat and laid it on the chair next to hers.

'Is this the kind of place you like?' she asked.

'I love this kind of place.'

'I come here all the time by myself. Do you know *bau* buns?' He shook his head. 'Then we'll try *bau* buns. You'll like them.'

It was the hour for *bau* steamed buns and 'purple kelp roll' and 'turquoise herbal pudding' downed with 'salt lemon water'. She added twist rolls and mini cage buns and then iced Vietnamese coffee with the filters resting on the glasses. The sun went out as they sipped coffee and she talked about her year in Paris, because he had asked her to. At the junction the traffic began to thin and a few raindrops hit the dust and speckled it. She ate her buns with her fingers and when she looked up her eyes were obscure and resilient, giving away nothing.

'I even had a boyfriend there, a French stockbroker. The stockbrokers love Khmer girls. He told me that. He used to take me on holiday to Morocco and Rome and all that. I never told my parents.'

'You're telling me.'

'I told my friends so why not you? You're not going to report me. It's a private matter anyway – we don't tell our parents everything these days. We keep it to ourselves. Claude still writes to me.'

'What does he say?'

'He says he loves me and can we go on holiday to Marrakesh again.'

'And you don't go.'

'Of course I don't go. *C'est fini.* He's not going to come and live here. If he's not going to come and live here it's out of the question.'

'You could go back and live in Paris.'

'No, like I said — when something's finished, it's finished. For me it's finished. I want to live near my parents. I want to live in my own country.'

'Unlike me, then.'

She smiled. 'It's a different circumstance. Are you close to your parents?'

'Not at all.'

'So there you are. Girlfriend?'

'*C'est fini.*'

'You've made a new start.'

'Yes, you could say that. I guess I have . . .'

'My father says one has to do that from time to time. Do you smoke?'

He took out a packet of the inevitable Alain Delons and she laughed.

'You're smoking those?'

'I got into the habit.'

'You'll be dead within a month.'

'I doubt it. They agree with me.'

'You're a strange one, Mr Beauchamp. My father says you're getting over a broken heart.'

'It's not the case. I wish it was.'

'I don't think it's the case either. I think you're just kicking your heels.'

'All right,' he drawled, 'you got me there. I *am* kicking my heels. It's not a crime.'

'I didn't say it was a crime. It's better to do it somewhere hot and cheap. Do you like the girls here?'

'I haven't got to them yet.'

She pulled out her own cigarettes, a Thai brand called Wonder.

'These aren't much better,' she said. 'But they taste good with Vietnamese coffee.'

He took one and they shared the smoke.

'If this was an American movie,' she said, 'we'd be censored. We'd be erased.' She mixed in four spoonfuls of sugar into her coffee and gave him a smile which had maybe been enhanced on that same street.

He said, 'Yeah, whatever. I find I'm smoking more now.'

'My father says it'll make me older by ten years by the time I'm twenty-eight. I'll give it up then.'

'You should give it up now.'

'I certainly won't.'

The afternoon began to wear down. Egg sellers on their bikes moved down 136 with their loudspeakers; the molar signs began to glow. One could feel the rain coming, the tingle on the tongue.

Sophal looked through him, but it was not coldly. She was merely curious about him. She had met men like him before in Europe, the subtly vibrating ones that have an uneasy distraction about them. The ones who are polite and impeccable and who never tread on your toes. They usually came from a little money and had been to good schools, but they were not happy or festive — it was not enough for them. They were brooding, internal men living in their world of ease and frost and corduroy and she found them attractive and chilling at the same time. The bright light here exposed them in some way. They became happier and more ghostlike at the same time. Some of them married local women and settled down and managed bad restaurants; others drifted about. One didn't know what to say about them. It wasn't pity exactly, it was more like a maternal anxiety. One wanted to save them, to put them right. She wondered if she had a sad propensity to be attracted to the exotic. Because for better or worse the Khmer boys didn't do it for her for some reason. She always said to her mother that she was 'spoiled'. The stint in Paris had ruined her for life and it was the world of the barang that now seemed richer in possibilities. She might once have felt guilty about it. But there is no guilt in the ruthless pursuit of happiness, there is just the pursuit. It's like moving towards the light. One crawls on all fours, if need be. One crawls on one's belly and whimpers, it doesn't matter. And in the end weren't the white men the same the other way round? What were they looking for? They didn't even know. Her father had a fine phrase for it which he had found in his history books: hunters in the dark. It came from medieval Japan and referred to the restless courtiers of the Imperial Court always hunting for their own advantage. But also, as her father liked to add, for happiness. The phrase was his favourite way of summing up younger people of the present age. His own ravaged generation were another matter.

She had intended to go back to the house and practise the piano, but as the skies darkened she lost interest in the thought of Brahms and asked the charming boy if he'd like to go to one of the Chineses place on Monivong and then maybe a bar on the other side of the river. He seemed an idle type, and not as busy as she'd thought at first. His days empty and long and confused; like hers, in other words. He said he'd love to.

As he smiled his consent there was a quick sympathy between them, a little flash in the dark.

They took another tuk-tuk up to Monivong. When she was alone, she said, she loved coming to the kitsch Chinese seafood places at the far end of this boulevard which lay well beyond the tourist city. They were places which her parents liked as well: Khmer, familial, with a touch of Chinese garishness. On the far side of Sihanouk, in the darker stretches of the boulevard, there were a score of these places identifiable by their stark white glare, their gold-and-red interiors and their fish tanks on the street.

There was Lyky, with its bright white interiors and glass-screened private booths and, further down on the same side, Man Han Lou, a place of nacre cabinets and palms with its live fish tanks outside. It was there, in the end, that they ate. It was like a spare Chinese tea room of former decades. They ordered seabass barbecued in rock salt and rice *prahok*, because, she said, he had obviously never tried the national dish.

When it was finally dark outside strings of blue lights came on in the windows. They were content to talk about food for a long time; the ordinariness of the subject was a relief. The *prahok*, meanwhile, was a little mound of rice with flecks of red in it and when he put a forkful in his mouth the intense fermented saltiness of the ground-up fish made his eyes water.

'That's — that's something else.'

'I think it's garum,' she said. 'Some people say the Romans brought it here once upon a time.'

'It's vile. But it's delicious-vile.'

'That's the supreme delicious.'

'Or the supreme vile?'

'It's both. My father has to eat it every day. I can't quite.'

'It's like eating dead eels made into a paste.'

'That's not far off. Afterwards we'll go for a drink and get the taste out of your mouth.'

Her eyes were merry, she had it all planned out.

'I'll be awake for a week,' he said. Tears were on his cheeks.

They went over the Japanese Friendship Bridge on motodops, struggling through the swarms of bikes which from the air must have looked like ants competing for traffic space on a single banana leaf. He was behind her and could see the slim arch of her back in its white cotton dress bobbing and weaving ahead of him and the flicks of her hair as the river wind caught them halfway across. It was later than he had realised. How much time had gone by chatting over Vietnamese coffee.

The sun had begun to change colour and dip towards the Tongle Sap, turning the water so bright that the longtails skimming across it were almost invisible. He felt a sharp exhilaration. The haze above the riverine construction sites burned a milky white, calm with a poisonous sultriness.

He followed her bike as it turned right on the far side of the bridge and moved quickly along a rural-looking road with small factories and warehouses and walls on either side. At its furthest end, where the road again turned right, there was a large beer garden called Golden Chroy Chang Var with the girls seated outside in silk gowns. They were just gearing up for the evening trade. Here Sophal slowed, looked back at him and made an obscene but friendly gesture at the girls.

The road met up with the river and shadowed it and soon they were close to the machines and the cranes and the half-built skeletons of girders. Between the road and the water there was a string of shack bars held above the river by stilts and beams. The riverside was being redeveloped, and half of them had already been destroyed. In a few months they would all be gone, to be replaced by a treeless, shadeless river walk where no one would ever go. They stopped outside the last one in the row and went into an open-plan bar alive with a brisk wind. There was no one there. They went out onto a balcony with old leather chairs and a coffee table and fell into them with their legs up on the rail.

It was a sundowner bar, with waving reeds around it.

'I should be home playing Brahms,' she said after they had been drinking beers for a while. 'But suddenly I'm bored with it. There's a party later at a friend's studio. A Dutch painter. Want to come?'

'All right, I could I guess. I don't go to parties much.'

'It's a small city, Simon. Soon you know everybody who you're ever going to know. It's either depressing or comforting – depending on how you look at it.'

'I'm just going to go along with it. If it's depressing I'll take a lot of pills – they're cheap here, no?'

'That's wisdom for you. That's what you ought to do.'

'I'm not leaving any time soon either. I like the sunsets here. I like a lot of things. I keep waiting for the homesickness but it never comes. It does come eventually, I suppose. Or maybe not. These old barang guys here don't seem to feel it.'

'I never asked them, myself.'

'I don't want to be one of them, though. That's my worst nightmare. I can't imagine turning into one of them.'

'But maybe they're happy – that's why they stayed.'

'Yeah, I guess. They feel at home, whatever that means.'

'That's a good reason to live somewhere – I *don't* think. You're like me, though, you're at a loose end. My father thinks it's a disaster. A generational disaster. He thinks we're all at a loose end.'

'Maybe we are. A generation of drifters.'

She blew between her teeth. 'That's a massive generalisation. I don't think it's true at all. Why, are you a drifter?'

'Well, I never thought of myself as one. God no. Anything but.'

'You *look* like a drifter. You feel like one.'

'Really?' he said. He was a little incredulous.

'It's just my instinct,' she said. 'My instinct is you're a bit of a drifter.'

He denied it again, but she was teasing.

'Look at you,' she said. 'Your clothes are all wrong. I *have* to take you shopping or something. You're dressed like an extra in a film. I should take you to Uniqlo or Muji or something. Unfortunately they don't have any branches in Cambodia. No, I'm teasing. You look very beautiful in your clothes. But I wonder where you got them.'

'A tailor,' he said. 'I don't want to look like the usual barang slob.'

'So that's it.' She laughed. 'No wonder my father likes you.'

The lights of the city came on over the far side of the river. Longtails with bales of okra passed underneath, the men looking up for a moment, and the wide power of the Mekong nearby could be sensed. The hour of sunset and they switched to sangria. He thought wistfully of all the people he had left behind in his old life. Now he began to wonder if any of them would notice his absence in the longer term. In the shorter term, of course, they would, but in the longer term, in the grander scheme of things, it was not so certain. As long as he kept his parents informed, meanwhile, nothing would happen. He was now sure of it. The friends and his job would all pass away. The friends, few in number; the job, minor. People walked out on minor jobs all the time.

It was an inexplicable callousness, but it had just come upon him out of nowhere. How had it come about so easily? It had not even surprised him. It's one thing to hate your life, but to merely dislike it – that was a greater mystery. There was no explaining that, because the dislike was total, not partial. There was no explaining *that* to even the most cynical Khmer girl. But somehow – a small miracle in itself – they understood it anyway and at a certain moment the questions died away.

They did now. Sophal told him about her father.

'He was a doctor for the Khmer Rouge, if he didn't tell you. He didn't choose to be – he was only thirty at the time. They overran his clinic and he had the choice to work for them or disappear. He chose not to disappear. As people usually do.'

'It must have been a terrible experience.'

'Everyone has their stories. His is not the worst, believe me. He and my mother came out alive.'

'I'm glad they did.'

'Ah, are you really a flatterer, Mr Beauchamp?'

'Not really. I mean I'm glad they're alive.'

'Because they're alive, I'm alive. Are you glad about that too?'

'Absolutely.'

'I'm hungry again. I have a place we can go and eat *arepas.*'

'What?'

'*Arepas.* South American things. And mojitos. *Arepas* and mojitos.'

He thought that sounded excellent.

'OK. We'll go South American.'

'*Sí, señor.*'

They walked back to the dusty and now-dark road and felt the cement dust on their lips. It seemed to be everywhere. The workers from the sites were walking through clouds of the same dust back to the main road, a long line of white eyes under the trees. It was like a street far out in the country, in the villages. The mulberry trees and the bats winging through them. She walked beside him with a soft apprehension, her bare shoulders inviting an initiative which he was too shy to take. They passed a school called the Chroy Chang Var, a tiled French building with a large garden. They wandered in for a moment to look at a curious circle of half-life-sized mythological figures in the middle of the garden. They could feel bats and sleepy guards momentarily stirred in the shadows. She turned to him for some reason with an enormous smile. At the bend in the road the karaoke girls were still there sitting on plastic chairs and lit by the glare of their Galaxies. One could smell fields nearby, burning hay and rubber. They walked past the clubs until they were among weeds and low white walls, alone in the dust, and the city was just an orange glare above the treeline. She brushed against him and something in him flared up silently. He was about to take her hand when she said, 'It's not much of an English lesson, mistah.' He shook his head and they smiled and entered their conspiracy as quietly as two people entering a church by the side door in the middle of the night.

On the other bank of the river they found the China House and went in happy and sweaty and dusty and sat at the bar and ordered the long-anticipated mojitos with the *arepas*. It was an old Chinese shophouse with red lanterns and wooden floors, the bar alive with ice buckets and mint and miniature straw parasols. They rubbed the iced towels over their faces and a dark red dirt came off on the material. Within ten minutes they had sunk down the second round of mojitos and eaten the mint. Within twenty, they were in a world of their own.

They went upstairs and lay on one of the covered divans with their shoes off and ate curries and jasmine rice with gin and tonics. They hadn't spoken for an hour.

'Shouldn't you be back?' he finally asked.

'No, we're going to Pontoon. I'm taking you to Pontoon. It's where the bad boys go.'

'Are we bad boys?'

'We're not bad or boys. But we're going to Pontoon anyway.'

He looked at his watch and then remembered it wasn't there and she noticed the odd gesture.

'You don't have a watch,' she cried. 'But you looked for it. That was quite cute.'

'Strange – I must have left it at the hotel.'

'Really? Maybe you don't have one, Mr Simon.'

'A man without a watch,' he muttered. 'Disreputable, eh.'

'It's better not to have one in this town. It'll get you into trouble. You should leave it at home every night from now on.'

'All right, I'll take your advice.'

Her foot had crossed over to his side and touched his. They were slipping downwards and the Chinese screens around them blurred in his vision. An hour later they were in a tuk-tuk to Pontoon, a fresh and bright rain falling all around them.

Outside the club was a small crowd of Khmer drivers. They pushed their way to the doors and the bouncers nodded them through after glancing at Sophal's ID. At the end of a dark corridor lay an immense horseshoe bar with sofas around it. They danced for a while, Sophal raising and lowering her arms with her fingers extended in the positions of classical Khmer dance, and then they sat at the bar among the punters and the girls on the make and the waify NGO men who moralised by day and picked up girls by night. She ordered a bottle of white rum and they drank that with huge pieces of ice and Coke and watched the aid workers and diplomat staffers from India and Africa and Europe elided into a great pleasure-seeking confusion which the Khmer girls preyed on with a nimble awareness of the smallest advantage and disadvantage. It was amusing for an hour. But without a watch, he reflected, there was no way of knowing how long it was amusing for. When they came back onto the street, in any case, it felt much later. The streets had gone into that delicious comatose state of the late nights, the pavements given over to noodles and fried squid and cats, the tuk-tuks moving through the rain more silently. The desultory, lazy atmosphere of sex and loose ends and straying curiosity. There was no violence in the air at all, just a rambling sense of restlessness and anticipation. Soon, later still, the street people would come out of the shadows, the scavengers and sweeps and drifters who sifted through the city's rubbish and detritus in the hours before dawn, but they too had a listless gentleness.

He offered to walk her home to her parents' house and as they walked along the boulevards the lights went out again and the roads filled with their indolent floods. They came to the gates and she said, 'We could go to Colonial Mansions instead — for a bit. I'll tell Daddy we couldn't find a driver with the blackout.'

Robert went along with it and they went back down to the boulevard and found a tuk-tuk who could be reasoned with. The lightning now came down in clearly visible forks but as yet there was no sound, no audible threat.

In his room they took off their clothes solemnly although there was no light to be had and no fan or cooler. He ran a cold bath and they lay in it for a long time. She had gone into his miserable kitchen and found some coffee grounds and mixed them with milk and brought the paste back into the bathroom. As they lay in the cool water listening to the rain she rubbed the coarse grains into his back, his shoulders and his arms, then his hands and fingers, filling every crevice of him with the mixture. Then she told him to do the same with her. He scooped the paste into both hands and then spread it across her back making it dark, then her tiny arms and the back of her neck. When they were both coffee-dark and grainy they lay back in the water and smelled the coffee and the milk and the rising sweat mixed together. The rain had reached a furious crescendo and hammered now on the half-open windows and the roof garden above them. They went to the bed only half washed off, still reeking like a coffee pot, and lay down in the damp sheets and kissed until they fell asleep for a while.

Even when they woke they were not entirely in the

world. The rain had stopped and a vast, anvil-shaped cloud had taken form above the city. At its centre, emerging hour by hour and with a ghostly uncertainty, a new moon finally forced its way into the picture. A halo surrounded it, a perfect circumference of surrounding atmospheric light. The cloud evolved around it also, frothy edges glowing with silver brightness. Inexorable and silent, it ballooned upwards like a sign of terrestrial war, its black core unaffected by the moon. Watching its outer edge progress into space, the observer felt a subtle madness. Far down the river, in fact, on the banks of the Mekong, the men who worked on the river looked up and made predictions. Some said it was a sign of good things to come, an omen that could be trusted, but by far the majority sensed that it foretold something evil and unknown. They said it was a cloud of dogs and vultures.

Dogs and Vultures

Twelve

In a dying hotel called the Tamarind Tree, Simon and Sothea also slept together in a $15 room. It was a small and unremarkable settlement on the river and there was a temple on the far side of the motionless water with a gold-leaf stupa and a radio tower that cast its shadow over a pond filled with decayed hyacinth. They had seen it for a moment before night fell, a vision of bright modernised faith. Through the air fell delicate snowlike ash from a plant of some kind, a crematorium Sothea had said when they arrived, though he knew it must have been a kiln. Across the street stood an office of the Sam Rainy Party where no one had been seen that day and the padlocked shophouses had not been opened after their arrival. The little town seemed to have fallen into a sleep, though cats sat erect and sarcastic under the yellow flamboyants. The sun sliced across it and failed to rouse any life. Only the birds screamed.

When Simon woke he heard koel birds whooping in dishevelled backyards and the half-abandoned park that lay against the river. He raised his hand to his eyes to block out the light. Where were they? He wrapped a towel around his middle and stumbled out onto a cement balcony where a laundry line held their drying underwear and Sothea's last good miniskirt. The owner of the hotel was in the mud yard below making tea with a hotplate, and a swarm of tanagers had come to pick off the pieces of bread that lay scattered around her. The woman looked up for a moment with amicable hostility. What did one say to such men first thing in the morning? A simple 'Get lost' wouldn't quite do. She smiled instead, and muttered the usual '*Sous'dey*' and her guest stepped back with his eyes squinting, as if still stoned from the night before.

He looked over the wall of the hotel into the street and saw the trees still wet from the rain and tractors dragging loads down it. He couldn't even remember the name of the place – they had arrived in the middle of the night and taken their dope within an hour. They must have passed out before midnight and gone into an impenetrable enraged sleep. His eyes felt dry and his mouth had emptied of saliva. What day was it? Beyond the town there were mountains, green jade hills that he knew. Smoke rose in wisps from fires set inside those hills, and he remembered those fires as well. They had seen them the previous day between the rains. His hand shook, a small vibration rather, and he went down to the ground floor in a cold fury to see if he could scrounge some coffee or, a worse option, venture into the street and buy some. The owner offered him tea and told him that they had Nescafé if he wanted to take that up to his girlfriend.

He woke Sothea with the Nescafé mixed with sugar and milk and they played some music for a while and made love in the glow of the thin orange curtains.

'Why are we here?' she kept saying. 'What happened?'

'You don't remember, baby? We got high after we arrived. We drove in our new car all the way.'

'Oh, the car,' she sighed.

'We still have the car. It's down in the street.'

'Coffee is good.'

'I made it sweet like you like it.'

'It tastes like Arabica.'

He laughed. 'It's Nescafé with Carnation.'

She was still half dressed in yesterday's clothes, as he was, and after the shared coffee they took a cold shower while the radio played. Sothea then stepped out onto the balcony and recuperated her miniskirt and dressed herself studiously in front of the bathroom mirror. She remembered nothing at all of the previous twenty-four hours. She thought Simon would remember it for her. If anything needed remembering, Simon remembered it.

While she did this, he packed their shared suitcase by simply throwing all the bits and pieces into it and placing the needles and junk at the bottom and the clothes on top of them. It was an inept concealment but it was instinct by now. They could wait until after lunch before taking a hit, or they could skip lunch and go into the forest when the heat came and get their juice. In the end, it would probably be neither. They went down at checkout time and threw the bag into the boot of the car with the money and strolled down the lone main street to get some *lok-lok* and beers. The soil had dried so much that the constant wind kicked up a fine dust. They sat at a metal table in their heavy shades and ate morosely, trying to clear their heads and feel human again. Gradually everything came back to normal. They had taken off without much planning and now they still had no plan. Simon thought about making a run for the border and going into Thailand for a while. He had friends here and there, and they could score some nice stuff in Bangkok while living free. But soon he turned away from the idea. The border was always tricky. He didn't know if the English boy had panicked and gone to the police. They wouldn't care, but they might figure there was a bribe in it for them if they caught him at the border and made things unpleasant for him. They were malicious enough to do that. Instead, then, he thought of a place he knew in the mountains where he'd been before to lie low. It was a lodge owned by a Scot who used to be a British soldier. It lay up among the minefields in the Cardamoms, on a track that was hard to find. He was sure he could find it.

'I've got just the place,' he said to Sothea. 'You're going to love it.'

'Hotel with swimming pool?'

'Not exactly, honey. But we have to lie low for a few days.'

'Low?'

'Yes, we have to be very quiet.'

She sulked while he paid the bill and they walked back to the car. It was an old second-hand Saber and it was on its last legs.

They drove out of the town into the bright hayfields where the old field guns lay on their sides like toys. Soon they were on the road to Pailin, but they were not going to go there. They took a turn-off and ploughed into low, rolling hills dotted with manilkara. They swept into a desolate village and stopped for a cold Coke at a tiny, swarming market. Thousands of flies descended upon them and they stood helplessly in the sunlight while cripples with blown-off legs, landmine victims, closed in upon them as well with an unerring instinct for barang money. 'I don't have anything,' he snapped at them in Khmer and they backed off a little, incredulous, before regaining their courage. Sothea swore at them and there was a stalemate. They went back into the car and drove on, up a long, wooded hill until the road divided and the left fork was a dirt track snaking between thorn trees. They took it.

'I remember the way,' he said, to reassure her. 'Don't worry, you'll like it. It's got a tree house. And a river.'

'I don't care no river.'

'All the same . . .'

She thought he looked a little crazy in the English boy's clothes. They didn't suit him, and they didn't even fit him, and he turned overnight from an elegant entrepreneur to a hippy on the run. He told her it was useful to change identities since he had stolen a lot of money and then he told her impatiently not to ask any more about it. She sensed at once that he was running away from a lot more than that. Whom, then, had he double-crossed? He must have double-crossed someone far more formidable than that English boy, but he wouldn't say. He didn't want to worry her. Now, however, he seemed agitated and lost and his temper was flaring. They bumped along the narrower track and soon they were rising steeply through fields bordered by yellow UN tape with signs warning not to walk across them.

There were little wood bridges with boys in *kramas* with weapons in their laps waiting to skin a wristwatch or a few dollars, and when they saw the Saber with the barang they perked up, stood and hoisted the weapons onto their shoulders and came into the sun squinting. It was two dollars a crossing. They had a famished, hollow look. They stared at the Khmer girl in the passenger seat and there was a tense unease in the stand-offish attempts at humour on the part of the American. In reality he was alarmed. He drove through quickly and up into slopes of burned grass and then a forest like England, the trees tall and willowy and silent in the hot sun. The track climbed up past lonely houses on stilts, their mud yards carefully swept, past Vietnamese tanks stuck for eternity at the edge of ravines of wild flowers. The car pitched left and right and Sothea held onto the overhead strap with a grim annoyance. At the edge of a larger, denser forest they came to another roadblock, this one manned by a policeman.

It was now midday. The cop was reading a paper in a deckchair under the shade of a monkeypod and, lowering the paper, he looked up with a calm, cynical clairvoyance as the ancient car rattled its way towards his two-lane bridge. He stood, like the others, and sauntered out into the heat and held up his hand. His two men were off on an errand and he was alone for an hour − all the more reason to assert himself with a certain amount of firmness. He stepped in front of the Saber and brought it to a halt and, without smiling, induced Simon's face to protrude through the opened window.

Davuth Vichea spoke enough English to wring a modest profit from a passing foreigner, and he knew enough to do it unobtrusively.

'Good morning,' he said, and dipped his head to catch sight of the Khmer girl in the seat next to the barang. So that was an inconvenience. 'Where are you going?' he said in Khmer to Sothea.

But it was Simon who answered in that same language.

'We're going to a lodge up the mountain.'

'You speak Khmer?'

Simon smiled and that was enough.

'What is that place called?' Davuth asked.

'It's called Moonrise Lodge.'

'The Scot?'

'The Scot is my friend.'

'Ah, so the Scot is your friend.' The policeman rocked back on his heels and laughed. 'His name is Michael, na?'

'Micky, yes.'

'Yes, Ta Mick. A dangerous man!'

'He's a little odd.'

'And he is your friend?'

'Yes. Did you know – he has a piece of shrapnel lodged in his head?'

'A piece of shrapnel?'

'Yes, a piece of shrapnel. It is why –'

Davuth rubbed his chin. 'I did not know that Ta Mick had a piece of shrapnel in his head.'

'In his frontal lobes, na. It is a war wound.'

'A piece of shrapnel – in his head. It would explain his behaviour.'

They exchanged a manly laugh.

'Well,' Davuth went on, 'what is your name, friend of Ta Mick?'

'My name is Robert O'Grieve.'

'Are you going there with your girlfriend?'

'Yes, sir.'

'Is she legal age?'

'Of course she is. She's twenty-five.'

'And you?'

'Twenty-eight.'

'Well, you'll have to pay the toll anyway. It's ten dollars this time.'

Simon didn't object at all.

'Are you staying the night at Moonrise?' Davuth asked.

'Maybe a night or two. We like the nature. My girlfriend likes the woods.'

'Is that right?'

Davuth smiled at the girl. She was, indeed, quite pretty and definitely under twenty-five.

'Is that right, miss?'

'Yes,' she said, not looking back at him.

'Well, isn't that fine?'

Pocketing the ten dollars, Davuth stepped back from the car and looked down its length, taking in the scratched doors, the dusty hubs and the fenders about to fall off. There was a smell of drugs about the whole thing. He thought for a moment of making this wretch open the boot and show him the contents and he was sure he would find the goods. The bribe then would be astronomical. The barang would beg and sweat. It would be gratifying, but the sun was now on his back and he felt an angry weariness and an indifference even to the prospect of quick money. The irritation of heat and weariness. One never knew with these people. They often had the strangest connections in higher places, one had to tread lightly with them. Whites were bags of tricks. They could die like a fly or kick up a fuss. His commander back in the day had killed one once with a pickaxe and it did not feel right. Now they were still rich but Davuth made his calculation and stepped back from the provocation. He waved at the road, and there was a curt permission in his hand, a tired relaxation of his authority. Yet his eye didn't miss anything.

'He's the bastard to watch,' the girl said as they went past him and she looked quickly over her shoulder and caught the sun shining on his pitted face and the leather of the holster.

The man even smiled at her.

'Never mind him,' Simon said.

'No, he's watching us.'

'He's just a cop like all cops. They don't pay them.'

The girl knew better, she knew her own people better.

They came into the upland woods. The road ran past a large house with a dog tethered in the yard and shiny black chickens and a Land Rover too grand for its surroundings. Further on there was a sign for Moonrise. The road there was like a mud footpath, the trees vaulting it.

At the top the forest cleared and they could hear the sound of a forceful river. In the clearing were a handful of wooden buildings and a tree house with vines falling down from it. When the engine cut they heard the river even more clearly, its rippling suddenly loud in the silence, and they saw the main house which must have been made from scratch by the owner himself. It was wide open with a kind of loggia festooned with wind chimes.

The Scot was in the sunlight in the middle of his property cutting blocks of wood with an axe. He was naked but for a Khmer sarong and his sweat glistened on the tattoos covering his white skin. He had noticed them but continued with his task. The axe came down and the splinters flew and then finally he stopped and turned and looked over at the Saber now parked at the edge of the clearing.

They got out and walked over to the loggia and the Scot came over with his axe and, after a delayed reaction, smiled at the American whom he now recognised. It was the shabby outfit that had thrown him. He took in the lovely but run-down Khmer girl and he got the picture at once and called over to his maid to make some tea and bring it out onto the loggia.

'We need to hang out for a couple of days,' Simon said matter-of-factly. 'I can pay this time.'

'I'm glad of that.'

'I got a lucky break and some cash.'

'Did ye now?'

'Yeah, I got a lucky streak at the Diamond.'

'Fuck ye, I cannae believe it.'

The bright heat of the day had reached its climax and now the rain would come back. They sat on cushions, in a vast woodland loneliness, and Sothea looked up at the home-made lamps that were hung above the tables. They were made out of old tank shell casings.

'Aye,' the Scot said to her, 'everything's made from munitions I found on my land.'

'You're crazy,' she said in Khmer.

'That's the truth,' he said in the same language.

'Look, Mick,' Simon began at once, 'I got some stuff as well which I might want to keep here. Are you gonna mind?'

'The wife says no to drugs from nae on.'

'The wife? You're married?'

'Got married last month to a farm girl. She's a right-on Buddhist.'

'Fuck. You don't say.'

'I do say and she says no drugs on the premises.'

'Well, Christ, Mick, look – I can't risk running around with bags of that shit, not after my win at the Diamond. You know how word gets around. Every punk in the neighbourhood will know it's me. It's like having a price on my head. You know that. Explain that to your missus.'

'There's no explaining anything to her. No drugs is no drugs.'

'All right, so you want us to die?'

Mick had his laugh and eventually so did the other two.

'Who's talking about dying, ye little prick? Just cart it around with ye. And don't get high every fooking day.'

'At least we can stay here two nights, no?'

'As ye can see, there's no one here. Though we're expecting an English couple tonight.'

'An English couple?'

'Aye, in case ye didn't notice, it's a fooking hotel.'

'Well, it doesn't matter. They're foreigners anyway.'

'You can stay as long as ye like. Just keep a lid on it.'

'Is there a cabin by the river we can have?'

'Aye, Robert Louis Stevenson is available.'

'What about Rob Roy?'

'Nay, it's for the missus.'

'All right, we'll take Stevenson. Is there a mosquito net?'

'Obviously there is. There's air con in the wee hours too.'

'Luxury. How much?'

'We'll talk about it later.'

The tea came and they relaxed. Sothea flirted with the Scot, and the Scot softened as if succumbing to the spirit of the place and soon the warm gin was out and they were recalling the last time they went to Phnom Penh together.

'But,' Mick said, 'ye've not been down there in a while.'

'No, I was renting a place on the river and liking it.

Sothea here persuaded me not to go down and she was right.'

'Aye, women always are.'

They were now aware of a group of Khmer girls and older women sitting by the kitchen and watching them while they peeled vegetables with knives. There was a cool sarcasm about them. The Moonrise was not, in the end, a casual or relaxing place. It had desperation written all over it, a desperate attempt to make a little paradise on land bought from a Khmer Rouge warlord. The bowls on the tables were, like the lamps, made from shell casings and the ashtrays too. Simon had always wondered how the mad Scot lived here with his Khmer groupies and his bastard children but it was not a question that ever needed to be answered. It was happiness of a kind and one had to end up somewhere. He had not done so badly for himself. Then he thought of the heroin and the cash in the car and he considered that the best thing to do was just carry them over casually to the cabin and not say a thing. He could see the path that led down to the river with the yellow tape on either side and the same warnings about landmines. The whole property was still mined and most of it was off-limits. One had to be careful about getting too liquored up at night and wandering back to one's cabin outside the marked paths. It was the place to be because it was so remote and so safe. It was alarming about the English couple arriving but one could, presumably, dance around their cluelessness.

Before the rain, Mick walked with them down to the cabin on the river. It stood on a steep bank surrounded by papaya trees. Its wooden terrace looked straight down into the black and ominous river, along which grew what looked like prickly poppy flowers. There was a musty scent in the air, a smell maybe of distant firesmoke.

They laid the suitcase on the terrace and the Scot opened the door for them and turned on the rickety A/C to take the edge off the stifling heat. Inside it was bare enough: a bed and a rocking chair.

'Dinner at six. I hope the English aren't here yet.'

'Me too,' Simon said. 'When are they supposed to be?'

'Nae way of saying. They're coming overland from Thailand.'

'Bloody bad manners. All right, we'll come up for dinner.'

'The wife is making haggis.'

'Christ.'

'Just joking, ye bastard. It'll be omelette with chillies.'

When he had gone, Simon and Sothea stretched out on the bed and decided not to shoot up. They could have sex instead. The calm and torpid river seemed to encourage this gentler course of action, its sounds now so close that they subdued all others. The windows had no curtains and so they watched the sky and fell asleep for some time. But Simon, in reality, was thinking continuously. How had his life fallen so low from such heights? He was not a bad person judged by ordinary measures; he had never harmed anyone physically. He had taken Robert's money, and indeed his name, but Robert had not worked for that money, he had chanced upon it by luck while gambling in a warlord-owned casino. It was hardly clean. A man who wins dirty money is not in a position to defend it from a moral position, he will do so only from self-interest. And so self-interests collide. So what? There will be merely a winner and a loser, those most inevitable of archetypes. One might as well be the winner.

Besides, he had done the English boy a favour. Simon could spot a would-be deserter a mile away. They usually just didn't have the courage to follow their less conscious desires. They needed a nudge and he had given Robert that nudge. It hadn't harmed him at all.

He kissed Sothea's naked arm with its dark superstitious tattoos. They had been living together for a year, brought together by dope, but he still didn't know anything about her. She had been a waitress in a bar in Battambang but she had ambitions to go to school and become a vet. Was it possible for her to become a vet? He didn't know. The country was an enigma to him, a forest of confusing signs. And yet it seemed like the easiest of passages from his life in New York to his life here — a matter of a few years during which he had managed to go through a large part, if not all, of his inheritance while doing little more than spinning in the dark. But for Sothea it was a different matter. For her, his self-indulgence was a ticket to somewhere else, though where that was, she had not figured out. Still, she could smell with an infallible instinct his family money, his ease and his self-confidence. There was no mistake about him — he was good luck.

How wrong she was, he thought. The only thing he had going for him was a good education and that was far in the past and as useless as everything else in the past. What a shame he had never taken her to Montauk or the lighthouse at the far end — or to a party overlooking the Park. As it was he had to tell her about it over and over. She could not understand why he had left that world for hers.

Soon, an electric bell rang out over the darkening forests. It was the Scot's eccentric dinner bell. He shook the drowsy girl awake and they dressed and went out into a heavy, rainy dusk with a mist rolling down the snaking river. At the loggia, the English guests had still not arrived.

'The driver called,' Mick said, 'they're still at the border.'

Let's eat quickly then, Simon wanted to say.

'They won't be here for an hour,' he did say. 'Let's eat now, if it's all right with you.'

The military lamps came on and the girls laid out mosquito coils. From the wall of trees the frogs barked unseen and raindrops fell from the higher branches with a commotion of their own. They ate a creamy coconut curry made with chicken legs and jasmine rice and with it tall Lao beers. Mick told him, for the thousandth time, how he had come to buy the land from a crony of the former regime strongman Ta Mok and how he had come to make all these handsome furnishings from military material. That piece of shrapnel – it came from a mine in Angola. He knew all about mines. Just as he explained this there was a distant, muffled detonation from far off in the forest and Mick and the girls began laughing. His wife came over and showed them their new baby and the baby was laughing too.

'It's just a deer,' he said to the other two. 'We hear one or two every twenty-four hours. They step on the mine and turn into clouds of blood. It's quite a sight in the day.'

Sothea turned a wary eye upon her protector. She didn't like it that deer were blowing themselves up.

'It's all right,' Simon said into her ear. 'They don't feel a thing. Just *pop!*'

'Aye,' the Scot said, 'a deer is not the smartest.'

'Clouds of blood?' she said.

Simon shrugged. Such was life.

He could sense that she was growing more nervous. She needed her hit and he had withheld it from her. Before long, however, they heard the drone of an approaching motor and a flash of headlights cut through the trees and lit for a moment the side of the main house. It also lit the lines of rain and the sweating bark of the ironwoods and one could see that it was a large, filthy local taxi. Mick stood up with a grunt and moved off to greet the car which had just arrived, bringing with it that rarest of gifts, paying guests. There was a hopeful spring in his step. He whipped a hand over his hair. Simon was furious but held his tongue, and he thought about how he could withdraw from the scene without too much fuss. It was, obviously, too late now and he would have to go through with a certain amount of formalities.

The doors of the car slammed and the figures of two shabby English tourists appeared in the confusion of shadows, and behind them the Khmer driver holding their bags. They came in a group towards the loggia and the whites had a look of frigid alarm, as if their calculation to trust the lush images of a website had suddenly been shown to have backfired.

'It's just a wee lodge in the mountains — nothing really,' the proud owner was saying, leading the way.

Simon and Sothea were obliged to get up and greet the newcomers and as they did so the driver put down the bag, at Mick's suggestion, and hung back at the edge of the light thrown down by the crazy shell-casing lamps. Simon looked down at him briefly and a shock went through his body, as if physically. He recognised Ouksa at once. Their eyes did not cross and Simon half turned and took Sothea's hand and pulled her to one side, to the rail which was darker than the table they were seated at. He was not sure if she would understand or even if she would recall the driver. There was no sign that Ouksa had looked over at them or recognised him. The barangs were busy making their arrangements and the man was paying him. The confusion of the rain might have helped. The transaction was completed and the driver turned away quickly and stepped back towards the car. He had left the engine running and appeared anxious to be on his way without ado. As the visitors struggled onto the loggia Mick stood at the foot of the small flight of steps and watched the car recede, lifting his hand once by way of farewell. It was entirely possible that he knew Ouksa or had had dealings with him in the past. Who could say. Simon came back to the table and they were introduced to Bill and Sarah Miles.

'Robert,' he said to introduce himself, 'Robert O'Grieve. This is my wife, Sothea. She's a vet.'

'Oh, a vet,' the Englishwoman cried.

'Yes,' Sothea said to her in Khmer, 'not a whore.'

'What did she say?'

'She said she's pleased to meet you.'

They were forced to eat all together and the meal therefore dragged on interminably. The visitors rehearsed all the tedious and entirely predictable dramas of their voyage overland from Bangkok. Was there not even one mishap that had afflicted them which he had not heard a hundred times before? Gradually, though, the rain died down and he suggested to Sothea that they go back to the cabin and get to bed early.

'It's one of those things about living in the country here,' he said to the Mileses. 'One goes to bed extremely early. It's like it can't be helped.

'At seven?' Mr Miles said, wide-eyed.

'Sometimes even earlier.'

'I'll be damned. It's worse than Chalvington with Ripe.'

'I am sure Mr Mick will offer you some of his home-made brandy. We call it Khmer brandy but it's nothing of the sort.'

'It's a fine drink,' Mick protested. 'And it's on the house!'

'Will it kill us?' Mrs Miles asked.

'It's been known tae happen.'

'Maybe it'll keep the mosquitoes away,' her husband suggested.

'That it will,' Mick said triumphantly.

Simon and Sothea rose and said their goodnights.

'Just don't go wandering about after four brandies,' Simon said. 'That's my recommendation.'

'Why?' from the Englishwoman.

'You might be mistaken for a deer in the dark.'

They walked back down to the river between the lines of yellow tape and Simon held Sothea's hand and then held her closer. Suddenly, for some reason, he felt a rush of tenderness for her, a desperate need to know that she loved him back and needed him as much as he needed her.

'Who are those awful people?' she said quietly.

'We call them Limeys. English. They're all right.'

'Are they angry?'

'I don't know. Did they seem angry?'

'They seemed like they were going to explode.'

'Maybe they will explode.'

Now, more than previously, he wanted to leave before morning. He had always got a strange feeling from Ouksa and seeing the driver again had raised an alarm deep within him. It was, like so many other things, an omen – and Simon believed categorically in omens. There had to be a meaning in such a coincidence. Naturally, it might not be a coincidence at all. It was a small region and people crossed each other's paths all the time. But still, there was something about Ouksa that was not blind. He seemed to know what he was doing at all times. He was someone who kept his ear close to all grapevines. That little slithering dark-eyed snake. He had come into the forest and seen them.

They lay on their bed and shot up with clean needles and then lay quietly in each other's arms listening to the tree frogs and the cicadas until the lights went off outside and the darkness augmented so that the river itself gave off a kind of black luminescence.

'Are we alone?' she said, thinking that she could hear things in the night.

'Of course we're alone,' he answered.

Though he was not sure.

'I don't want to stay here tomorrow,' she said.

'Nor do I. Maybe we'll leave.'

'Can we leave when the sun comes up?'

'We won't sleep anyway.'

'Then let's leave.'

He lay awake wide-eyed. The Cambodian jungle had never made him feel at ease. It had a depth and velvety density that suggested something being concealed and withheld. The birds speaking to him but not saying anything he could find pleasurable. A realm of dinosaurs and reptiles, musical and lilting but also filled with ghosts. It gripped him and yet it left him cold, mentally suspended.

When fear came to him, indeed, Simon always relished it in some way. Fear was the most intense feeling by far, and the most complex. But he was not sure what he was afraid of now. It was just the smallness and madness of the room itself. His life had boiled down to rooms, it was spent entirely in rooms on the roads, but mostly in rooms. A suitcase stuffed with money that was not his, a few items of unwashed clothes and his 'happiness gear'. It was vagrancy taken to a fine level.

All his life, considered from a certain perspective, had been leading up to such an outcome. Vagrancy had become second nature to him from an early age. His dropout from Yale had been the warning sign which even he had not heeded. His family had merely taken it to mean that their pessimism about him – formed during his early years – had proved to be accurate. Old New England families had a strong and tight-lipped fatalist streak. They were personality realists.

They were a bit like Buddhists in that regard. His father had not argued much with him about it; Simon had made the argument that he was better suited to scriptwriting out west. It was a very original aspiration but he had duly gone off west and written some garbage in a rented house in Twentynine Palms and then moved into Los Angeles and gradually discovered that he had even less industriousness at his disposal than he had talent. Those, however, were the fun years. He went through all the prescribed experiments of the American middle classes. He circled around the Burning Man trust-fund girls in San Francisco, he did the peyote inductions and the Esalen retreats. It was better than nothing.

He tired of it only when his internal restlessness produced the inevitable surfeit and the drugs had begun to wear him down and make him desultory. At twenty-five he found himself in Mendocino making olive oil and living with an Iranian girl. He had plans to write a screenplay based on the life of Carlos Castaneda and his harem of deranged groupies; but it frittered itself away among the olive stills and the garden dinners sweetened with home-grown marijuana. It was hopeless, he realised.

Life was far too enjoyable to waste it working at the mid-level of things. He gave up the idea of writing and wondered instead about travelling for five years, dropping everything and folding up the wigwam. But even that required too much planning. When the old man called him a 'worthless sonofabitch' he internally agreed and wondered if there was a remedy to being one.

It was rumoured among his horrified family that as a boy of eleven he had tried to burn down a dorm at his prep school in Vermont. Through a series of hysterical confrontations he had gradually persuaded them that it was a lie, a defamation on the part of his hated schoolmates, but the reality was that he *had* tried to burn down the dorm and kill all the sleeping boys whom he loathed. The strange thing was that through those hysterical confrontations he had come to doubt his own memory of the event and to start believing that he really was innocent and persecuted. Moreover, he enjoyed this slippage, this moving from one version (the true one) to another one (the false one) which cast him in a better light. It seemed to him more truthful to the spirit of things, not the letter of things. He was not a real arsonist, any more than he was a real dropout from Yale.

He had just suffered a mental breakdown during his second year. He was diagnosed with clinical depression and began to take the medications. But the chemistry did not agree with him; he was going down to New York every weekend and hiding out in a place on Rivington which he kept secret from his family. He began going over to Brooklyn to score his smack and 'China white' in the streets around the Gowanus projects.

It soon became his favourite area of the city – he sometimes picked up from his dealer on the Carroll Street footbridge overlooking the canal or on Butler nearby where there was always a strong smell of roasting coffee from the warehouses. He would sit in the Thomas Greene park after hours, watching the trucks shooting down Third Avenue and the crack whores walking alone up from the darkness of Douglass Street. He was always there, half high or mostly stoned but with enough money to keep them happy.

When he went down Nevins they called out to him 'Skinny', because everyone on the street had to have a name. They took him onto the warehouse rooftops for blow jobs or into the empty Douglass and Degraw swimming pool. Years later, when he first arrived in Phnom Penh, it made him think of that half-forgotten place.

That was his secret life at Yale. On other weekends he went to family dinners out on Long Island or at the Pierre Hotel. He insulted his sisters after a few bottles of champagne and then he took the last train back to Newhaven. There must have been something about these extremes that he relished. It was easy for an upper-class boy to slum, many of them did, but eventually they grew out of it and took the jobs desperately being offered to them on Wall Street by their alarmed kin. He had no intention of doing the same.

When his grandfather died, the old ladies' footwear

manufacturer from Worcester unexpectedly left him a sizeable amount of money. There was nothing his father could do to thwart the transfer, and Simon packed up his bags and left Mendocino without a second thought. He always left without a second thought. He was always free to roll in a leisurely fashion downhill, as he thought of it. For how can you roll uphill?

He drifted back to New York, then Paris and Barcelona and a few other cities suitable for rich boys who didn't need to engage with the local economy. His funds began to diminish but he had not paid attention. His fleeting businesses rose briefly and then failed predictably, and as each one failed he moved on to a new one with his own money and then his grandfather's money and then, at long last, the money of an uncle here and half-forgotten cousin there. His family began to think of him as a wastrel, though the word was old-fashioned relative to what he actually was. But throughout it all he never lost his taste for reading and beautiful things and his careful, attentive visual snobberies, which were applied to everything from female make-up to chessboards and bespoke shoes. He knew that such things didn't save you but that they did pass the time. It was only in the East, however, that he had finally come to understand that he was good at nothing and that being good at nothing did not prevent him from being a success. He had learned to make money in new ways, he had adapted to his own failure and turned it into a way of being happy.

They did not sleep, as he had foreseen, and during the night a storm broke over the mountain and they came outside onto the cabin's porch and smoked. They dressed and packed the suitcase again and Simon wrote a quick

note to his friend. *Pressing matters, no time to explain.*
He left money for a night's stay with the note and left
it on the bed and then they whiled away the dark hours
coming out of their high. Simon had no idea where they
would go next. It was just a matter of disappearing for a
few days and it was likely better to move than stay in one
place.

Perhaps they would go to the north and find a village
to hide in. He had done it before after a drug sale had
gone wrong. He had once sold cocaine to a Khmer club
owner who had decided to kill him because he thought it
wasn't pure – a jolly caper. He had learned all the tricks
of evasion, the thousand and one ways of disappearing.

He wondered what his dead father would think
seeing him in this pitiful condition. That thunderous
and silky Wall Street man would have been amazed
more than outraged, but deep down he would not have
been surprised. He told all his friends that Simon was
'scum'. His only son had never worked properly for a
living and his tastes had always been dubious. A violent
death in Cambodia would not have struck the old man
as unexpected, Simon thought bitterly. It would have
seemed logical. A body floating in the river at dawn in a
pair of Brooks Brothers socks.

It was about five when they got going at last. The rain
came down with a lazy savagery as they struggled up to
the house and threw the suitcase into the back of the
car. Everyone was asleep, and the cicadas roared in the
forests that Mick had reputedly bought from Ta Mok,
Pol Pot's most trusted man. They sat in the front seats
for a moment and began to laugh. They were still half
stoned and the effects of the heroin had not cleared from
their senses. Nevertheless, they started the car and drove

quietly back down the slippery hill towards the track that curved down the mountain's side. The first light was about to reveal the papaya trees stark and burned in the near distance.

Thirteen

Ouksa drove down the same track with a stunned disbelief in his own luck. Standing by his car and staring into the loggia he had noticed and recognised Simon at once, but controlling his instinct to make himself known or extend a greeting he had turned away as if nothing had happened and driven away as coolly as he could manage. In the driving, bestial rain the act had been easy. But he shook with excitement.

So the barang con man had made it up to the Moonrise Lodge. It was a place which all the cab drivers around the border knew, even if they had few reasons to ever go there. He had come up there with his girl to hide out while the landlord went through his abandoned rental by the river and the locals whispered about the scandalous goings-on which had gone rippling through their lives for months.

It was said the American had thrown a man into the river while high on Ecstasy. They said, too, that he went asking for the bodies of barang suicides so he could pay for their funeral expenses in exchange for going through their pockets. No one could imagine how much money he had made this way. Thousands. People had seen ghosts walking around his property, the souls of the dead walking through the wild fields that surrounded Beauchamp's house and sloped down to the river. It was an evil business; he was an evil man in his way. Gently spoken and mannered but off on the devil's business. The Ap was close to him. Now he had ripped off the nice young Englishman and he had heard about that too. The boatman who took Robert south had returned north and talked about the matter high and low. Paid to keep his mouth shut, he had duly opened it for nothing.

It was one hot Sunday that Ouksa had heard about it in Battambang and he drove down to the river to seek that man out. The boatman was drunk in a run-down bar and he bought him a drink and took him down to the water so they could talk.

'Hey, brother,' he said to him, 'can't you keep your voice down a bit? Just let me buy you some drinks and talk to me. Just you and me.'

'What's it to you, brother?'

'It's something I should know about. I know that barang kid.'

'You do — how's that?'

'I was his driver for a day.'

'That English kid?'

'Yeah, the shy one. So you took him downriver?'

'The boss paid me to take him.'

'The American?'

'Him. We carried him out and put him in the boat.'

'Funny business. Where'd you drop him off?'

'A place I know. He went into the city.'

'How'd you know that?'

The man looked at him with cold and vapid eyes.

'The drivers told me at the jetty. Where else could he go?'

Ouksa bought him a second Saeng. The man was tottering, the sun in his face, and flies danced around them and shimmered against the water.

'Was he able to walk?' Ouksa said.

'He walked. He woke up during the ride.'

'What was it all about, brother?'

The man laughed. 'How the fuck should I know?'

'He must have said something.'

'The American didn't say anything. The English kid asked for his bag on the boat, but it wasn't there.'

'A bag?'

'Yeah, his bag was missing.'

Ouksa bit his lip and looked down at the river.

'Did you come back to the American's jetty after?'

'I did. The American and his girl were there. They were getting into their car.'

'A sweet job for you.'

'I'll say. I didn't have to kill anyone.'

The joke went nowhere.

'No,' Ouksa said grimly. 'You didn't have to kill anyone.' Then he said, 'What's your name, brother?'

'Thy.'

He walked back to his taxi and thought. It was clear enough to a clear mind. The man had followed him and pestered him for another drink so he gave him a buck and got into his taxi. He then drove off angrily, feeling that he had missed out on something. He had got to the two grand first but he had let it slip through his fingers like a fool. The American had not been so stupid. Eagle eyes, that one. He remembered the blue eyes that had tracked him, dismissed him and yet knew everything about him.

For days he lay by the river in the afternoons watching the boats go by. When it rained he lay on the back seat of his car and slept and when the evening was dry he went to a bar he knew and sat there impassively slinging back brandy shots and following the girls with his eyes.

He trawled the temples looking for soft touches, preferably elderly Europeans always ready to overpay. Campy blonde girls who might be up for some extra fun. They never were. They didn't come here for sex. And the sights were not visited much in the rainy season.

One day that week he had a Buddhist group from Vancouver who wanted to see Wat Sampeau and he took four of them there for an exorbitant price. He walked up with them to the sinister caves and took them down to see the carved Buddha where the dead were remembered and the shrines sitting on top of their spurs of rock with prayer ribbons fluttering in lines all around them. He didn't like going there, or any haunted place, but the money was good. It was not, however, enough for him or his crippled wife. She could no longer work and for six months he had been driving the roads every day to make enough money to keep them sane. What use had the prayer flags for her? She had smashed her leg in a metal workshop.

The Buddhists would never understand such a thought, though they would certainly empathise with it. So he walked with them down the winding path that looked over a sea of dark green jungle with the loudspeakers of the wat by the road echoing up, and he talked amiably about all the temples he knew while his mind raced ahead into a dark and sinister future that would certainly be his. His wife's smashed leg seemed insignificant next to the memorials to the thousands murdered on top of Wat Sampeau but he had not even been born in that period and it didn't mean as much to him as it apparently did to the rich Canadians. They gave him a handsome tip for the day and bought his wife a pair of new shoes which she could hardly wear.

He thought about her asleep in their house at the edge of the fields as he waited in the bend of the road below the mountain where Moonrise stood. It was still raining and he turned off the car's lights and waited with all the patience of which he was remarkably capable. He had called at eleven and told her to go to sleep, he was on a job for wealthy Chinese. She knew he was often with the Chinese, even though he loathed them. They were essential to his fortunes but they disgusted him.

Often, in fact, his clients filled him with a bottomless and directionless contempt. Especially the gamblers who rolled around Pailin while he waited for them for hours outside casinos and karaoke joints. Those parasites who thought his country was a genocide museum and a playground but nothing too serious. Who behaved as if he didn't exist. He hated the way they threw money at him, with a flick of the wrist, as if he was an extra in their shimmery theatre of lust and poker. Well, I exist all right, he said aloud as he sat behind the wheel of his taxi. I exist *a lot*. A car's lights had appeared.

It was the Saber which had reached the bottom of the mountain track and had nosed its way onto the main road. It hesitated and Ouksa heard the engine tick as the driver let it idle and dithered. Finally it turned towards Pailin on that lightless road and when it did so he saw the red tail lights move off at a fair clip. He started his own engine but left the lights and followed. The rain helped him, because nothing could be seen in a rear-view mirror without lights.

Simon drove at about fifty towards the east and Sothea

soon fell asleep on his shoulder. They had the radio on and it was old Khmer pop from the seventies. Ouksa followed a quarter of a mile behind and when the Saber slowed he slowed as well, judging the distance expertly. The Saber was slowing again as if it was about to stop. Simon indeed was looking for a spot to pull over so he could pee and take a breather. Sothea had woken and he told her he was going to stop for a few minutes and they could clear their heads. She rubbed her eyes and felt with a quiet instinct that something was behind them and turned to look through the muddy rear window. Seeing nothing, she was half reassured. They then pulled over into a muddy verge beyond which stood tall sugar cane. They turned off the engine but kept the lights on and got out into the rain, which had lessened, and walked to the edge of the cane, which trembled gently in the rain. She went on a little ahead and entered the glade of cane that reached above her head. She was exhausted but she needed to pee as well and her head was still spinning from the dope. It was, from Ouksa's perspective, the moment of opportunity.

He had stopped his own car down the road and crept along the hard shoulder until he was behind the parked Saber. He had taken out of his boot a baseball bat he always kept there. Every driver in that semi-lawless place had a weapon of some kind and his was a mild one. He saw the white man standing with his back to the road at the edge of the sugar cane and the girl slipping into the thicket ahead of him. He crept up to the car and hid behind it and then moved silently around it – still covered by darkness – and like a classical dancer aimed his pitch with the bat with an elegance that surprised himself.

Simon, at last, sensed that something was amiss and

began to turn, his eyes wide, and the bat smacked against his head and sent him reeling downwards into the ditch that separated the verge from the plantation. He rolled down there with a wild grunt and his arms flailed about for a moment and then he lay quite still as the blood poured into his eyes and he saw something for a moment – the clouds of course – and Sothea, seeing the whole thing, let out a cry that reached his ears just as they were disappearing.

Ouksa knew that he had achieved everything with one blow. He jumped over the ditch and plunged into the cane in pursuit of the girl. The stalks were so pregnant with water that as he crashed through them he was showered with drops. But soon, as the girl shot ahead of him, surprisingly fast and nimble and quiet, he passed out of the beam of the Saber's headlights and the total darkness gradually got the better of him. He began to curse and lash out at the sugar cane with the bloodied bat. He could not afford to leave the two cars and the body like that by the side of the road, visible to anyone who happened to pass by. Soon, therefore, he slowed down and felt short of breath and dizzy and he dropped the bat and rested his hands on either knee while he caught his breath. He listened as he straightened himself up and he knew the girl was faster than him and had disappeared entirely into that sea of vegetation. He couldn't hear her but he knew that she was still running, because the prey will always try a little harder than the predator. He wanted then to call out to her softly, in their language, and tell her lies, recall her and draw her back in. He had nothing against her, after all. He wanted to tell her sensibly that he was only doing this for his crippled wife, and it was no one's fault that she had broken her leg in a metalworker's shop.

It had nothing to do with her, but by the same token it had nothing to do with him either. It was circumstances, little one.

Abandoning the hunt, he returned to his car and threw the bat back into the boot. Then he looked up and down the empty road and went over to the Saber and turned off the lights. All the doors were open and he went through the car thoroughly. He found the passports and the suitcase which was on the back seat and when he opened it and tipped out the clothes he found the money wrapped in a plastic bag and the heroin equipment. There was some dope he could sell but some instinct told him to leave it well alone and just take the dollars. It was the simpler path. He also had a distaste for drugs and their culture. He therefore left everything except the cash and the passports – they indeed might be valuable – and he went back to his car and put them all underneath the front passenger seat. He rested again, drenched in rain and perspiration and anxiety, and then returned to the Saber, closing its doors. He went back down to the ditch and stood above the body and wondered what he should do with it. This, at least, he had not thought through very well. He could leave it there with the heroin in the car – the local cops would likely shrug – or he could drag it back into the car. Or he could drag the body far into the sugar cane. In this way it would not be discovered for a while longer, though it would imply the existence of a person who had dragged it there.

The best would be to dispose of it in a grave but he didn't have a shovel. He turned and walked to the Saber and took the keys and toyed with the idea of taking it instead of his own car, but the stupidity of that move dawned on him and he put the keys back. He returned to his own car and the urge to just drive off took hold. There was no trace of him at the scene, nothing connecting him. Sometimes it was better to leave things as simple as possible, and he knew too that the girl had not even seen his face. He was about to take off, but as he opened the car door a pair of lights came into view on the road and he was caught in a moment of doubt.

It was a car moving quite quickly up the road towards him and there was not time to do anything but get into his taxi and try to get away before it caught up with him. He turned the key, the engine started, but it was already too late. The other car, a black SUV of some kind, had already drawn level and then swerved brusquely into the verge and interposed itself between the taxi and the Saber.

Ouksa backed his car into the road but a man had already descended from the SUV and was walking around the front of his vehicle and into the road ahead of him, his hand extended. He could sense from this authoritative gesture alone that it was a policeman and the life went rushing out of him. Everything in him went slack and despondent and he let go of the wheel and slammed on the brakes and wild thoughts moved through him. A few miles away, his crippled wife woke up suddenly and opened her eyes and for a moment she had a premonition of disaster, a certainty that things would turn out badly for both of them.

Fourteen

Davuth had held up his hand and the frightened driver
he could see behind the wheel had instinctively obeyed
the silent command and stopped the car he was reversing.
Davuth went up to him and showed him his badge and
asked him what he was doing. It was in a cool, disdainful
voice, the voice that stopped all comers, and there was
no need to ramp up the pitch. He knew already that the
driver had no ready explanation and he knew already
what had happened because all the signs were there and
logic dictated that Ouksa had done what he had done.
He told him to park the car and come over with him to
the Saber and he told him to do it slowly. Ouksa did as he
was told and they walked together across the muddy open
ground to the edge of the cane field. Davuth asked him
his name, and all the rest.

'It's a barang, isn't it?' he said to him as they came to
the ditch.

The policeman had a strong torch and shone it down
as far as the white shirt and the paralysed blue eyes. For
Ouksa everything looked at once very different. The
frogs sang right across the vast fields of cane and there
was a gentleness in the rain.

'I didn't know him,' he said quietly.

'You followed him here from Moonrise. I know all about him.'

'He threatened me — we pulled over.'

'No, no. Nothing like that. Shall we go have a look at what's in your car?'

'You don't believe me,' Ouksa said.

'There's nothing to believe.'

Ouksa could do nothing but go with Davuth back to the car and show him everything that was under the seat. The policeman took the passports and the money and simply walked to his car and threw them in the back. He was feeling rather pleased with himself. It had been, after all, an extremely easy trap to load and spring and he had done no work but wait and observe. The driver was a simpleton. He told Ouksa to shut up and stay by the Saber and he went through the car himself until he found the clothes and heroin equipment and the dope itself. It was to the driver's credit that he had left it behind. He took that as well and threw it into his own car and then returned to the shivering and terrified youth.

'Where are you from?'

Ouksa spilled everything about himself.

Davuth said, 'You're probably wondering what I'm going to do.'

'Yes, sir.'

'I'm not going to do anything. I'm going to give you a shovel and you're going to take all their belongings and your bat into the sugar cane and bury them.'

'Yes, sir.'

'Then you're going to go home to your wife and shut up about everything you've done. It's not difficult to understand, is it?'

Ouksa shook his head, and his misery was tinged with relief. Davuth could sense his insolence and his fear jostling in the atmosphere between them. It was a small struggle and he had to impose himself more fully.

He said, 'If you ever say anything I'll come down there and shoot you myself. I'll blow your head off like a chicken. I'll come and shoot you in the head and say you were a suspect in a murder and that's all, you'll be forgotten.'

'Yes, sir.'

'We're clear then.'

Davuth relaxed. The worm was a worm now, but he was not yet properly crushed.

What about the barang?

'Where did the barang get all this money?'

Ouksa said he had no idea.

'No idea? You're a liar, you —'

Davuth stepped up to him and took him by the throat. He had been a guard all his life, since he was thirteen or fourteen. He knew how to make fear abundant. He knew how to shake them up and make them think of the afterlife in a mass grave.

'Where did he get it?'

Faltering, Ouksa said, 'He stole it.'

'He stole it? Who was he? Who was that rich fuck?'

'He was a drug dealer, sir.'

'From where?'

'American.'

'American —'

'Yes, sir.'

'And he stole it from who?'

Now Ouksa found a petty courage.

'I don't know. From a barang.'

'You don't know? Then how do you know he stole it?'

'I heard from the boatman.'

'You're a liar.'

'No, it's true. They said —'

'What did they say?'

' — he took it from a barang.'

'Where is that other barang?'

'He left.'

'Who was that boatman, brother?'

'His name is Thy.'

To Davuth it seemed probable enough. He relaxed his grip and the tension ebbed. His point had been made and the driver had been shaken down.

'I'll give you a hundred,' he said. 'For digging that hole and burying their belongings. It's fair.'

'It's not much of a deal,' Ouksa dared answer.

'You little worm. You're the one who did it. You deserve nothing. I could shoot you now — nothing would be said.'

'Yes, sir.'

'Shut up and get digging.'

Davuth went to his car and took out a shovel and threw it at him. He turned on the Saber's headlights and sat on the bonnet and lit a cigarette. In response, Ouksa looked up at the sky: three hours of dark remaining, maybe two or less. He didn't know what time it was. He went to the barang's car and took out all the stuff that was in it and rolled it into the suitcase and dragged it out. It was a task intended to humiliate him and he knew it. Before the belongings were disposed of, however, Davuth sifted through them one last time. There were two shirts and he turned the collars and saw that they were from a tailor in Phnom Penh called Vong.

'Dig the hole properly,' Davuth said, 'and don't be lazy. Dig it a good way in and make it deep.'

The rain had now lessened but the ground was soft and sticky. Ouksa went into the cane a fair way and threw down the shovel, then went back to the ditch and began to drag the suitcase over to the same spot. It was an infuriating struggle. His feet slipped in the mud and he was not strong enough to drag it effectively. He couldn't understand why it was so heavy. It took him the better part of ten minutes to pull the thing out of view of the road and close enough to the shovel. He cursed the policeman and his devious and well-timed arrival and picked up the shovel and began to drive it into the sod between the thick sugar-cane stalks. It was a bestial task even if the rain had ceased. When the hole was finished he was exhausted and wiped his face and stood still with his ears alert. Far out in the sugar cane he could hear a distant, tiny sobbing. It was almost like the wail of a small animal, but it was certainly human. The girl, lost and bewildered and alone out there in the sea of cane. He wondered if Davuth heard it too. It was only now, surprisingly, that he thought of the Ap and a cold fear gripped him and he rolled the suitcase into its grave with a furious urgency. He filled it in with the same earth, smacked it down with the back of the shovel and dragged himself to the verge as the light was beginning to change. The policeman was still sitting coolly on the bonnet as if lost in thought and around him lay a circle of cigarette butts. His cowboy boots had been polished by someone else and they had not lost their lustre. Ouksa went up to the SUV and laid the shovel against its side and said that it was done.

'Did you pat it down?'

'It looks like nothing there.'

Davuth threw the cigarette he was smoking into the ground and then said, 'Pick up all the butts and put them in your car. Burn your shoes when you get home. I'm going to say I found a car by the roadside.'

'Yes, sir.'

Ouksa crawled about picking up the butts. Like a dog, the policeman thought. Like a vulture.

Davuth said, 'Did you hear something out there?'

'I heard an animal – an animal was crying.'

'There it is again.'

The policeman slid off the bonnet and walked up to the cane. The sobbing, again. But now so far off they could hardly hear it.

'There was someone else,' he said sharply.

He went back to Ouksa, who had stood up, and slapped him hard in the face.

'There was someone else here.'

'Yes, a girl,' the driver stammered.

'She ran off?'

The driver nodded.

'That's not very good news.'

'She didn't see my face.'

'How the fuck do you know what she saw?'

Davuth remembered. The cute Khmer girl who was under twenty-five. Did it matter that she had seen Ouksa's wretched face?

He pulled out his pistol and walked yet again to the cane and thought about going in and finishing it. But it would be impossible to find her. It was going to have to be the way it was and by and large it would work well enough. It might be more practicable to dispose of Ouksa.

He considered it. But no. It would only complicate things further. He re-holstered the gun and strolled back to the SUV and smiled at the muddied youth and told him to just drive away and pretend that nothing had happened. He wasn't very smart, he said to him, but it was better than being the American. He should thank Buddha for being alive and with all his limbs.

'And a hundred dollars better off.'

'Yes, sir.'

'It could have been you,' Davuth said, looking down at the ground to make sure that Ouksa had picked up all the butts. 'You'd be reincarnated as a cockroach.'

'I understand,' Ouksa said and bowed his head.

'Now help me carry the American into my car.'

They struggled down into the ditch. With difficulty they dragged the body back to the SUV and rolled it into the boot. It had a leaden sadness, a pointlessness. Davuth covered it with a towel and then he walked Ouksa over to his car and shone the torch into his face. He saw how colourless and soulless it had become, how his fear had grown and was now uncontrollable. It was gentleness that would seal the affair now. He turned off the beam and sighed and gave Ouksa a cigarette.

He said, 'That was a stupid thing you did. Now you'll have to live with it. Go to the temple and ask forgiveness. Pray and make merit.'

'I will, sir.'

Ouksa was now sobbing, his whole frame shaking.

'I didn't do it for me —' he began.

'It doesn't matter who you did it for. You have to make merit.'

'Yes, I know.'

'Make merit and think about your sin.'

'Yes, sir.'

It's pathetic, Davuth thought, and walked back to his car. Pathetic and necessary.

He took out the passports and looked them over. He had expected one to be the girl's, but it was not. An Englishman. He turned to Ouksa.

'Who is this?'

'Don't know, sir.'

'*Robert*. You know this one?'

Ouksa shook his head.

'Why was his passport under your seat?'

'I found them together in the barang's car. I don't know —'

The face was open. It was childish and blond, with wide-open slightly crazy eyes, those of a man who did not believe what had just happened to him. Was he alive or dead?

'Why did he . . . ?'

Davuth stared out at the sugar cane as if the answer might be there.

One can feel a human heart from a great distance; the hunter feels his prey even in a great darkness.

'They must be friends,' he murmured. 'In any case — you don't know.'

'No, sir.'

'It doesn't make sense. But you can go. I'm getting sick of looking at your miserable face. Wash your damn hands when you get home. Don't talk to your wife. Don't talk to your children. I'll know if you did.'

Davuth waited for Ouksa to drive away before walking thoughtfully around the scene. Tyre marks and footprints, yes, but that day's rain would wash them away quickly. There was just the Saber. It was best left where it was, untampered and abandoned. It was a rusting hulk anyway, it would be scavenged by midday. He walked down to the cane again and listened for the sound he had heard earlier.

The stalks, defying him, waved back and forth in the breeze and disclosed nothing. The horizon was lit. Everything had returned to normal. He thought it all through as slowly as he could and soon he realised that the less he did the better. There was no one above him in the police hierarchy at that local level who might look over his shoulder or ask him an inconvenient question. He was magnificently alone.

He drove down to the river amid the cock crows and went to a sand spit he knew and dragged the body down there and let it go gently into the water and waited until the current shifted it and bore it out into deeper water where it could move. He felt a quiet satisfaction doing it. He was familiar with death, there was nothing magical or awesome about it. It appeared and it disappeared and in that respect it was very much like life.

Fifteen

Davuth's station lay seven miles downriver from that place. It was an old French schoolhouse with perforated cement windows in some rooms and a dusty yard shaded by dying trees. There were two cars and a motorbike and a servant cleaned the rooms and made the two men meals when his other officer was there. There was a desolation about the road the station stood on. A few women had food stalls there during the day and by the gates there was always a tray of split chicken pieces and fish roasting slowly in the sun. The pale blue sign with the words *Police Station* in English and Khmer was slowly rusting at the edges and beginning to look unimposing. He sat alone for many hours in his office with the blinds down smoking bad cigars and reading horoscopes in the local papers.

When the Internet was up he played online poker and lost small amounts week by week, but indifferently and with a kind of method, and when it was down he played patience with himself and talked on the phone with the business owners he shook down now and then. He called his daughter at her school and told her to be home on time and thought for five minutes every day of his dead wife and then rode around the area in the SUV looking for what he called 'signs'. His days were usually empty and serene. On most of them, he went to the river and sat there quietly with a packed lunch and waited for the bodies of barangs to show up. It was quite a rare occurrence but there was one every month and then he would be busy.

They were mostly young, early-middle age. Europeans, Australians, a few Americans and Canadians, people drifting eastwards, doping up in Laos and Luang Prabang and coming down in the dry season to the places in the kingdom where they could winter for a few dollars and party among themselves. They picked up Khmer girls and Yaa Baa and Burmese heroin and went their merry way en route to enlightenment. The curious thing was that he had seen more of them in these last years.

They were middle class and unemployed, or so it seemed, their education now of little value, and they seemed to be able to scrounge enough money to take leave of their senses for months on end. Once upon a time, the Khmers had been in awe of them. But now their dirtiness and scruffiness and unruliness had dimmed their image at the very moment that the Chinese and the Thais had come into considerable amounts of money. The barangs no longer seemed as formidable as their grandparents, even if their grandparents had been hippies in the sixties. At least the hippies back then had class – though the sixties were an age that seemed prehistoric from the perspective of a Khmer of fifty-four, precisely because he remembered its peaceful wonders. Back then the kingdom had been a paradise on earth. The king upon his throne, the guerrillas far away in their jungles, the war in Vietnam not yet close and callous in the day-to-day. The streets were filled with girls in miniskirts. But he, to tell the truth, had mightily enjoyed the Revolution.

The barang grandchildren of that age now wandered the East with no prospects and they dropped like drunken flies into his river, forcing him to scoop them out. Naturally he knew all about the American (though he had pretended otherwise to the gullible Ouksa), but even the American could not pay for all the cremations. He, Davuth, did his best. He went through the possessions that were left behind – usually little more than a few rags and useless books but with a family heirloom ring here and there – and then went through all the desultory procedures. The call to the relevant Embassy, the filling-out of the report forms, the inventories and then, lastly, the sad and lonely cremation at the wat with only himself present.

He would wait for weeks for relatives to appear; they rarely did. The remains were forwarded to the Embassy and nobody looked very seriously at the paperwork. But he was paid nothing and it was expected of him. Over the years he had taken advantage of the situation. The missing rings and wallets and brooches and credit cards were never a subject of inquiry by his superiors. Quietly, he sold them on the black market and saved up his daughter's college fund. Everyone has to live, no matter how they do it.

He made himself a coffee in the station kitchen and called the maid and told her she could stay home that day. He knew that someone would call from the river in about two or three hours and he waited patiently for that call while he sipped his coffee and watched the sun rise over the dust-blown road. His officer was away for the morning having a medical examination. He went out into the first rays of the sun and sat in a chair and looked over at the SUV which he had cleaned thoroughly. While it was still dark he had driven to his house, burned the towel and the newspapers from the back and then taken the money and the passports and put them in the safe in his room. Before coming to the station he took out the passports, looked them over again and decided to take them with him to the station. He looked at them again now. The American's was covered with stamps from many countries. The Englishman's had nothing in it. They looked like men who were polar opposites and yet their passports were together. There were not together for reasons he yet understood, but the face of the Englishman had something sympathetic and unnerving about it. The eyes were so straight, there was no deviance in them, and he was only twenty-eight. His passport had been issued in London that same year. He did not look like the usual drifters who passed through Battambang – far from it. He looked like a wide-eyed innocent from a small town somewhere, but even the innocent can be driven mad by experience.

Now the American was dead, and where was the Englishman? No one would ever give up their passport willingly.

The American and his girl – he had seen them somewhere. At one of the bars on the water maybe long ago. A man spinning in his happiness in expensive clothes. He remembered the clothes, as one does in this country. A well-tailored man stands out.

'They all die like that,' he said aloud. Casually, as if it were nothing.

He looked at his watch, and as he did so, the phone rang and it was the owner of a riverside cafe saying there was a body near the piers under the temple at a place he

knew a mile downriver. He drove there calmly. The body
had become entangled in the beams of the jetty and
hung there while a swarm of construction workers fussed
around it trying to disentangle it. Finally they succeeded
and the limp rag doll was brought to terra firma. The
American's skin had changed colour and something had
taken a bite out of his left shin. They laid him on the
mudflat and Davuth stood there and took notes and asked
everyone to clear off and go stand further away. Then he
had an ambulance called and the body was transferred to
the police station. There it was laid in the garage while a
few photographs were taken and the coroner came and he
and Davuth talked alone in the field behind the station.
The man was an old collaborator and they saw eye to eye
in these matters. Autopsies were obligatory but sometimes
they were slyly overlooked. The man observed that the
American seemed to have suffered damage to the head
but it might have happened in the water. Indeed it might,
Davuth agreed, and they had a smoke and talked about
other things and soon they walked back to the garage and
Davuth suggested they cremate the body that day and
have done with it. The coroner was in agreement. Another
barang who had got high and thrown himself into the
river in a moment of ecstasy or despair — for were those
two states not often one and the same? They would quietly
split any proceeds between them and life would flow on
and the usual busybody from the Embassy would drive up
and ask about those same belongings. 'We couldn't find
anything,' Davuth would say and life, yet again, would
flow on nowhere towards its mysterious and nihilistic
destination.

Late in the afternoon he took the body to a wat and had

it cremated by the monks he knew. They said prayers and he gave them a small donation out of the money he'd made and then he waited patiently while the ashes were packaged and he asked them to keep them there for a week while the paperwork went through. He had his customary cheroot and walked back out into the early evening and he saw that at the top of the hill the young monks were lounging about outside their dorms and looking down — as if at a sport — at the bridge that was being built across the river. He went up there out of curiosity and sat on a wall and looked at the same thing. The half-built bridge, the curve of the river. Women washed clothes in the shallows, their long hair unfurled. A horse stood there with them, its head dipped towards the water, and young boys swam in a deeper pool near the bridge. The workers were drifting away at their day's end. Some had built fires and were cooking fish in the open. He looked up at the huge trees that towered above the dorms and one of the boy monks offered to show him something unusual for a little tip.

They walked in among the trees and it was as if night had arrived here first, bringing with it the stirred nocturnal insects and the stillness. Yet the sky was blue; there was no rain. The boy took him to the densest part of the trees and made him stand still and look up and then he abruptly clapped his hands and there was a generalised stirring in the treetops and, as if with one will, the thousands of bats hanging there erupted into life and rose into the air with a noise like locusts.

The boy turned to see his reaction and the policeman rolled back on his heels for a moment and a dark superstition came into his mind and wrecked everything there.

But then he let out a laugh and shook his head. The monks were watching them and their faces, by contrast, were immensely grave. To them it was not quite a joke or a stunt. Davuth controlled his fear as the bats then came whizzing down into the lower parts in a crazed confusion and when they had finally calmed he strode back out to the embankment and walked down to his car with something resolved in his mind. He drove back to his house and saw that his daughter had returned from school. She was seated at the kitchen table doing her schoolwork. Calm and self-contained, like many girls at that age.

He kissed her forehead and she looked up for a moment and he passed into his room where the safe was and closed the door. He took a quick cold shower then opened the safe and looked at the money and then at the passport of the Englishman. It was not avarice he felt as he went through the possibilities that had now opened before him. Something told him that a road lay ahead of him and that the road was made for him and no one else. The Englishman was also on the road and the money Davuth had inherited was not the end of the money that could be had. That barang was now a non-person, a man who had ceased to exist. Did that not make him uniquely vulnerable? He, Davuth, on the other hand, would be invulnerable when hunting him down. The idea gave him a twisted pleasure.

Then he locked everything in the safe and went into the kitchen and made his daughter dinner. They had a housekeeper who could come whenever needed and the old woman often looked after the girl when he was away on cases. He would call her in the morning. For now he made fried rice heavily sauced with *prahok*, the fermented fish paste. His daughter looked up and watched him with big cool sceptical eyes. She sensed everything about him.

'What did you do at school today?' he asked.

She told him, unconvincingly.

'I might be going away for a few days,' he said as he sat down with the rice and the *prahok*. 'It's just another job.'

'Are you looking for a bad man?'

'Not really. It's just a job.'

'But is it a bad man?'

He shrugged. 'What is a bad man?'

They ate in silence and he glanced through her exercise book. It was filled with figures of algebra, simple calculations, diagrams he could not understand. His own schooling had been interrupted by the Revolution and never resumed, but those abstractions, he always felt, were reprieves from the relentless realities of life, small delusions that paid no dividends. They had never been of any use to him, but later they would be of use to her. Education was a magic that some could use.

'Never mind about bad men,' he said, and stroked her hair. 'You don't need to think about that.'

He closed the book and gave her permission to watch television for a while. As she did so he took a beer from the fridge and went out into his little garden. He sat there looking at the clear moon and its portentous halo – a sign, surely, of ominous things to come. He felt the pressing smallness and meanness of that garden now, the evidence that he was just scraping by for all the perks he creamed from his profession. It was never enough. He wanted a house with a swimming pool and an iron gate, many things that did not come easily to lowly men. He would have to retire soon and then his slowly augmenting fund for his daughter would come to a standstill. It was not far off and he had to make the most of his remaining days of corruption and opportunity and profit. They were numbered like the fingers of his hands and as his commander had taught him to do long ago, one had to chop those fingers off one by one without thinking too much about the pain.

He thought about this later, too, when he was alone watching DVDs after his daughter had gone to bed. An HBO series called *Vikings* which he had grown fond of. The Vikings, barangs of the far north in a distant time, went about with their axes assailing the English, cutting into their flesh with pleasure. Had it really been like that, the killing days? The men with blades smiling like the Vikings – seemingly all the time – and wading through fields and villages of wattle with an intention that was, after all, inscrutable. How they hated the English Christians. They loved to spit on their crucifixes. It was fascinating – the pleasure of the desecration. Did they really enjoy the releasing of blood and the insolent disturbance of Dhamma?

He had to think this over since it had been such a theme in his own life. And it was at night that his memories came alive again and when he became aware that the ghosts of the murdered came alive as well and roamed across the land. It was known to everyone in the villages. His own past, too, was re-enacted nightly in this way. He sometimes thought that in a demented way his past was very short, almost non-existent. He had been a child in the sixties, in the happy time. But what did he remember of that?

The devious King Sihanouk in white and the music of Ros Sothea. The song called 'Venus'. But the Angkar said it was all an illusion. There was no happiness then, it had all been a facade.

Later, it seemed that his life had begun with the Revolution and many men had said the same thing. Their lives began on 17 April. It began then on that day, but when would it end? Where would his soul migrate to?

I'll be an ant, he sometimes thought. I'll be crushed by the heel of a schoolgirl on her way to school. I'll be the size of a crushed seed.

'The blood debt must be paid with blood,' the Angkar used to say. 'To show you mercy is no gain, to destroy you is no loss.'

Even before 1975, before he had become a *kamabhipal* for the Angkar, visions came to save and destroy him. They lay in the fields in terror when the B52s came upon them. They avoided touching the ground with their faces so that the vibrations of the bombs would not give them nosebleeds. On the far horizons of those summer days the red dust rose in a wall to the height of half a mile. Beautiful, astonishing. Silent and sombre beyond the cassava fields. It was like the oncoming of Vishnu, destroyer of worlds.

Through his village in the midst of these dust storms of bombs came the spindly boys in black with their weapons. The servants of the Angkar. So it had begun for him a long, long time ago, the eradication of his heart. Long before the war and the camps and the triumph of the Angkar. Life, then, was a mystery, but it was a cheap one. 'We are all under one sky,' his father used to say, meaning that all suffer the same in the end. But it was not true.

When he became a *kamabhipal* he saw every day that the 'old people' survived and the 'new people', the '17 April people', the doctors and the university people, the ministers even and their families, were crushed and dissolved with whips and their throats were cut with palm fronds. He worked for months at a secret camp in the forest, learning the new ways. He learned to lie under floorboards and listen to the conversations of villagers. The next day they could be denounced, dragged down to the river and cut apart with machetes. Their bodies went downriver.

Davuth was a peasant and so he had been one of the 'old people'. His class were the builders of Angkor long ago, the salt of the earth, the wielders of threshers and fish traps. The ones whose faces were carved in stone a thousand years ago. People were not all under one sky.

The ghosts now walking quietly through the tobacco knew that better than anyone. The killers lived under a different sky. He looked up now and saw that the stars had reappeared and their glacial brilliance made him frown. It felt as if he could look right through them into the meaningless chasm beyond, and when he did he felt strangely reassured. It was not nothingness that instilled fear in him, it was the morbid idea that life had meaning after all.

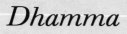

Dhamma

Sixteen

Sophal watched the halo around the moon and she ran her hand along the curve of Robert's spine and her thoughts moved back and forth like a comb moving through thick hair that it cannot disentangle. Hours passing in repetition, and there was no forward movement. She couldn't sleep and the rain distracted her, it never seemed to give her a break. The streets slowly filling like saucepans, the rot beginning again and the men wading along them looking for small opportunities. But still the moon was there despite the clouds (there was no accounting for that) and she watched it drily, wondering if it would explode one fine night and finally leave her alone. The English boy slept like a miner. He slept like that but he never did any real work. Some part of her regretted her rashness in sleeping with him so quickly, but she had drunk too much too quickly and as the evening had progressed she had felt how lost and childish he was. But now she seemed to feel him more clearly. There was something also off-orbit about him, something spinning without wheels. She didn't believe in his name, and his descriptions of his past did not quite ring true.

Did such things matter? No one ever knew much about another person. Charm was sometimes more than enough. She got up and went to the bathroom and for some strange reason began brushing her hair. Naked, she looked oily and burnished in the mirror, like something distant and far-off, and she could not recognise herself for a moment.

The previous year, she had been a medical student in Paris. Her father could imagine nothing better than her one day becoming a doctor like himself. A doctor with French qualifications. One night she had been called out to accompany a medical team who wanted her go with them to the hard suburb of Kremlin-Bicêtre to unlock the apartment of a Khmer man who had gone missing seven years earlier. She went at three in the morning, the same rain. The social workers broke down the door and found a neat and orderly apartment, very Khmer in its tastes, and in the centre of the small kitchen the caretaker from Takeo who had been made redundant in 2002, hanging by a gardening rope.

The electricity had been cut off and the place was cold and dark and the body, by some chemical miracle, was perfectly preserved. They held up torches and took notes and waited for the police to arrive and cut down the body. A lonely and unknown Khmer man of forty-three made redundant during a management restructuring. They knew his name. Chann Ong. His name meant 'the moon'. The surname, Hokkien Chinese. He had killed himself and his body was discovered that night, seven years after the event. Her superstitious mind pondered it, though she said nothing to the Frenchwomen with her.

She touched the naked foot, like the foot of a mummy which has not lost its colour entirely. They catalogued everything in the apartment. His twelve Buddhist books, his dusty toiletries, the old Pan Ron records. His bed had been made and the towels folded and left on it. A doll's house for a dead man.

No one could explain how a cadaver could remain preserved for seven years. Before hanging himself Chann Ong had sealed all the windows tight and placed a towel under the door. So the room had been almost airless. No flies, no air, no bacteria? But still they could not explain it. She thought to herself, 'It was his death wish,' and something in her stirred, she suddenly wanted to go home. It was not a feeling she had had before. They cut down the body and she felt like crying in front of all these quietly appalled French people, for how could they understand anything that had gone through Chann Ong's mind as he sealed his death chamber and climbed that kitchen chair? It was not just the despair of losing his job and writing the dozens of angry letters to the management in order to receive desultory brush-offs. There was an anterior history, a shared history that was written upon the unconscious, and she understood it.

When she told her father this story he immediately asked her his age. Then he nodded and said that it was self-explanatory. Chann Ong was 'one of us'. One of the people of Year Zero, the first year of the Revolution – or the 17 April people, as the unindoctrinated or 'old people' were known.

It was brushing her hair in the Englishman's mirror that made her think of Chann Ong and so he was not, then, entirely forgotten in his own land. Where was his ghost, then – here or there? Wandering the boulevards of Phnom Penh or those of Paris? She stood up straight and stared into her own eyes and remembered the crinkled soles of his feet and the certainty that it was a sign from the afterlife to her.

That night she drove home to her flat in Marx Dormoy along empty streets and her gloom deepened. She wanted to be home. It was she who wrote to the Khmer Embassy and told them about Chann. No one knew what to do with a perfectly preserved corpse – superstition had entered the equation. In bed, she told her French boyfriend about it and became slightly hysterical. But nerves never healed a situation. He told her, in his calm European way, that ghosts didn't exist and she thought cruelly, the divide between us is enormous, isn't it?

Later it seemed to her that this might have been the moment in which she decided to leave Europe, but in reality she had never been quite happy there. Easy to love Paris, yes, easy to love Sunday-morning walks on the Île de la Cité with her Frenchman and the pastries at Stohrer on the Rue Montorgueil and a hundred other things great and small. But even with Claude she always felt alone. She was not really in love with him. Her favourite place in the city, after all, was the church of Saint Gervais and Protais near the river, whose back door was always left open late at night. She would go there and sit alone in the pews and feel the musty medieval ghosts in that Gothic nave. She was sure she could have been a psychic if she had wanted to. An upper-middle-class Khmer girl with a little family money but no inner reason to be in that world apart from a medical education and a taste for escape. What she had escaped from was her own family. The gloom that surrounded them like an invisible miasma. They were people who frequently liked to quip, 'It's a miracle we're alive!' But if it was a miracle, who could explain it, and why should other miracles not exist?' 'Do I believe in miracles?' she began to ask herself. 'Me, a doctor in the making, a rational agent?' Could a body really remain perfectly preserved for years in a sealed room? Her father said yes. But it was a miracle anyway.

It was now her own life as a temporary emigrant that began to feel insubstantial. All along, it had been her father who drove her from behind, who constantly admonished her to succeed in Europe. She was doing it for him. Even listening to classical music − it was his urging, his idea. It was he who had driven her to be ambitious and study in Paris. In reality it had been his own dream and she was the one who now had to fulfil it. Not being her own dream, however, it sat uneasily with her. She was not, in fact, ferociously ambitious. She wanted to drift and roam and roll through childish adventures, not get up for 9 a.m. lectures and dissect cadavers in cold rooms. Yet she also thought having dreams, the very concept of having a dream, was childish and absurd. Why did one need to have illusions like that in order to just live? Living was not a project with a propaganda film driving it. It was pulled along by mystery and pleasure, not by a desire to have a big house in Neuilly by the time she was forty.

And increasingly, finally, the enchantment of Paris began to wear off. The sullen bitterness under the surface, the men pissing in the streets defiantly, the feel of quiet decay. It was a slow-motion decay which had gone hand in hand with a slightly hysterical campaign of urban renewal and antiseptic respectability. But the men were still pissing in the street and there was still a feeling of stasis and creeping old age. Europe dying on its feet of torpor and smugness and debt. Half the people her own age were unemployed, living in a state of dependency. At the hospital they were continually handing out free antidepressants to middle-class brats who didn't want to pay for them. It would have been morally shocking in Phnom Penh of course, and privately she *was* shocked. But her boyfriend scoffed at her. Why shouldn't they have free Paxil for their imaginary mental disorders? 'You're all brainwashed to accept it,' she retorted. 'You have no connection to real life. You're on life support and you don't even know it.' Work isn't everything, he would sometimes say, thinking that she would agree with him, given her wonderfully lazy proclivities. And yet she knew it was false. Work indeed was everything and she began to wonder if she would ever have work that meant something to her. She didn't want to be a doctor, however. Working full-time as a doctor in Paris had the vague feeling of living as a tourist in an expensive boutique now designed merely for other tourists. What her father didn't understand because he lived mentally in another age was that now it was Europe that was adrift and listless. Her sense of moral superiority was also adrift – how often Sophal had to listen to overheated journalistic lectures about trafficking and servitude in her own country from these fleshy know-it-alls, who in reality knew nothing at all about anything. Thank God, she began to think severely, you're here to save us. To make us more like you.

She returned to the bedroom and kissed Robert on his cheek and walked back out into the fresh, wet early morning and downstairs to the lobby where the boys were all asleep like figures in a painting. The rain had finally stopped and she walked down to Norodom and went along the boulevard in the lonely coolness, glad to be alone again and wondering about what had happened. It didn't occur to her to think about whether she had enjoyed it. Enjoyment was not the issue yet. There was something graver at stake. But this grave thing was — apart from being grave — distressingly unclear. It was about whether she had thrown herself into a well.

She found the first cafe open in a side street and sat at an outside table with a double espresso and a croissant and smoked her Wonders as the traffic began to thicken and a pale light spread across the facades of the travel agents and two-bit boutique hotels and chic bakeries. There must be a moment when happiness begins — an actual, precise moment — and she began to think that she was experiencing that moment now. She let the smoke calm her and still her shaking hands.

When they had calmed she remembered other moments like this in the past. When her French boyfriend had asked her to come with him to see his family in Avignon. But on that occasion she had refused. The prospective happiness had been too elaborate, too planned, and her prim refusal of it had made complete sense only hours afterwards. One wasn't happy so easily. She was convinced, perhaps childishly, that it had to be unexpected. That was the problem with her whole European phase: where was the unexpected?

Simon was the unexpected incarnate.

She walked home then and let herself in through the outer gate and went through the dripping garden as the maids were beating the carpets in the damp air. They looked up her with amused complicity, those two old women who had known her since she was small. She went up to her room and fell onto her bed in her clothes and slept into the late afternoon, and when she woke the koel birds were announcing an early evening of mosquitoes and low sun and drinks with ice at the edge of growing shadows.

Seventeen

She went out that night to a party at the house of a
French artist on a street not far from her own house.
She walked there along Pasteur, past the upscale lounge-
style restaurants and the Japanese bars. Like her father's
house, it was a massive old French villa which the owner
had restored with his personal fortune. In his garden, the
Frenchman had placed artworks by several well-known
Khmer artists and surrounded them with an open bar lit
with Vietnamese lanterns. Inside, the ground floor had
been converted into the evening's playground and there
she whiled away a few hours drinking vodka cocktails
and finding her friends. It was the sort of evening she was
becoming used to during her time of 'unemployment'.
With no pressing financial worries, no rent to pay, she
could do what she wanted with her evenings and she had
consequently fallen into a lulling rhythm of long nights
and late risings and mild hangovers. She knew it would
pass eventually, but for the moment she felt it was exactly
what a twenty-five-year-old should be doing with her
life. There were no pleasant surprises, but no unpleasant
surprises either. She was now in her own culture and she
could float or sink according to its own laws of gravity.

She went up to the balcony that looked down onto the garden and a friend of hers found her at eleven, sitting alone and looking down at the handsome boys in the garden. It was an old school friend, a girl who now worked at the American Embassy as a translator, a girl who had suddenly become fatter than herself. The wearisome chatter began.

'I haven't seen you in a while,' the girl began.

'I've been looking for work.'

'We thought you had a boy. Someone saw you with a boy – last night.'

Sophal gave a slight start and then laughed it off. 'That was quick!'

'Someone was at China House and saw you with a barang boy.'

'I can't wriggle out of it.'

'So, who was it?'

The girl snuggled up closer.

I'm not going to play games, Sophal thought grimly.

'An English boy I met. He's my English tutor.'

A ripple of laughter. 'No way!'

'My father hired him.'

'But you had other ideas. That was a fast move.'

'It wasn't a move. We just hung out.'

'Uh-huh. Is he here?'

'Of course he's not here.'

'Why of course?'

'I didn't ask him anyway.'

The girl was sure she would know him. She knew all the eligible barangs.

'What's his name?'

'Do I really have to tell you, Arunny?'

'Of course you do.'

It was tiresome, but in the end it was better to get it over and done with. Sophal didn't really care either way.

'His name's Simon Beauchamp. He's teaching English for a year, I guess. He used to work in a bank.'

'It sounds familiar.'

'Really? He's only just got here –'

'Is that what he said?'

'Pretty clearly.'

'I could have sworn – I've heard the name before. But it was last year. More than a year ago.'

'Then it couldn't have been him.'

'Is he blond?'

'He's got blondish bits.'

'I think I met him.'

Sophal put down her drink and her weariness vanished. 'You met him?'

The girl tittered and rolled her eyes.

'I think I did. Simon – yes, I'm sure I met him.'

'Where?'

'At a party somewhere. On a boat in the river. Some German guy – you know those parties.'

'Who was he with?'

'I think he was with some Khmer girl.'

So that was it.

'But you're not sure?'

'Well,' the girl snorted, 'I couldn't swear to it obviously –'

'What could you swear to?'

'Nothing much. It just rings a bell – the name.'

Sophal was angry for a moment.

'I find that hard to believe.'

'There's nothing to *believe*,' the girl retorted. 'I'm just telling you what I remember. Lighten up, Sophal. These guys are all the same. They tell you what you want to hear.'

Sophal supposed this was true.

'So you mean he's been here longer than he said?'

'Well, yeah.'

'It's a possibility, isn't it?'

Her voice was sad for a moment and the girl flinched.

'It's no big deal,' she offered. 'I just met him at a river party. I mean, I didn't do anything with him!'

'I didn't say you did. It's just annoying.'

'Men *are* annoying, didn't you know?'

'I don't find them that annoying. It's myself I find annoying.'

'Why don't you invite him now and I'll tell you if it's him?'

Sophal threw up her hands.

'God, I hate things like this. I don't care if he was here last year. He had his reasons to lie.'

'I dare say,' the girl said sarcastically.

'I knew it. I had a feeling —'

'One always does.'

'It's true.' Sophal paused. 'Shall I invite him?'

'No. Let's get drunk. Invite him later.'

But for the rest of the evening Sophal let it prey upon her mind. The one thing that had never occurred to her was that Simon had lied about the length of his sojourn in her city. That lie seemed more fantastical than others he might have told and deep down she didn't quite believe it. Naivety is hard to simulate. And if Simon was one thing, it was naive. She had never seen naivety like it.

It was like snow with only a tinge of dirt.

The following day she called him and when he didn't

216

pick up she sent him a text message. She invited him to meet her at a venerable French restaurant called Van inside the old Banque d'Inchochine building. She said it was her treat and to wear a nice shirt. He accepted. She stayed in all day studying, then told her father that she was going to Van for an English lesson. 'With Simon,' he said with a smile. She went back upstairs and dressed in an Agnès B dress she had bought in Paris and which fitted her perfectly and a pair of steely pearl earrings. It was a different look, a rich girl's look, and she knew how to do it. It was a look that had a bit of thunder and lightning to it. She had never been glamorous or even pretty in her own estimation but she knew how to carry the colour black. She put on a thin layer of lipstick.

That night a few protests erupted around the city. She heard the staccato pop of sporadic gunfire, the far-off din of violence. On her way to the restaurant she passed the remains of shattered barricades littered with shoes, bloody T-shirts and tear-gas cartridges. Police stood at the corners in their plastic face visors, weapons tilted on hips. The acrid taste of the gas had not yet dissipated. Yet a few blocks away it was as if nothing was happening. Van, in any case, was one of the older and pricier French places which ambassadors, sundry diplomats and businessmen liked to frequent when they wanted to sink into no-nonsense old-school French food. Tournedos Rossini, as at Le Royal, with wedges of foie gras and perch quenelles and *timbales de crevettes* downed with bargain-price bottles of Duhart-Milon. The restaurant was wainscoted and the floors creaked when the shy, silent Khmer waiters dared to cross them. It was almost always half empty but its small outdoor terrace overlooked the wide square by the colonial Post Office.

She got there first and was shown to the outdoor table which she had specified. She ate there with her parents and they knew her well. The square was alive with motodops and streaming crowds. From the table by the wall she could even look down at the nocturnal girls sitting on stools outside the wild bars on Street 102. It was an alien energy which threw the quiet European terrace into relief, but it often happened that it still unsettled the diners' subtle feeling of superiority, especially if they were visiting Europeans. Not Sophal. She sat there now and ordered a Kir Royale. They made them thick and sweet here and she liked them that way. She could smoke outside and she liked the slight swish of the mosquitoes around her bare shoulders. She had, in fact, been coming there since she was little, and the waiters were subtly indulgent to her. One of them lit her cigarette for her. Then she saw Robert walking across the square with his shoulders slightly hunched, in the same linen trousers he always wore. The shirt he always wore. Men did love their lazy uniforms. He even saw her on the terrace and they waved and she saw for a moment the dirty-snow naivety in his face. She was becoming surer that her friend had made a banal mistake. They always took too many drugs at parties with foreigners.

Robert came into the monochrome tiled downstairs lobby with the old heavyset green doors of the bank. There was a shrine there and a kitsch statue fountain of a European angel. Inside, Khmer statuary, a droplet chandelier and steep polished wooden stairs which led up to a claustrophobic landing where the glass windows of a fridge displayed to passing diners prime cuts of Australian beef. The chandelier-lit main room was robed with sashed cotton curtains and there was an ancient phonogram on a pedestal, but no guests except a table of elderly French tourists. A waiter escorted him to the terrace. There was no one there either but Sophal and he was for a moment taken aback by the almost brutal elegance of the black dress and the earrings and the colour of the mouth that was smiling back at him.

He had been walking along the river all day. His face was burned and tanned at the same time and it made him look older and more rugged, more worn-in. It was a look she liked in white men. When they burned off their pallor they seemed to come visually alive, and alive in other ways too. He made a quick joke about the formality of Van and she shrugged and said it was her father's favourite restaurant.

The terrace seemed submerged in trees, in frangipani flowers; the walls of the building exactly the same sorbet yellow as her father's house with the same white stucco. An Italian villa of some kind. Only the vast and violent clouds gave away the true location.

'Steak Rossini?' Robert said.

'There's nothing wrong with it.'

'I ate it last time with your father.'

He sat and took her hand and turned it for a moment and kissed the back and the light sweat came off on his mouth.

'You look like – I don't know what.'

'Don't say princess.'

It was the word he'd been about to use.

'Something *like* a princess.'

She called the waiter.

'Two Kir Royales. Actually, no, this time I'll have mine *de mure*. I always go from blackcurrant to blackberry.'

Robert glanced at the empty glass in front of her.

'I'll have the blackberry one as well then.'

'Yes, sir.'

'You can have it with red too,' she said. 'It's called a Communard.'

'I think not. Anything with a name like that here —'

She took his hand back and kissed it in turn.

'It was probably the only cocktail allowed in the seventies. I'll ask my father about that.'

Fireworks began over the river, half obscured by the Banque d'Inchochine building. People stood still in the square and watched. A fairy atmosphere descended and the chemistry between them had slightly altered; a night's sleep, a few hours to reflect. It was now a closer bond, to their surprise. It was she who talked. Some *amuse-bouches* came and they attacked them with little silver forks. Beyond the glass doors the rich old tourists ate by candlelight, sepulchral, and their motions with knives and forks were in comical slow motion. The chandeliers twinkled with a subdued melancholy which suggested that they had been there far longer than even these ageing tourists had been alive. Robert, in any case, was glad to be above and beyond the sweaty real city for an hour and with someone else paying. He had walked for miles that day, past the Sofitel and along the jumbled river, and he couldn't really tell her why. A confusion, a disorientation. An incoherent desire to walk out of the city altogether. He had sat on a bank of weeds some miles out of the centre and felt each minute passing like a miniature century. A migraine throbbed through his head and he felt himself wishing that he was somewhere else. Vietnam, perhaps, or even China. Just somewhere *further on* where not even one person knew him and where he could be himself again. Sooner or later he would have to do that anyway. When he looked at Sophal's face he felt a sullen guilt and he wanted to just tell her everything in a few brutal sentences. But it would never happen. The deeper he sank into his own lie, the deeper he would drag her until they were both so deep in, it would no longer be worth trying to crawl out of it.

'My father likes you more and more,' she was saying. 'He likes the idea of you more than anything, I think. I've always thought the idea of a person and the person himself are more or less the same.'

'I wish I could talk him out of that. I don't really understand —'

'He says, by the way, I should take you to Phnom Chisor. It's only an hour away and we could take the family driver. Like a picnic. Would you like to do that?'

'A day trip?'

'Yes, and you might even like it. Of course I don't know what you like. It's a ruined temple, like Angkor but lonelier.'

'I like ruins. Or I *think* I like them.'

'We're famous for our ruins. People who come here are more interested in our ruins than they are in us.'

'They have to be interested in something.'

'But not you — you don't seem interested in anything.'

'I'm a bit aimless, it's true.'

'I know you're a pathless wanderer. I can tell.'

'Is that your phrase?'

She said, 'That's my phrase, yes. I'm always right too.'

He threw up his hands and smiled. 'Then I'm a pathless wanderer. Is there a cure?'

'Marriage.'

'Then I'll have to be pathless for a while —'

'You'll be thirty soon. Then it's almost too late.'

'Is it? Not in my country, it isn't.'

'You're not in your country.'

He put down his knife and fork and said he wanted to buy her a bottle of wine. A Bordeaux, no?

'Big spender!' she cried.

The Duhart-Milon, then.

It was a mad expense, but he calculated he could just about manage it and survive. He ordered the wine and she told him it was entirely unnecessary but that she was glad he had. She needed a serious drink and a bottle of Duhart-Milon was it. When it came they went quiet and it was poured and they raced into it with a childish pleasure.

'I love getting drunk like this,' she said. 'In the dark on a terrace. With a silly boy.'

'So now I'm silly too?'

'Yes.'

In fact, the wine had gone to his head immediately.

'Shouldn't I be teaching you English?'

'Go ahead.'

'I forgot the lesson.'

'Then there is no lesson today. You'll have to make it up to me.'

'You've been speaking English since you were three.'

'Two.'

'So your dad is wasting his money.'

'Isn't that his problem?'

'Well, I suppose it is.'

Robert cut into his timbale and he thought ahead for some reason – to the following day, to the following decade.

He said, 'It seems quite unreal here. Has your father

been coming to this place for years? It seems like his kind of place.'

'All of us have been coming here for years. It's our place.'

'Your father seems very kind. He didn't need to give me that money. I didn't want to take it —'

'I wouldn't worry about that. He wanted to help you.'

'That's just the thing — I don't understand why.'

'There's nothing to understand. It's a feeling — he has a feeling for you. It's enough for him.'

'I'm not even teaching you English. He knows perfectly well you speak it perfectly.'

'*Perfectly.*'

'So it's just a ruse, isn't it? Perhaps I shouldn't mind. I should just shut up and take the money.'

'That's pretty much what you should do, Mr Beauchamp.'

'In a way I did.'

She fed him a forkful of green beans.

'You have a charmed life. There's something charmed about you. People do things for you — don't they?'

'I wish they did. I don't think they do.'

'You land on your feet anyway. They think you're helpless and have to be helped.'

'I *am* kind of helpless.' He looked at her archly.

She said, 'It's your greatest asset. You never know what's going on. There's a definite charm in that, but I'm not sure it lasts forever. For the moment you're doing very well.'

'You make me sound rather awful.'

'Awful's an old-fashioned word. You're not that, you're something else. The maids say something amazing about you. They say you have an aura of disaster about you.'

She covered her mouth with her hand as she laughed.

'Jesus,' he sighed.

'They're country women. They can see these kinds of things.'

It was probably true. He was disaster incarnate, lumbering through the world without a clue and destroying everything around him without knowing it. But the idea that this quality projected an aura — it might have been true.

'But then,' she went on, 'there are disasters and disasters. What kind of disasters do you bring on?'

'None that I am aware of.'

She pouted. 'I don't believe it. You're a disaster on two legs.'

'On four legs,' he said.

They ate clafoutis for dessert. His body broke into an uncontrollable sweat. It ran between his eyes and he looked up at the clouds and caught the far-off lightning. He felt a hundred years old and he drank most of the bottle without remembering his manners. All his life he had drunk when he felt nervous and now he felt nervous again with her. Any minute, he had decided, she was going to unmask him and then there would be a miserable and wretched scene. He had decided he wasn't going to grovel and apologise. He was going to laugh it off and be a boor and tell her a tall story and that would be that, they would part and it wouldn't matter.

'I think I said before,' she was saying, 'that you don't seem like a teacher. I never asked you what you teach — it's rude of me.'

'It's all right. English literature.'

He didn't say it with much enthusiasm.

'Is that a hard one to teach?'

'I have the feeling it's a dinosaur subject. The children aren't interested in it any more. I feel like I'm just talking to a wall most of the time.'

'They're more interested in the Internet?'

'I don't know what they're interested in. It's not like I'm so much older than them — but it feels like two or three generations. They're on a different planet.'

'Then you should change job.'

'There's something sad about it,' he admitted. 'Do you know who John Donne is?'

Slowly, she shook her head.

'You think all the time that these famous writers are universal and then you realise that no one outside of a very small culture has ever heard of them, not even in your own country. If Khmers read John Donne I'd be delighted and amazed. But when fifteen-year-old English boys don't know even know the name . . .'

'Is it surprising?' she asked.

'That they're forgotten? Maybe. Then what am I doing with my life? Teaching forgotten things to those who won't remember.'

She shook her head. 'No, you're a teacher. That's your mission.'

'Not now anyway. Let someone else do it. I've decided to be in the present and nowhere else. Like everyone else.'

'Maybe you could teach John Donne in Cambodia — be the first one.'

'A brilliant idea which no one will go for.'

But long ago the French had probably taught Alfred de Vigny and Victor Hugo to little Khmer children in stuffy schoolhouses. It could be done for a while, futilely and nobly. He thought of the room where he taught in Elmer with its walls covered with pop posters of Great Writers intended to make them more appealing to teenagers who would never, in fact, find them appealing. Shakespeare in a hip beard, Wordsworth in psychedelic colours. The hint that they took drugs and had orgies. The hard, yet wandering look in those teenagers' eyes as he walked back and forth with an open book, reading paragraphs of George Eliot. It was comical, but there was no other way. His rage built up over a long time but it was a rage against the years he himself had spent mastering this material. He had to justify it somehow. He could not just admit that it had been a waste of life and time.

They went for a walk in the rain by the river and it seemed like the first night they had been together, only the city seemed larger and brighter and fuller. They planned out their picnic to Phnom Chisor as they sat on the promenade wall and looked up at the white kids eating pizza at the FCC.

'Are you really going to find a job here?' he asked. 'I got the feeling you missed Paris.'

'I went for an interview at a hospital today. It went well. I can find a job – they need doctors here – but that's not the problem.'

'What's the problem then?'

'I don't know. I'm never happy in any one place. Perhaps the world got too small.'

'That's exactly the problem.'

They walked down to 130 and got ice creams on the street. The Quay was lazily alive with drifters and amorous strollers dragging their feet under the frangipanis; they walked over to a man selling toy birds on the kerb, transparent birds filled with throbbing coloured lights which gave off a manic chatter like an aviary of living animals. It was astonishingly realistic and yet the birds glowed red and blue and violet. It was there that they ran into one of her friends, a Dutch artist who was walking home with two models for a night of painting. His name was Horst and it was not his name. They tagged along and soon they were climbing up a dark stairway to a terraced studio with paintings all over the floors and jam jars filled with fresh joints. They sat on the floor of the terrace with the glow of nearby neon flashing on and off and the sound of real caged birds in the unit above and the Khmer girls took off their clothes and posed and they drank a lot of vodka together. Horst was a small man filled with electric energy. He had been married four times to courtesans, three of them in Africa, and had washed up on the shores of the Tongle Sap in search of further illuminations. He paid his girlfriend, who was not there, two thousand dollars a month to share his bed and his canvases, though the canvases were more important to him than the bed. His career was successful and he made a small fortune selling his work in upscale galleries in Amsterdam. At night he trawled the bars and clubs looking for faces who could fill his nightmare paintings and by and large he found them. Now he sent one of the girls down to get them oysters and she returned with a vast plate of crustaceans wrapped in cellophane and bedded on crushed ice. They ate them on the floor with lemons and iced beers and hot green dipping sauce. Horst took off his clothes as well and soon they were all naked and smoking the joints while Horst painted the two girls. It was three in the morning when they came down. They went home separately and agreed to meet early the next morning at Colonial Mansions.

*

She was there with her family driver at seven. They had a coffee by the pool amid chattering pintails.

'I didn't sleep,' she said cheerfully. 'And yet I don't feel tired at all.'

'It's far too early – but I don't feel tired either.'

She had brought her swimsuit and they went into the pool for a while and sipped their coffee at the edge with their bodies submerged. Then, at about eight, they headed out of the city in a clear blue morning tinged with yellow dust and found the long, straight road that swept past the darkened temples of Ta Phrom towards Chisor.

Eighteen

At Ta Phrom they stopped and walked away from the dusty car park into the piles of stones and soon they had come to the great back wall which seemed to be shored up with wild flowers. A group of children had followed them with expertly desperate eyes and they murmured continuously to Sophal in Khmer as they wandered across to a new temple in the short shadows of morning. It was the hour when the grass is alive and butterflies swirled around them. She took his hand as they circled back to the ruins and picked their way into a sanctuary lit by a high skylight and then back to the car park where the driver waited. Between the pale yellow straps of her dress the shoulder blades had become lustrous with moisture and the silver watch on her wrist sparkled against a skin that now looked as dark as cinnamon bark. At Chisor, the vendors were not yet there and the vast steps leading to the top of the little mountain were empty. They began to climb and when they had cleared the treeline they stopped and sat on the steps next to a home-made shrine and felt their heartbeats. The horizon was flat and green, slightly hazed, and at its furthest limit the mauve clouds gathered in a line of tension.

'It's the end of the rains,' she said, holding out her tongue. 'I can taste it.'

The slopes were forest, singing with insects. Higher up, the surrounding plain appeared as a partial circumference with no signs of the present century. The sky's blue flesh became richer and out of it poured a blinding sunlight. The steps ended in a cluster of temple outbuildings and a path that crested and then fell downwards towards the ruins. At the highest point they rested again and Robert looked down at the endless flight of steps and he thought he saw a man standing there in the shade of a few trees. The figure was in a shabby dark suit and he was talking to a monk who had appeared out of nowhere and the two men were gesturing to each other in some manner. He squinted and then shaded his eyes and he thought, in this light one could hallucinate anything. He turned back to Sophal, who was looking the other way towards the ruins which could not, in fact, be seen from that vantage point.

'I love it when there's no one here,' she was saying.

'I wonder how many people have heart attacks on those steps.'

Leaning in, he kissed the glistening space between the shoulder straps. She flinched slightly.

His lips moved against her hot skin, 'I think we're being watched.'

'There's always someone watching.'

No doubt it was true. Or half true.

She raised her eyebrows and her smile was slight, as if she for one didn't mind being watched. As if that was a norm she could accept.

The downward path passed by some handsomely maintained new buildings, including a quadrangular pond. The paint white and gold and fresh. There were donation plaques from Buddhists in America. They came down into a kind of square with ancient trees and old people lying on the benches seemingly oblivious to them. Prayer flags moved in the wind and from the square they could look out over the dark green plain where the oval shadows of clouds moved like grazing cows. Behind them rose the ruins. Temples of Vishnu long toppled and scattered. They moved between the buildings in a gathering and claustrophobic heat and eventually climbed up through a weathered portal and onto the top of a flight of steps that led down to a terrace. Here they lay in the sun for a while. The wind flowed over them and there was no sound but that. Humans seemed not yet to have arrived in that landscape or to have left long ago – you couldn't tell which. He reached over and laid his hand on her breast and the smile came back, the same slight, stone-carved smile that made her face so serene-looking and ancestral. She turned over and they began to kiss. Soon, however, he heard voices in the square and they got up and walked to the end of the terrace and sat there for a long time enfolded in each other until the clouds on the horizon advanced halfway across the plain. He could see her features in the stone faces above them. The bloodlines, ancient and unbroken, and the mouths with the same smiles. It was a matter of observation not romantic fantasies. Then, as they watched the plain darken and a roll of thunder reached them, he felt a sudden wave of cold fear overtake him and he turned his head and looked up at the walls. There was no one there but it didn't matter. There was something there, if not something in human form.

He said, 'It's going to rain, isn't it? We should beat a retreat.'

He had never believed in the supernatural, but as they wandered slowly back through the ruins he permitted himself the feeling that comes with the nearness of ghosts. Inside the sanctuaries, candles had been lit which had not been lit before. There were flowers, dishes of sweets and incense, and the air had become denser with perfume. At the square the old people had roused themselves and watched them with less indifference. A few monks also sat there eating from plastic plates, though no tourists. They sauntered back up the hill to the covered platform where the steps began and sat there in the shade with some cold water they had bought from an old lady with an ice box near the pond. Sophal was thinking ahead to dinner with her parents that night. Should she invite the English boy as well? She was a little confused. She could never gauge how much her father could guess about her.

'What are you doing tonight?' she finally asked.

Robert shrugged and he was conscious of the gesture being lame. He was about to add something when she said, 'You can come and have dinner with us tonight if you like. It's a bit boring for you, but I'll be there!'

'Then I'll come.'

'I'll call them when we're driving back. You sure you don't have other plans?'

'I never make plans.'

'Look,' she said, pointing to the steps below them.

The monk was still there, seated under an orange parasol, and it reminded him at once of the temple near Battambang where he had seen Simon. The other man in the shabby suit had disappeared but he had the feeling that this disappearance was not genuine.

'I'm so glad to be back in this country,' she said quietly. 'Are you surprised by that?'

'Not at all.'

'This place is special. Don't you think?'

'I can feel that.'

'I'm happy you can. But somehow you seem anxious. What are you anxious about?'

'I am?'

She had noticed all along that when she looked at him from the side his cheek twitched as if his jaw was clenched. His foot always tapped, his eyes always moved quickly.

'Yes. You are always nervous in some way.'

'Am I really nervous?'

'Yes, you are. There's something nervous about you.'

Indeed, it was why she didn't quite trust him.

'You're always on the lookout.'

'I don't think so —'

'You haven't done anything bad, have you, Simon?'

'What do you mean?'

'You haven't cheated any of your other students?'

He said, slightly annoyed, 'I think I'm pretty relaxed. By English standards anyway.'

'Well, you are not a relaxed people.'

'We are what we are.'

'If you're in trouble —'

'Why would I be in trouble?'

But his laugh was obviously forced.

'People,' she said, 'get into all kinds of trouble.'

'Not me.'

On their way back, he was agitated. Sometimes he felt that he was inside a huge broken machine and that there was no exit from it. You're out of my mind, he thought, remembering a poem about William Burroughs, or was it a line of Burroughs himself? I'm out of your mind. You're out of my mind.

He slept alone for a while at the Mansions and then walked over to the Sar home to have dinner with the family – it was their specific request. The servants had laid out a table in the garden since the rain had not returned, and dull, dusty-looking stars twinkled above the city's orange glare. There the three of them sat around candles in glass shells and their faces had a curiously conspiratorial look when he observed them from the windows of the house. The mother was holding forth about something, her hand rising for a moment to emphasise a point then sinking back to her knee. There were tall glasses of white wine. They were an eccentric family, without a doubt; but what made them eccentric was not eccentricity in itself. When he appeared the doctor rose and he made the same gesture with his finger that he had made at the Royal restaurant. They were sitting under a mango tree that looked to be at least a hundred years old, and as if reading his mind the doctor said, almost at once, 'See, this is our tree that has been here since before the house was even built! The servants say a spirit lives inside it. They are correct, as it happens.'

It was very different from the meal of the first night. The food now was Khmer, delicate and smoky. *Lap khmer* salads soaked in lime and *kdam chaa* crab fried in Kampot green peppers and served with baguettes. The wife, for some reason, retired early and the doctor took out his cigar box and waxed philosophical. It felt to Robert as if he had many things bottled up inside him and that he had not expressed them to many people. As he drank, he became sharper and moodier, and the subject of conversation turned with baleful inexorability to the nation, to the nation which he wanted to explain to a young and impressionable foreigner.

'I have been reading a new book about the seventies, by a man who I greatly respect. A film-maker. Perhaps you know him?'

The name Rithy Panh, however, meant nothing to Robert.

'No matter. He wrote it in French. He made a film about the S-21 camp. He is interviewing the commandant, Duch – a mass murderer – and he makes a remarkable observation.' The doctor sat back in his chair and looked over at his daughter, waiting for her to say something. He had drilled these things into her since she was little but he seemed to want to know if she understood it after all. 'He says that Duch hated Vincent van Gogh but had a noble love for Leonardo da Vinci, and in particular the *Mona Lisa*. Why does Duch the fanatic Communist and killer love the *Mona Lisa*? Because, Duch says, she looks like a Khmer woman. There's something Cambodian in her portrait. An heiress of the kingdom of Angkar perhaps? Or is it because the works of the Renaissance are so mathematical? Duch, you see, was a maths teacher before he became one of the world's most famous torturers. It's so strange to me that someone like that would have an opinion about the *Mona Lisa*. He then says that Vann Nath, the man who painted all the images in the museum today, a man who survived the prison – one of only seven people to come out alive – was not a great painter. I think that made me angrier than anything. Vann Nath owns a restaurant these days – we should go over one day and eat there. He is a gentleman.'

'Daddy – ' Sothea began.

'What is it?'

'Don't you think Simon might be a bit overwhelmed by all this?'

'He lives here, doesn't he? Don't you, Simon?'

'Yes, sir.'

The 'sir' was a little absurd, and the doctor laughed.

'You don't have to call me sir, Simon. Are you overwhelmed?'

'Not at all.'

'See, he's not overwhelmed. I can talk about my own country, can't I? I want to tell you about this book. It's a remarkable book. He talks about the nation. He says the nation is mysterious to him − as it is to me. What can you say about a nation that killed a quarter of its own population in three years? Such a nation, he says, is enigmatic, impenetrable. It's a sick nation, maybe even an insane one. I quote word for word. But the world, he says, remains innocent. That's the strange thing. The crimes of the regime were still human all the same. Those crimes were not a historical oddity, a geographical eccentricity. Not at all. The twentieth century, he says, reached its fulfilment in Cambodia in the Year Zero. The crimes in Cambodia can even be taken to represent the whole twentieth century. They were committed by the most educated people in the country, people who'd studied in Paris. The scholarship boys. The lucky ones. People who knew they were right and educated and well travelled. It was in the Enlightenment that those crimes took place. That's what is so hard to understand.'

The doctor began to light his cigar. He smoked too much, that was his indulgence in late-middle age, and a customary one at that. It made him feel more French, more relaxed.

'I think it was here that all the tendencies of your culture, Simon, reached their maximum point. Do you see what I mean? It all came from you. Had those boys not gone to the Sorbonne, if they had stayed in Buddhist schools, they'd have had the usual South-East Asian corrupt monarchy with a few minor crimes here and there, but nothing more. There would have been no exterminations, no total control. We would have stayed sane. At the prison here they used to conduct experiments, draining all the blood from women to see what would happen. They had already marked "to be destroyed" in the margins of their files. But it was not just us; it was a very European experiment. You destroy people in order to make ideas live. It's a uniquely Western kind of behaviour. Pol Pot was a good student, remember, and a very good carpenter. A gentle boy. He lived for ideas, which is why you had women being drained of all their blood in a converted school. We may have been insane then, but the insanity was not all ours. It was a way of looking at history that completely denied history. There are those who say we've always done that anyway – but not with an end in mind. We never wanted to make a perfect society. We are fatalists. We don't believe in future perfection.'

When you thought about it, the domination of the nation by Western ideas and moods and movements and moral ideologies was a devastating spectacle. The doctor, however, was not recriminating. It was a salient thing about the Khmers, the lack of bitterness they had about it.

'First, you drop half a million tons of bombs on us, then you give us a deadly ideology like Communism which exterminates a quarter of the population, then you send your missionaries here to lecture us about our sexual behaviour. I saw on CNN – it was Mira Sorvino, some actress I am sure you know, weeping outside a peasant's house and screaming at them not to sell their children into indentured servitude. It was all for the camera. The peasants had no idea what she was talking about. But white people are remarkable people – they love charging around on crusade saving everyone. The carpet bombing and the missionaries and the NGOs – all unconsciously connected. You know all these anti-trafficking types. Most of them are evangelicals, missionaries. They seem wonderfully unable to find any trafficked people, but when they do get someone they force them into twenty hours of Bible study a week. No one ever mentions that. We're like Africa in the nineteenth century to the men from Texas. We're the place they do their conversions and fund-raising. They themselves live very well here of course. Tax-free. I'm not saying they aren't nice people who want to do good. But Duch was a nice boy who wanted to do good. They all think they are right and want to do good. It's irrelevant. You've turned us into your experiment, that's what I say. We're just Cambodians after all. Too poor and weak to say no. We always need something from you. It's only my daughter's generation that is starting to say fuck off. I see a change in them – a stirring. I am very relieved to see it. They don't seem to want to be your victims and experiment any more. Am I talking rubbish, my dear Simon? Forgive me, it's the wine. My wife says that not only do I smoke too much, but I drink too much as well.'

'It's perfectly all right,' Robert said.

He was enjoying it immensely.

'Well,' Sar said, blowing out a complete smoke ring, 'time will tell. If I am talking rubbish time will tell. And I never talk to anyone anyway. The white people would be horrified if they heard. But we came to help – we're sincere. You know how people think.'

The doctor laughed and flicked his ash. They began to eat chocolates and brandy and the stars became noticeably clearer. The talk became gentler and more personal. Robert felt more at home, and for a moment he thought that he could also belong to this family one day. It was far from being an impossible idea.

Nineteen

Davuth came down to the river at about noon and began his search for the man called Thy. He was not difficult to find. 'He's always up in the bar getting drunk,' the other boatmen told him.

There indeed Davuth found him, sitting alone and drinking shots of Sang Som diluted with dirty ice. He collared him in a friendly way and they got talking. The rains had held off that day and the whole room, the whole dishevelled river hamlet, was filled with burning, corrosive light. Davuth was in his one good suit, neat and combed and shaved, and he had the look of a mildly respectable contractor on his way to the city. He had been up since dawn and he felt sharp and prepared. He had left his car with a man he knew and walked unnoticed into the jetty area. It was a new adventure, and it was more than a mere adventure. It was the beginning of a new life.

'You can take me down to the city,' Davuth said to the drunk now, 'and I'll pay you what the American pays.'

Thy looked away and into his dirty ice as if mention of the American was mysterious bad luck.

'He pays better than anyone.'

'Yeah, well, I'll pay the same.'

It was a deal and Davuth asked him sternly if he was sober.

'Of course I'm sober,' Thy said defiantly.

They went down to his boat tied up at the jetty and set off with the sun at their backs. Davuth sat next to him in the cabin and they chatted with rum and cigarettes and Thy told him all about the young barang he had taken down to the city a short while ago.

'How about that American?' Davuth asked. 'I heard about him. Wasn't he some drug dealer down here?'

'He was but he took off. I heard —'

Thy's face tightened and he glanced down at the hands of the policeman which were resting passively but somehow dangerously in his lap.

'You heard what?'

'I heard they fished him out of the river.'

'They did?'

'He must have crossed the drug dealers in Pailin.'

'I guess he must have.'

'It's not a smart thing to do.'

'It's the stupidest thing to do all right. But you had a few dealings with him. Tell me about him.'

'Why?'

'I'm just curious. I heard a lot of stories.'

Thy was now drinking heavily. There was a chance, surely, that they would capsize at some point but it couldn't be helped. Davuth poured out the booze and Delons.

'He was a dealer, I'm sure. But I liked him. He was all right. He paid me good. You can't ask more than that.'

'No, you can't ask more than that.'

'He paid me for odd jobs. Between you and me —'

'Yes?'

'A few drop-offs, you know — that kind of thing.'

'I see.'

'Yeah, it was all right. He wasn't a tight-fist.'

'You can't ask more than that.'

'You bet you can't. He paid dollars.'

Davuth said that was the best a man could hope for: dollars with no questions asked.

'You got that right,' Thy said.

'And that British boy you took down to the city —'

'Ah, he was a queer one.'

'Why so?'

'Slept most of the way. Maybe he was stoned when we loaded him on the boat.'

'You and the American?'

'Yes.'

'Why would you do something like that?'

The boatman looked over Davuth and his eyes went blank.

'Don't ask me!'

'How strange,' Davuth drawled. 'Did the kid know where he was going?'

'He seemed to have no idea.'

'I'll be damned —'

'He just got off at the jetty where the American told me to let him off.'

'Then take me to the same place.'

'You said you'd pay the same.'

'It's a promise.'

They drank a fair bit more on their way to the jetty. Somehow the day had passed altogether by the time they got there and the lights had come on in the waterfront shacks and birds swarmed the mulberry trees with a deafening chirping and fluttering. Davuth paid and they went together up to the bank, the boatman staggering and mocking himself, and Davuth took his leave as brusquely as he needed and went in among the drivers who were hanging out under the babbling trees. He sifted through them asking about the English boy and seeing if any of them remembered him. Since there were very few of them it didn't take long for him to find the one who had driven Robert into Phnom Penh. Davuth took him to one side and used all his matey charm on him. He offered a pretty good tip if the man could take him to the same hotel he had taken the young barang.

'Sure,' the man said cheerfully. 'It was the Sakura if I remember correctly.'

'Then let's go to the Sakura.'

It was a chaotic drive. The road was clogged with long-distance trucks. The dusk came upon them. The man chatted glibly. Davuth listened to the stories about his family and then casually asked him if he had noticed anything odd about the young barang he had taken to the Sakura that night. The driver caught Davuth's eye in the rear-view mirror and he wondered if the barang had contracted a debt he couldn't pay. The man in the back seat looked like a genial enforcer. The driver prevaricated and then admitted that he couldn't remember much about the foreigner except that he looked quite broke.

'I see,' Davuth said quietly. 'But he paid you all the same?'

'He did pay me. He paid twice what you paid.'

They laughed. Davuth leaned over and passed another two dollars to the man. When they came into the city the driver remembered that it had not been the Sakura after all but the Paris on Kampuchea Krom. When they got there Davuth asked him again about the Englishman and the driver said he had had no bags with him. It was an extraordinary thing. A barang with no bags.

Yes, Davuth said to him, it's an extraordinary thing. With that, he turned and walked boldly into the lobby of the Paris, ignoring the drivers outside. The two girls on duty at the reception desk looked up with an instinctive alarm. Davuth gave off an energy that commanded alertness and wariness, if not a slight distaste that the person seeing him for the first time could not quite pin down. A briskness in the hands, a crisp gait that was nevertheless rarely hurried. He never put women at ease. He set down his bag and smiled, however.

'I'd like a room,' he said.

One of the girls took him up to the fifth floor.

'Have you been here before?' she said to him as they climbed the stairwells. On the higher landings the dolled-up girls parted for them sullenly.

'I don't come down much to the city these days. My daughter's at school and I never have the time.'

'Lucky you.'

'She's a lovely girl.'

'Here on holiday?'

'Business.'

'Ah, I see. Business . . .'

They came to the fifth-floor landing and its row of tarnished doors and smell of ashtrays, and as they went down it he said, 'Did you have a barang staying here recently. A young kid called Robert?'

She stopped and their eyes met in the semi-gloom near an exit light.

'No, I don't think so.'

'Maybe that wasn't his name.'

She took out the key and continued walking to the door, which she opened quietly.

'Maybe it was Simon, his name.'

'I don't remember all the names,' she said.

'You have a lot of young guys staying here for the girls?'

'All ages.'

'But not a lot of young barangs?'

'A fair number. They like the girls too.'

Davuth smiled.

'So it's rumoured. But you'd notice a good-looking young one.'

He closed the door behind them and threw his bag onto the bed. He went up to her and passed a ten-dollar bill into her hand.

'He hasn't done anything wrong,' he said. 'I just want to know if he was here.'

She nodded and absorbed the bill.

'Which room?'

'The one next to this.'

'Can I change room?'

She hesitated. 'I think there might be someone in there.'

They listened, and the comical nature of the pause made them both smile. An old Chinese guy getting off with one of the spinners?

'I think it's empty,' she said. 'Let me call down and check.'

When she had done so she took him next door to the other room and let him in. He threw his bag onto the bed a second time and strode to the windows, pulled open the curtains and looked down at the boulevard alive in its evening glory. The trees glittered with a golden light. The KTV was lit up. One forgot how both Chinese and French parts of the city felt as night fell. He thanked the girl and asked her again if she remembered anything about the barang occupant of the room and then asked her, in a different tone, if she wouldn't mind keeping this all between them. He assured her that there was no sinister reason for him asking this. It was just discretion, which benefited everyone. She agreed and he watched her slip away with a malicious satisfaction in the power of ten-dollar bills. Then he locked the door and set to searching the room on his hands and knees.

The carpets had not been cleaned in a while and yet after half an hour he had found nothing. He went through the bathroom, found nothing again, and then showered. Drying off, he lay on the bed and smoked and looked up at the yellowed furnishings. So the English barang had moved on, but to where had he moved? Davuth had refrained from asking the girl point-blank; it would make him look suspicious. Now he went down to the lobby and found that the girls had left for the night and a male clerk was there. Man to man was a little easier. He tried the ten dollars again and got the man to talk about recent arrivals and departures and soon he had found S. Beauchamp in the book but no onward address. The man told him to try the drivers outside. The same guys were always there.

Davuth went into the street and the drivers tossed him a few words. He lit up and puffed a bit and waited for them to calm down. He strolled over and asked if they knew the English boy. One of them said that he had taken him around a bit.

'A blond kid about twenty-eight?'

'I took him to Colonial Mansions'

'What's that?'

The man offered to take him there.

'Then let's go,' Davuth said. 'Is it a hotel?'

'It's a serviced apartments.'

'Fine,' Davuth cried, and patted the man on the back. He was rather enjoying himself now.

They drove through a dry, early-winter evening with the rain now holding off. The boulevards swarming, the lights temporarily reliable and on. The rain would come later that night, but for now it was merciful. The lovely nights of winter were coming.

The new karaokes overflowed, the Koreans and Japanese and Chinese abundant. The tuk-tuks filled with barang families and haughty Khmer-Chinese girls in long silk dresses studiously turned away from eye contact.

He had come along that same boulevard many times thirty-five years earlier and he always remembered whenever he was there. The people alive now, the young, did not understand anything about the city they inhabited. They didn't know its underlying nature. It was as if centuries had passed since then. In Year Zero of the Revolution that same teeming city had been almost entirely empty. The government ministries, the S-21 prison, a few posts here and there – at night it was as dark as the countryside, you could walk through it without meeting any human life. It was a city of torches and whispers. There were fires at the corners, patrols threading their way through the labyrinth. Strange to recall, he had felt very safe there. It was not unlike the village from which he had come. On sandals cut from old tyres, one could walk silently, one could go unnoticed.

Even the electric light of the present incarnation of the city struck him as faintly incredible, absurd. A complicated joke designed to humiliate the previous generations. When he thought of the things he had seen as a teenage soldier along those same wide streets it made him wonder if sanity was even possible in this world. The men casually shot at street corners during comatose sunlit afternoons and taken away on carts. An eighty-year-old grocer begging for his life under the trees on Street 19, then bayoneted by teenagers. Just momentary visions glimpsed for a split second, like the signs on playing cards. The nights when the city sank into silent darkness, seemingly unpopulated. The buildings emptied out where they roamed and slept and played cards and shot dogs. Rumours: a foreigner being held at S-21, one of two Australian yachtsmen captured off the coast, forced into a tyre on Mao Tse-tung Boulevard and burned alive.

Davuth had been attached to the M-13 camp in the jungle so he was already habituated to this system. To save you is no gain, to kill you is no loss! The blood debt! He wondered now — speeding along this capitalist boulevard — if he had ever believed in Communism. For what was Communism? The movement had begun one fine day in 1968 with the attack on Bay Daram a few miles from his parents' house in Battambang. It even emerged, then, from his own region. He was only ten but news of the attack went around like wildfire. It was the first modest move of the Angkar, the first blood drawn. But the Angkar was deeper than Communism; it came out of the distant past. Under the Angkar, sleep itself was prohibited. Ever since he had had trouble sleeping. He thought of it as 'rest', as if the illegality of sleep had been established in his subconscious and could not now be uprooted. And so for rest of the life he had been almost continuously wide awake. How many nights he and his patrol had wandered across the city hunting in the dark for traitors, for bourgeois elements, for saboteurs and trash who he already knew did not exist. They had freedom to kill whoever they wanted. If they heard a noise in an empty building they went in and killed the rats and the dogs, and sometimes an old woman sleeping on newspapers. The hunt itself was the meaning of Angkar.

The Leader had been right, cities are whores. They put on their gay make-up and forget. Davuth didn't mind; it was the way of the world.

At Colonial Mansions he paused for a moment and glanced up at the cream facade. In the lobby there was no one there. The reception gave him a cool and unwelcoming stare. It was a barang dormitory, for sure.

'I'd like to see a unit I could rent for a week.'

'We'd need a deposit,' the boy said indifferently.

Davuth agreed to it and they went up and looked at a unit on the fourth floor. He asked if the place was full at that moment.

'Ninety per cent,' the boy said.

It was much more comfortable than the Paris. The barang had money. When they had left the unit Davuth stepped to the balcony alcove and looked down at the pool. The windows opposite were lit, comfortable sitting rooms and bedrooms with bright tropical curtains. Around the pool the deckchairs were empty and in it a Chinese woman, as always, swam lengths, making no sound whatsoever. A curious place. The best thing would be to book the unit for a week and take his time.

He resolved to do that, then went down with the clerk and sat in the lobby cafe and ordered an orange juice. It was still quite early and from time to time guests and residents came in through the doors and walked up to their apartments through the swimming-pool area. He asked if he could smoke, was told that he could not, then demanded an ashtray and smoked anyway. Two hours passed. Young Korean girls came in and out, employees of some large construction company nearby, and a handful of ageing barangs with Khmer girlfriends. The usual trade. He flexed his fingers and thought to himself that his daughter was right and that he really ought to give up smoking. Now was the time.

When it was clear that he was waiting for nothing he booked the unit at the Mansions, paid for it in cash and took the same tuk-tuk back to the Paris. The rain exploded over the streets. The driver asked him if he really wanted to go back to his room.

'You have a place to go?' Davuth said.

It was on Street 282, the driver said. Near the Stadium.

All right, Davuth said wearily. A long time since he had enjoyed himself with anyone. Months, maybe. Now was the time for that too.

The downpours always caused the traffic to knot up and paralyse everything. They crawled through chaos towards the Stadium and even on the lonely streets leading to it the vehicles were trapped in slow-motion convulsions, the surfaces suddenly turned into water. Down came the plastic wraps on the tuk-tuk but he was soon soaked anyway. He gave in to the moment. One got soaked and there was nothing to be done. At the end of Street 282 there was a darkened corner where it met the main road alongside the Stadium and there on the left was a doorway with a group of men huddled under plastic ponchos. There was an entrance with a doorman holding a torch and roaring gutters all around.

He ran into the doorway and the face shone the light into his face and ushered him into a corridor. At the end of it rose a flight of steps and a single light fixed to the wall. The man told him that the power might go out at any moment but led him all the same to the stairs and swung the beam of the torch up them, indicating permission and normality.

Davuth shook off the rain and wiped his face and waited to regain his composure and then went up the steps to a landing plunged in darkness and stagnant heat. At its far end, reassuringly, the pink lights projected their aura of harmony and calm.

Twenty

He went to the end of the landing and turned into a larger room where the mama-san sat with her pot of steaming tea behind a desk with a good-luck cat and a gold Buddha. The only customer in the rain, he caused a mild stir and the mama-san told him how brave he was to venture out in such filthy weather. She took his ten-dollar entrance fee and told him amicably to just wander down and look at the girls behind the glass window. They only had a dozen in that night, most of them had stayed away because of the difficulty in getting around in tuk-tuks. Take your time, she said, and went back almost immediately to her knitting. He wandered down towards the window which was lit softly and he saw the girls sitting on two rows of seats, one higher than the other, texting into their phones and not looking up until they saw him in front of them.

The rain was loud here and he stood there indecisively while some of them smiled at him and waved and made come-on motions with their hands. There was a minder on his side of the glass to help him with his choice. He scanned the faces one by one and he found a girl that he liked and motioned to the minder; it was a slightly plump girl with a glossy fringe. The minder went into the room and pointed to her and she got up.

Davuth went back to the mama-san and asked her how much it was.

'It's between you and the girl,' she said flatly.

He knew it was about twenty dollars for a local for an hour. The mama-san gave him a room key and said the girl would bring towels. He could go to the room now and wait for her.

'You can even take a little more time,' she said. 'There's no other customers.'

Davuth took the key with its number tag and went back out onto the landing. His back was still soaked and his hair was dank. I must be repulsive to such a pretty girl, he thought. The rooms were at the other end, arranged around the stairwell, and he went up to the next floor and found the room. It was a stifling, tiny hotel room with a tiled floor and a wooden bed. He turned on the light in the bathroom and then the ancient A/C unit above the door and then slowly took off his soaking clothes and laid them over the television. Then he sat on the bed and waited.

While he was doing this, the girl had risen from her chair behind the glass and was about to exit the room when a girl at the end of her row held up her hand and asked her if she could take the client.

'What?' the minder began to cry.

'I'll give you the fee,' the other girl said to the one Davuth had chosen.

It was such a surprising offer that the girl chosen simply looked at the minder and shrugged.

'Well, all right then,' she laughed.

The minder looked over to the mama-san.

'What if the client is angry?' he whispered to both girls.

The intruder said, 'He won't mind. He won't care. There'll be a blackout any moment now anyway.'

There was a general burst of cynical merriment and the girls nodded and one of them said, 'Try it and see if he complains. He's probably a cheap bastard anyway.'

The replacement girl had the Thai nickname Pom, a ruse to make the Japanese men think she was Thai. There was little similarity between them and so there was a risk that the client might throw a fit but she was determined to try it anyway. She went into the bathroom and powdered her face and took one of the condoms and a towel and went back out and arranged everything with the mama-san. They were allowed not to tell management how much they obtained from a client and so it was up to them to get the most they thought they could. The Koreans and Japanese overpaid and so they were the most popular clients. Obviously, Khmers paid a lot less and consequently they were much less desirable, though they were more likely to accept a darker-skinned Khmer girl. It was why the chosen girl had relinquished her client so readily. Pom knew what she could get from a Khmer man dressed like this one and as she made her way down the corridor she made that calculation easily. She would ask him way too much and see what he did. But there were other considerations at work. The reality was that she had recognised him. Her heart was racing and her skin had gone hot all over her face and neck. She had seen him only once before, though it was not a face one could easily forget. She came to the door and she paused and listened. He was sitting quietly in the room doing nothing. She wondered if she should wait until the lights went out, as they surely would. Then, deciding to risk it anyway, she put her hand on the handle of the door and pushed it. At that very moment, as if the gods had been listening all along, the lights did go out and there was an amused groan from the ground floor. She slipped into the room as the air con gave out and closed the door behind her and locked it. The man looked up and saw little more than a shadow carrying a folded towel with a condom placed upon it.

'Blackout,' she said and they sighed together and the mood was not at all bad between them. She put down the towel and went to the bathroom and opened the little window above the sink.

'It's just my luck,' Davuth said, and sat there quite sadly, waiting for his small miracle to come and go.

'The girl you chose,' she said. 'She got sick suddenly. Headache. So I came instead. Is it all right?'

As she had expected, he shrugged passively.

'Doesn't make much difference now, does it?'

'I guess not!'

'What's your name?'

'Pom.'

'It's a Thai name.'

'But I'm Khmer. It's just for the Japanese.'

'Everything for the Japanese,' he muttered.

She came onto the bed after a cold shower and rubbed herself dry with the bare towel. He had already done the same. His muscular body lay on the bed expectantly and he did nothing but try to see her face as she came next to him and placed her hand on his chest. He could feel how emotional she was and he tried to figure out why. But there was no explaining it. She asked him where he was from, what his name was. He didn't lie. There was no point lying to a girl like that. They spot a lie in a second or two. They know men better than they know the backs of their own hands.

'What do you do?' she asked as she laid her head on his chest as if listening to his insides.

'I'm a policeman up in the country.'

She asked him if he was down on business and he said, as vaguely as he could, that he was. She asked what town he was from.

'Near Battambang.'

'I guess you need some entertainment,' she said.

'I need some entertainment, as you say.'

Yet he didn't make any move, he sat there in the dark as if thinking.

'Are you tired?' she asked after a while.

'Sure I'm tired. What does it look like?'

'It's fifty for the hour,' she tried.

'Don't try that on with me. It's twenty.'

'It's fifty today. Today is a special day.'

'What's special about today?'

'It's blackout day — didn't you notice?'

It took a while for the heat to come back into the room. About thirty minutes before they began to sweat and feel short of breath. That was the moment he chose to agree to her fifty and pull her on top of him.

It was not as perfunctory as she had been expecting, and she didn't care either way. She wanted to know something about him that could not be obtained in any other way. It had not been that long since she was running alone through the sugar cane and when she had run about half a mile she had stopped and crouched and waited until the unknown figure appeared at the trench where Simon lay and calmly smoked a cigarette. Even from such a distance his face was unforgettable and when she saw it again she felt a nauseating surprise but no real astonishment.

He paid and took his shower and came back to the bed.

She said, 'Where are you staying?'

He told her and even gave her his apartment number. The implication was that she could come and visit him any time she liked.

'Maybe I'll come by then,' she said.

'It's better than me coming here. I don't like these places.' The slight disdain in his voice enraged her.

He rose and got dressed and she did the same. She had what she wanted, but she was not sure why she wanted it. She didn't know yet how she was going to use it.

Fifty dollars was left on the bed.

Picking them up, she escorted him to the stairs where the rain was now pouring in uncontrollable torrents.

'That was very nice,' he said humbly.

'You're welcome. Do you have a phone number I can call you on?'

'I got a new number yesterday.'

When she had taken it down she kissed him on the cheek and told him to be careful in the flooded streets, making it clear that she wouldn't come down to the pavement with him. Davuth stumbled into the rain and saw that the tuk-tuk had patiently waited for him, the driver huddled between the plastic flaps with a soaked newspaper. That night, he slept beautifully and his dreams were not even the usual nightmares – just the elegant forms of Viking longships and the mountains of stone and wild grass through which the cataracts of Scandinavia fall like those of Hawaii or Java.

*

The next day he took the unit at Colonial Mansions and passed the morning sitting at the balcony with his smokes. The unit was furnished and there was nothing to worry about. No one remembered him from his previous visit, not even the boy who had shown him around. People were so unobservant; they missed every passing clue. By midday the Englishman had not shown up and Davuth walked instead to Vong.

The tailor was at his table and Davuth had no trouble getting affable and quick-talking with him. He gave Vong a facile line about meeting a young Englishman in a bar who had recommended him.

'I'm sure you remember him,' he joked. 'Blond and rather good-looking. I'm sure he throws his money around a bit.'

'It could be.'

'He calls himself Beauchamp and gets his clothes made here.'

'There's one by that name who comes here. There are two of them, in fact.'

'I know all about it. Two of them. Were you not a little curious?'

'It's none of my business, now that you mention it. Is it your business?'

'It could be my business.'

'Are you a detective?'

'That I am. One of them has run away —'

'With some money or some drugs?'

Davuth laughed in his homely way.

'I don't know yet. Does our English friend have a lot of money to spend on clothes?'

'Not that much.'

'When was he last in?'

'Last week.'

'Colonial Mansions, isn't it?'

'You know already.'

'But which unit?'

'It's 102. You could always ask them.'

'That wouldn't be very discreet.'

Davuth asked him what Beauchamp had ordered.

'Shirts, trousers. He wasn't very particular.'

'He's a nice young man, isn't he?'

'As nice as they make them. The other one, though . . .'

'Yes, he's a different kettle of fish. Still, they all look the same, don't they?'

'They certainly do.'

'I feel I should order a shirt – just to say thank you.'

'Shall I measure you up?'

'No time. Maybe next time.'

Davuth looked quickly through the window into the street. His eyes shone a dark mahogany as the blue outer light hit then. The tailor felt that he had done something vile without realising it, but it was too late. The detective was already on his way, cheerful and smooth. Vong watched him amble down the street without any pressing urgency. An odd bird, and a calculating look in his eye.

Davuth walked back to the Mansions and went up to the first floor. He walked down the line of doors until he was at 102. There he stopped for a moment, looked along the corridor and peered through the patterned lace curtains into a largely invisible room.

Lingering only for a moment, he carried on down the corridor then climbed up to the floor above and circled round to the opposite side, from where he could look down at the same door. His own unit was on the floor above this, the third, and from his own balcony he had a fair view of 102. How easy it had been. He went up to that balcony then and sat there for an hour and saw no one come or leave. But patience was one of his hard-won virtues. He had honed it during years of sadism and war. In soft and comfortable times its power was magnified tenfold. He could sit there for days if he had to, or even weeks. He was crocodilian and he rarely felt tired or bored: those states had been made alien to him long ago. And so he waited for the light in 102 to come on or the door to open or a tall and slender blond to appear on the landing, wearing the clothes of Simon Beauchamp who was now dead and turned to dust.

Twenty-One

When he did so, Davuth was not at his balcony but downstairs in the lobby where he sat at a table by himself with a glass of Sang Som. He had asked the receptionist to go into the closed cafe and get him some ice for his glass and he sat there with the glass, the ice, his own bottle of Sang Som and an ashtray, placid and watchful and totally sober. The rum burned his tongue and he enjoyed its ferocity, the way it seared the inner lining of his cheeks then gave up the ghost as it slithered down his throat. The cursed rain was back and the lights around the pool were going off one by one like a city closing down for the night. He always enjoyed those moments of closure and incoming darkness and it was usually when he took to the bottle in his cold and controlled way. He was raising his glass, in fact, when Robert and Sophal came through the glass doors and swept across the lobby arm in arm. He knew at once that it was the Englishman though he was surprised to see him with a very young and attractive Khmer girl. They always managed to snag one, didn't they? He lowered his glass and smiled at them with his eyes and they could not fail to notice him. 'Good evening,' he said in English and tipped his glass as if toasting them.

'Good evening,' Robert called back and they paused for a moment before crashing through the doors into the pool area.

'So that's what you look like,' Davuth said to himself. The boy was not as shy or furtive as he had expected, not as weak. He had no experience with the English, only a few Americans and Germans and the odd Frenchman, and most of those he had met when they were already dead. In one sense, it was the ideal way to get to know them. The dead reveal everything about themselves without any artifice, or so it seemed to Davuth.

Half an hour later they came down in their swimsuits and jumped into the uninviting water and swam to the far end, where Davuth saw they had positioned a bottle of wine. There they bobbed about drinking and laughing and caressing each other, the young in love with being young. He watched them with a detached fascination that – for a while – had nothing to do with his intentions. But, in any case, when he considered his intentions he found that he didn't have any. He was making it up from day to day, adapting to what happened or didn't happen as the case might be. He could tell from their cursory glance at him (it felt as if it was distinctly *downward*) that he had registered in their eyes as little more than the usual country bumpkin. It enraged him for a moment then he settled back and admitted that in a sense they had a point and there was nothing he could do about it. That's what he was and he minded it much less than anyone else. The Revolution, at least, had taught him not to be ashamed of his origins and he kept that feeling alive day by day, decade after decade, secretly and malignantly. The girl especially had looked at him with a sudden contempt, as if he didn't even have the right to speak up as they walked across the lobby. 'Who is he?' she would have been thinking as they climbed up to 102. That bumpkin who so insolently wished them a good evening in an English he obviously didn't speak, alone with his cheap and tawdry Sang Som, the drink of truck drivers and policemen. That little snob had not even concealed her surprise and resentment. She didn't even know who she was really with, in all likelihood.

He left them there and went up to his apartment and later, still curious, he stepped out to the balcony and looked at the two heads in the pool. He had formed the unconscious idea that the Englishman had money locked up in his unit, money that was in some way connected to the dead American, and he was certain that he could be blackmailed or intimidated to surrender it to him without too much fuss. But all was uncertain and vague. He didn't know either way; it was a shrewd and logical guess relative to the circumstances. He obviously had enough money for clothes at Vong and an apartment at Colonial Mansions and he had no passport. There had to be reasons for these things.

He made up his mind to get to know them, but in a very casual and unobtrusive way. The next day he watched them go out together and he again sat in the lobby with his bottle of Sang Som and waited for the boy to come back to the Mansions. He did so after lunch. Once again, Davuth raised his glass and because it was the second time the boy stopped and came over with a lopsided smile and cocked his head and said, 'I'm sorry, do I know you?'

'No, sir,' Davuth said in his gimcrack English. 'But I saw you last night with lovely lady friend.'

'You did, yes. But do we know you?'

'Me? I think not.'

'I just wondered —'

'Have a drink. I am all alone in this Mansions and always drink alone in this lobby. I have my own bottle, as you can see.'

'I don't know,' Robert said.

'Sit and have a drink. So what?'

There was a playful finality to those last two words and so Robert gave in, slightly curious anyway. His instinct told him that it was best not avoided or refused rudely. The man had level, steely eyes that gave off an indistinct heat.

'All right,' he said, 'I will.'

'Please,' Davuth shouted across the room in Khmer, 'one more glass for my friend.'

It was brought.

Davuth poured, and then used the tongs in the ice bucket sitting on the table next to him.

'I like mine icy cold — and you?'

'I like it cold too.'

'My name Davuth. And you?'

'Simon.'

'It's nice American name.'

'English.'

'You holiday or business?'

'Holiday,' Robert said. Then, 'Well, business too. I am thinking of living here.'

'Very nice and welcome. Well, chin.'

'Chin-chin.'

They tapped glasses and sipped.

'You look like a bright young fella,' Davuth said.

'I don't know about that.'

'You found nice Khmer girl all right.'

'I don't know how.'

Davuth gave him his brightest smile.

'You are young, handsome. They will love it.'

'Are you staying here?' Robert asked, to change the subject.

'I am tour guide. I have a deal to stay here.'

'A tour guide?'

'I know everything.'

'Everything?'

'If you want Angkor Wat, I can take you. Vietnam, I can take you.'

'That must be good business.'

'Yes, sir. I can take them to every place and translate for them. This is why I wait here in the lobby.'

'I see.'

Robert accepted a second shot almost at once.

Davuth said, 'I wait here and they come and find me! The Americans are the best. They pay upfront – unlike the Chinese who pay downback. It's my joke. They pay after and never happy. What about you?'

'I don't really take tours. I'm sorry.'

'But you will change you mind one day.'

'I will?'

'You will. You will take a tour somewhere with Davuth. It's the best one you can have. And it's romantic for your girlfriend.'

'She probably wouldn't find it romantic.'

'Oh, we'll talk. I have a lot of options. Good price for you. Very romantic.'

They drank on, and Robert began to like him. He was unlike any Khmer he had met so far, rough, fast-talking, manly in his way. He seemed quite ancient although not yet out of his fifties. The eyes and their crow's feet had gone ancient and shrivelled and yet they were also intensely alive and witty and through them Robert felt himself mocked, but gaily and without deep judgement or animosity. Davuth, he felt, was much deeper than himself because he had lived a much more dangerous life. The gift of a dangerous life: swiftness of thought, a fine capacity for hatred. You didn't meet that type in developed countries any more. In rural southern Italy you might, wandering the roads. You might in Serbia or the darker French towns where strange military types still surface for a moment, veterans of wars they won't admit to. You might come across one in the poorer islands in Greece, mending nets. But Davuth, although Robert didn't know it, came from a recent war and it was a native one. He had come through it and he had learned how human beings worked on the inside. He looked right through Robert and into empty space and appeared unsurprised at how transparent an educated man can be, how docile and primitive and ignorant. There was no respect in his attitude at all. Davuth, for his part, had seen educated people begging for their lives from armed illiterate children by burning roadsides and he had not forgotten the looks on their faces, the way they had tried to explain why their palms had no blisters. It was one of those pathetic things you never forget. The children would listen, uncomprehending, then shoot them in the head with Kalashnikovs and laugh as the bodies went into convulsions. All that education and restraint for nothing. A demented child can blow all that classical music and Marx and mathematics out of you in a split second, just because he feels like watching your convulsions. Look to your own salvation, the Buddha said. He wouldn't look out for yours, there was just yourself and your inner compass and the ability to plan ahead.

'All the same,' he said, 'I can fix thing for you around town if you tell me what you need. I'm a fixer as well as a tour guide. Everyone here needs a fixer — I mean every barang like yourself.'

'You can give me your card if you like.'

'They're up in my room. But I can give you my number.'

Robert hesitated for a moment but took it down anyway. There was no harm in it and one *did* need a fixer. It would be doing a hard-up local a favour if he could ever afford to do it. What would it cost, anyway? Fifty dollars? He could do that at some point. He even asked Davuth point-blank now what a trip down to the Mekong near the Viet border would be and the guide poured him another drink and just said that he could give him sixty for the day and his meals and all would be fine with him. It wasn't much, he added, to take the girl on a romantic trip and there was a temple down there that no one knew about, the temple of Phnom Bayong near the village of Kirivong. They could hike there for hours and look down on the Mekong and feel like they had come somewhere different.

Robert began to agree with him, though outwardly refusing.

'I'll run it by the girl,' he said.

'I think that girl — that girl will say yes.'

The Englishman thanked him for the drinks — it was far too much — and said he might see him later.

'You might see me later,' Davuth said. 'In fact, I'm sure of it.'

'Then I will.'

Robert went up to his room, drew the curtains and lay on the bed in a slight stupor. He hadn't realised that Sang Som was so strong even with ice. Despite the

A/C he felt hot and damp and something in the chance encounter had rattled him. The fingers, perhaps, fat and powerful and elegantly assured. The eyes full of humour and doubt. An hour later, he went to meet a Vietnamese businessman he was giving lessons to and didn't return to Colonial Mansions until nightfall. This time it was Sophal who was waiting for him in the lobby and he told her about the tour guide he had met there a few hours earlier.

'It was the same guy from last night.'

She frowned and there was a sudden anxiety in her voice.

'Him?'

'Looked a bit rough to you?'

'He looked like a con man. I wouldn't talk to him, no.'

'Not at all,' Robert protested. 'He's a riot. You should meet him.'

'I don't want to meet him.'

'I'm sure he wants to meet you. He suggested taking us on a tour.'

'You said no, I hope?'

'Of course I said no. But he's sort of funny. I quite like him.'

'You're not even thinking about it?'

They went up to the room and made love. The heat of the day seeped through the flimsy curtains and made them feel washed out and spectral, but the thread of the conversation begun light-heartedly in the lobby was not broken and sure enough it resumed eventually.

'I said no to the tour, as I said. But all the same –'

She said, 'What is he doing hanging out in the lobby like that? It doesn't feel right.'

'He says he's fishing for clients.'

She snorted. 'That's one thing to dislike.'

'Maybe. Maybe not.'

'Remember, you're not local. You don't pick up on these things.'

'What things?'

'The vibe. He looked at me —'

'He's just a horny old man. I'm sure they all look at you like that. We can't hold that against him, can we?'

'You think I want to be holed up in a car with *that* for hours on end?'

'I suppose not,' he admitted reluctantly.

Moreover, he was not sure why he wanted to go on that tour now. It just seemed like a fairly good idea for a romantic weekend, but more than that it was an added layer to his disguise, a distraction from the question which he now imagined was turning inside Sophal's mind about his identity. The more normal things they did together, the less she might brood about Robert and his loose ends. This was how he was thinking, in any case, though it was more a blind probing than a train of thought. He thought it would be clever to kick up a little dust and commotion because of late he had begun to feel a quiet suspicion in her. It was her instinct cutting in and the only way to foil instinct is to spoil, entertain and divert. She lay now against his chest with her hand resting on the area of the heart and he could feel her aroused attentiveness and wariness. He was correct. Sophal had bristled at the mention of a tour in the east with a man like that and she began to wonder at once why he had suggested it. His breath still smelled of that cheap rum and it was obvious who he had been drinking with. Why, though, would a man like Simon sit down and drink rum with a man like the tour guide? What would they have to talk about?

How annoying men were, there was always this collusion which even they didn't understand.

'You should be more careful,' she said quietly. 'You shouldn't talk to strangers so easily.'

'Why not?'

'You just shouldn't. It's quicksand.'

'Quicksand?'

'That's what my father says. It's quicksand for naive boys.'

'Oh, I'm not a naive boy.'

'You're not as naive as you seem, but you're more naive than you think. That's what matters. If I can see that, so can Mr Tour Guide.'

'Come off it,' he sighed, smiling to himself. 'It's not that easy. I'm not that easy.'

'You're wrong — it's that easy. You should stay away from him.'

'Bollocks,' he muttered.

She didn't quite get Britishisms.

There's a long road that goes east to Vietnam and at the end is a mountain with a temple and views over the Mekong. He wanted to go see it and make her see it too. It was surely feasible. He turned and looked through the open door into the living room which was now almost dark, the lights of the swimming pool transforming the drawn curtains into a square of dark gold. A wave of nostalgia came over him and he thought of his parents going quietly about their honourable and unrelenting lives in a council house in Bevendean at the edge of the Downs. It was six in the morning there perhaps and his father might well be already in his surprisingly fertile English garden cursing the onset of frost. They ate their porridge together listening to the *Today* programme on

Radio 4. He had sent postcards by now to calm them and keep them, as it were, on his side. The postcards would be on the mantelpiece, displayed for some reason. So his disappearance was not yet total and his parents were not yet looking for him and lying awake at night wondering if he was dead. They were maybe worried about him leaving his job and soon the school and his English girl would be dropping by to ask them if they knew anything. They were reticent people who understood the laws of discretion and it was possible they would fend off those questions artfully. He didn't know. His mother, certainly, would not be convinced by his assurances. She knew how unhappy he was. The first thing that would emerge in her mind when she woke would be her son. Just then, as his eyes were adjusting to the dark and just as he was imagining his mother rising into a cold English dawn, a shadow crossed the gold square and stopped for a moment and seemed to look into the room. Then it moved on and he heard the curious whale-like snorts of the swimmers who always did laps at that hour. He rolled over and his mouth was dry.

'What's wrong?' Sophal said.

'It's nothing. I was just thinking about my mother.'

'Does she know where you are?'

'I sent her a postcard —'

She suddenly felt awake again. Did people still send postcards?

'It's better than nothing, I suppose. If you disappeared tomorrow would you send me a postcard?'

'No.'

'I knew it. I'd use telepathy.'

He thought, would I really not send one?

They went out later and had dinner at a Viet place

called Ngon near Victory Monument, an open-air place with frangipanis and fans and tables with bowls of spices and stone mortars. They ate bowls of *boun* with vermicelli and fried *nem* and chilled coconuts with the tops lopped off. There was nothing more to say for the evening. Finally he did say, as if it didn't matter and he had not been thinking about it for a while, 'You know, I think we should go to Phnom Bayong after all. Your father will approve.'

Along the river an hour later the lamps burned in a soft and solitary splendour, their stationary light enabling the eye to see the motion of the unlit waters below. They walked arm in arm underneath them and from the river came the sweet humidity that raised their spirits and made Sophal want to empty a bottle of vodka. High clouds soared above the city in monochrome, hammer-headed and seeming to swim like sharks upwards towards a dimly present moon. At the horizon the pink flashes of lightning silent against the same clouds. There was no rain yet and the young girls sat with their boys in the gloom eating ice creams and watching them pass. The grass sloping down to the river made him dreamy too. He told Sophal about the river his father used to take him boating on. The very evocation of it in words made it materialise anew in his mind, from where it had been absent for a very long time – for a period, in fact, that felt emotionally like centuries. The river, the home country and its dull and heavy memories. The river was called the Ouse and it ran through the Sussex countryside from the village of Piddinghoe down to the sea at Newhaven. And, long ago, his father took him sailing on a small catamaran to show him how. The river ran between mud and chalk banks and in high summer there was a feeling of death and stillness upon it, abandoned tankers rusting in the shallows, the dragonflies playing over it just as they did here. The cemeteries dated from the Middle Ages, from the age of Stephen's War 'when God and his angels slept'. The river smelled of salt and stewing algae. If only he had known it had been a premonition of Phnom Penh. Both places had an atmosphere of decay but the decay of each was different. The English kind was the sweet torpor at the end of a long and successful innings; it was recent and slightly weary. It was a kind of refusal to live violently and intensely. It was smugly moral. The Khmer decay, on the other hand, was long-standing but the Khmers themselves were quickly emerging out of it. There was no weariness or old age about them. At least that was his way of interpreting it. Perhaps mistakenly. The Khmers didn't have time to lecture either themselves or others. They were young and wounded, but their wounds were so deep that they could be ignored for a while. Their sadness was of a different kind, too. It was from the 1970s, a time that every fifty-year-old could remember vividly. It was the sadness of generations which had entirely lost their youth for nothing and who had no choice but to forget. The sadness of England, however, lay precisely in her tremendous memory, in her refusal to forget anything. Increasingly, and now definitively, he felt that his affinity lay with the Khmers. They were indefinably alive. In their faces, in their eyes, there was the constant surprise of life itself, that horrifying and sweet wonder. Their ancientness took a different form from his own. It was almost as if it was physical and unconscious, thousands of generations compressed into gesture and speech patterns and quick understandings.

They were more subtle than the English, but they were less cerebral. They were more alive, but less consciously joyous or boisterous. For centuries, and even now, the whites wanted to improve them, drag them into a future which for the whites themselves no longer existed. But the project would always fail. The pale ones would never understand the real substance. They floated like water-boatmen on the surface of the Khmer pond, the glassy, fragile consciousness of this race whom the whites despised and whom the most philanthropic among them subconsciously resented.

As his father's catamaran sailed quietly down to the open sea, he used to feel a kind of death wish, the urge to keep sailing across the Channel towards Dieppe and another life as a crook. It was as if when you didn't know what to do with your life, a river could save you by making you purely unconscious. Even the way his father taught him nautical knots seemed to be a silent preparation for something furtive in the future, and his father was aware of it. When they were alone out at sea riding waves, his father asked him about his school and his friends, and everything that Robert said in reply to these questions merely served to illustrate how hopelessly alone and isolated he was. Nor did it seem that anything could be done about it. He was a lonely kid and his teachers often remarked upon the fact. He sometimes missed school altogether and went walking through the woods until it grew dark and he had to make his way home. He always lied about the reason for his lateness. 'You're a funny little bugger,' his father would say, and his bafflement was tenderly neutral. Looking back on it now, it seemed to Robert that everything had been a sign pointing to a future liberation far from his own home –

because already then, all those years ago, he had been in the peculiar situation of not loving that home but of feeling that it didn't suit him at all and never would. And so it had turned out.

Twenty-Two

Robert and Sophal parted ways by the Psar Rus and he headed back down to the river in a quiet mood, eventually turning along 106 and walking up in the drizzle alongside the lawned gardens. To the right, by shambolic tin walls and shaggy trees, the girls stood at the corners waiting for people like him and men slept inside waiting tuk-tuks as if the night was already over. Higher up the street turned to rubble and grit and litter and the dogs stood there watching him, assessing his strengths and weaknesses. An alley swung rightwards towards 102 and as he passed into it he saw a young woman ahead of him picking her way gingerly through the long oblong puddles and scattered refuse from the day market. Thrown together inside the claustrophobic alley they walked a few yards apart until she turned left at the large trees and into the pool-like darkness around them and up towards the golden lights of the Mansions. He hung back a little to let her ascend the steps and then followed her into the lobby, where she didn't stop at the reception desk, breezing past into the corridor that led to the stairwell.

He went the opposite way, up to his apartment, but on the first floor he stopped midway and waited for her to reappear on the floors above him. Something about her was unusual. Not the shiny black dress or the heels, nor the tight white summer blouse and the careful pinning of the hair. It was that something about her was not unfamiliar.

When she did appear it was on the third floor. Her hand was on the rail and then she stopped as well, halfway down the landing, and she saw him standing below her, looking up. When their eyes met he recognised her and she him and she flinched and stepped back from the rail, but not entirely out of view. Sothea, for her part, was astonished more than anything else and she didn't know what to do but go forward until she was at Davuth's door. Robert turned towards his own door, unlocked it and hung back, wanting to change his mind and go up and speak to her.

He couldn't think of any conceivable reason that she had appeared out of nowhere in his own building. He glanced back up at the third floor but she had slipped from view.

Feeling rash, he decided to go up and find her. Once on the third floor, however, he found himself in an empty corridor with no Sothea. He walked down it slowly and peered through the windows of each unit and as he did so he felt a sickening giddiness and inertia. Here was a person who could expose him easily, but whom he could expose as well. And if Sothea was there, wasn't Simon likely to be there as well? Perhaps even in one of these units on the third floor!

There was only a faint echo of old Chinese music coming from one of these and he went down to the ground floor and out into the street to wait for her. He went across the street and sat on the bags of cement that were stacked outside the Korean construction site and waited for some time until it was late enough for the motodop drivers to sullenly drive off empty-handed. The long wait began and as one o'clock came he heard, as if hours in advance of themselves, cocks crow in the gloom behind the Embassy. The silent lightning kept him company, but even so Sothea did not re-emerge until well after three. She was obviously still shaken and nervous because as she stood at the top of the steps she looked up and down Street 102 and when she saw that it was empty she started off down the same alley through which she had come a few hours earlier.

He followed her, almost in disbelief, and they walked briskly into the long, humid lawn bristling with crickets. She slipped into this darkness so effectively that he could barely see her until they came out on the far side. There was a bar there with a few drunken old Frenchmen sitting outside on cane chairs with their women and Sothea darted to a corner just behind the market, not looking behind but seeming to know that all was not well. He caught up to her as they turned into the smaller street and when he was a few feet from she turned and saw him and her eyes went wide with horror and she began to run. He called out, 'No, wait!' and ran after her and to his surprise she relented almost at once because she couldn't run in her heels.

She slowed and then stopped and turned a second time, and this time she was composed and cold and ready to hit back.

'It's all right,' he said, and held up his hands, and she saw that he was not nearly as angry as she had expected.

They took each other in for a while and then she sat down on the kerb and he sat down as well and he felt the sweat massing on the palms of his hands. He had prepared nothing to say and now that he had to say something he couldn't find any words at all. It was pointless demanding explanations, they both knew what had happened. Moreover, he knew that Simon had done all the planning and the execution. She had had nothing to do with it. Finally he said, 'So where is Simon?' and left it at that.

'I don't know,' she said.

'I know he's at Colonial Mansions — I followed you from there.'

'He's not there.'

'I think he is. I need to know which apartment he's in.'

'No, it's someone else. Simon and me broke up.'

'Then where did he go?'

She shook her head and there was something final about it that was very real.

'So you really don't know?' he said.

'Maybe he's dead.'

'What about my money? What about my passport?'

'I dun know about that.'

'You must have been with him when he spent the money.'

'He spent some . . . We spent some — I am sorry.'

He suddenly flew into a small repressed rage.

'You two — you really fucked me over.'

'Yes. It was bad thing.'

'So *now* you say it was a bad thing.'

It wasn't even really my money, he thought.

'I think you better make merit,' he said, half joking.

'Yes, you right. It was bad thing.'

'It was bad thing and now we're here in the same city.'

'Yes, it crazy.'

'Is that all you can say?'

'I said it crazy.'

'You think it's just crazy and that's that?'

'Yes, it crazy.'

'Then it's OK, it's just crazy and not, you know, evil or malicious or anything really bad?'

She shrugged and looked down at her feet and soon he calmed down and it was he who felt sorry for being a bully. He ought to have known – it was a small country, you ran into people again quite quickly, and Phnom Penh was small as well, for all its secrets.

It was Simon he needed to find. But then again, did he really need to find him now? What would he do?

'I see,' he ended up saying, and his hands went limp.

She, however, roused herself and began to get up.

'I'll walk with you,' he said.

They went slowly through the dead city and he asked her what she was doing now. She looked a lot more elegant than she had upriver, more composed and in command of herself, and she said she was working in a club and living with a friend of her mother's in Toul Kork.

'Why were you at Colonial Mansions?' he said.

'I have a friend there. You know what I mean.'

'It's a coincidence, isn't it?'

'Lot of people live there.'

'Yes, but still . . .'

It was vexing, but he couldn't push the issue. She strode on ahead of him and he had to quicken his feet to keep up with her.

'Where are you going now?' he said.

'Home.'

'But – when was the last time you talked to Simon?'

'Some time ago. I not gonna see him again.'

280

'You can't know that.'

'Yes, I know.'

'But if you see him —'

She let him come up level with her and she looked at him carefully and she felt sorry for him, but she couldn't tell him the truth. She had felt sorry him when she saw him at the river house, so lost and clueless.

'What?'

'Well, I want my stuff back.'

She sneered, 'You never get it back. Get new stuff.'

'Can't you help me get it back?'

'No.'

'Maybe I'll go to the police then.'

Finally she stopped.

'Maybe,' she said, 'the police are already near you. Did you know that?'

'Why shouldn't I go to them?'

'I'll say you liar. You won't go to them — they are after *you.*'

'They are? Why are they after me?'

'I don't know, do I? I think they are.'

'You didn't answer my question.'

He was bluffing and they both knew it. She suddenly stepped into middle of the street and raised her hand — she had seen a motodop far off under the glistening wet trees.

Then, as if relenting, she turned back to him.

'Where you stay?' she said.

'At the same place we were. The Colonial.'

She seemed immensely surprised, though it had been obvious enough.

'You better leave there,' she said adamantly.

'Why should I?'

'I said you better leave. I'm giving you advice.'

'I won't leave.'

'All right.'

The motodop swept up and, almost without stopping, scooped her up onto the back seat where she sat side-saddle and flashed him a parting look before the bike turned and roared away towards the boulevard. She stared at him as it did, and she smiled and waved and there was a strange innocence and fatalism in both the smile and the wave. It was as far as he was going to get with her, even if he did see her again. He gave up and walked back to the Mansions, defeated by her agility, and went up to his apartment and stewed in his brooding uncertainty for a long time, smoking cheroots and eating pistachios as he often did late at night. He walked about the room spitting the shells aimlessly and he circled around the great and ominous idea that his enemy was only a few metres away from him on the third floor, incredible as it seemed. Simon, asleep on a bed identical to his own and under the same roof. But it was not clear what he should do. He could ignore him and they could carry on with their exchanged identities for as long as they needed. Otherwise he could go up now and confront him and they could have it out and bring it to an end and go back to being who they were really were. He could get his passport back and return to Elmer and nothing would be said about it. He could do that, but as soon as he understood that he could do it, he didn't want to. It was just that he was forced to. He couldn't ignore Simon for long. They would meet in the street, word would get around and everything would be ruined. It wasn't much that would be ruined, but it was something he had created by and for himself and he didn't want to let it go so easily. He began to feel agitated and paranoid the more he thought about it, and soon he had wandered into the kitchen and picked up a knife from one of the drawers. He wrapped it in a tea towel and slipped outside onto the landing. Then he went to the stairwell and up to the third floor. He then went along the third-floor landing, past the flowering balconies with their French-style iron tables, and past the series of darkened and curtained windows where not a single light was on. He had a feeling that one of these doors would suddenly snap open and a confused and sleepy Simon would stick his head out and he would have him – for a moment – at his mercy. But since he didn't know which door it was, he could only pass it, and then pause by the stairwell at the far end and feel his hand shaking. The sweat dripped onto the floor and a cloud of moths crazed by the landing lights danced around his head while he collected his thoughts and realised that he had better go back down and replace the knife in its drawer. He locked his door and turned off the lights then sat by the window and looked up at the third floor. But then again, maybe he had leaped to an absurd and exaggerated conclusion.

Sothea – he knew nothing about her. Perhaps she had told the truth.

That bitch, he thought more calmly.

The following day, when he called Sophal, he told her that they ought to leave the city as soon as possible, even if it was only for a few days. In fact, having got up late, he went down to the lobby for his coffee and found Davuth almost at once. The policeman was dressed in a pale blue shirt and he looked much more handsome than he had the day before.

Twenty-Three

'I've thought it over,' Robert said as he sat down opposite Davuth and ordered bagels and cream cheese with his coffee. The policeman looked up from his paper calmly and there was a faint merriment in his eyes, an unflappable disdain and patience. He knew at once that he had him. Robert fumbled with his words and they tumbled out too quickly. The sun distressed his eyes and he felt a headache coming on. 'I've decided that I'd like to take you up your offer to go to Phnom Bayong. Can you give me a decent price? I'd pay you upfront if you could bring it down a bit – I know you can. Can't you?'

'I said sixty, didn't I?'

'Yes you did.'

'So how much would you like me to bring it down by?'

'What about forty?'

Davuth was drinking a tall, ice-filled Coke through a straw and the crushed ice burbled as he sucked on it now.

'I don't like bargaining about my prices,' he said coolly, looking Robert in the eye. 'It's not what I usually do.'

'Of course. But the thing is – my girlfriend and I are a bit hard up right now. However, we might need someone later on too. I mean –'

'I see what you mean. I like you, Simon. I've enjoyed our talks. So it's fine by me if we say fifty. Can you do fifty?'

'I suppose I can.'

'Fifty is for a whole day. And there is a strong possibility that we will get stuck down there for a night, in which case I will not charge you any more than fifty.'

'Stuck?'

The policeman grinned and opened his palms. 'The Mekong is flooded at this time of year. It's a flood plain. We'll have to take a boat part of the way.'

Robert's face fell. 'Oh, a boat. I hadn't quite bargained on a boat.'

'Of course, the boat will be extra. Boats are not cheap.'

'That rather throws a spanner in the works then.'

'It's all right. I have a friend down there who can throw in the boat. He owes me a favour.'

'Well, if you say so . . .'

It didn't seem quite right and Robert was about to cancel the whole thing, but then he thought of his desperation to get out of the city now and he nodded and went along with it. It didn't seem particularly advisable to owe something to a man like Davuth, but now there was little choice.

'If the waters increase we might get cut off. We might have to spend a night down there. Or we might get back too late and have to spend a night in Takeo.'

Robert said he didn't really know where that was.

'Never mind. You're not the guide! I know where it is and I know where we can stay if we have to.'

Takeo. The word had a dismal ring to it.

'You seem to be saying,' Robert ventured, 'that it would be better to spend a night in Takeo and make it a two-day affair.'

'That, in fact, is what I would recommend.'

'But we can't afford that, because that would make it a hundred dollars.'

Davuth smiled again. 'I might be able to give you a special break. But you pay my hotel that night and petrol for the next day.'

Since that was reasonable, Robert agreed.

'It's not very much,' the policeman went on affably. 'Just a few more dollars. I can give my time for you and your lady friend.'

'I didn't realise there would be a boat, though. I hate boats.'

'It's not a long ride in the boat. You and your girl will enjoy it. Unless it rains!'

'It will rain.'

'Then you can sing in the rain.'

'Sing in the rain?'

Davuth laughed and his head rolled back a little.

'Simon, have you seen a series called *Vikings*? It's on HBO.'

The Englishman seemed irritated.

'No, not yet.'

'Ah, it is very good. They terrorise the Christians and have human sacrifices. They shave the sides of their heads. But you know they are *good guys*. They are like a loud football team.'

'*Vikings*?'

'Yes, it is barang history. I thought about it a lot.'

'I can't believe you watch HBO.'

'I found it in the market in Pursat!'

'It's amazing what you can find in the market in Pursat.'

'Everything.'

'Well, never mind about Vikings. When d'you think we can leave for Takeo?'

'Tomorrow morning will be sunny. No rain.'

Robert thought it over. Then he called Sophal and they talked. She sulked, but it was clear that her previous opposition to the idea had somewhat abated. She could sense that he wanted it and finally she agreed. 'I'll have to tell my father right now,' she said. 'He won't be thrilled.' He closed the phone triumphantly and said to Davuth, 'You're on. Let's get out of here early. Say six?'

'Any time you like.'

The rest of the day Robert went swimming at Le Royal where he lay low, ordering sandwiches from the bar and drinking tonics with lemon, apprehensive at the idea of running into Simon or Sothea. He was the aggrieved party but now he had no wish to see them at all; it would be an unpleasant scene anyway and nothing good would come of it. Far better to let sleeping dogs lie and for all their cards to fall where they might. He no longer cared. He didn't even care about his passport because if he ever needed a passport again he had resolved to simply go to the Embassy on Street 240 and say he had lost his. But in the meantime he was Simon, and Simon had an easy life. Simon had time on his hands and did not worry about the clock. He had spent his whole life not working so he was used to this regal idleness. He took it in his stride.

As he did laps in the pool he eyed the rich barangs dozing on the loungers and he felt that in some way he belonged in their company. It was not a bad life out here when you got a little cash rolling. There were, in any case, far worse lives out there. After a while, it became sinister, the soft edges, the senses of timelessness, the lack of struggle. You went to seed quite quickly, but by the same token you didn't mind as much. You looked in the mirror less and less and, in fact, you thought about others less and less. These were positive developments. But you couldn't escape the going to seed. It was mental in the first place, which meant that it couldn't be corrected. You woke, Robert continued thinking, every morning in the beautiful heat to the sound of the koel birds and you took your coffee in the sun among the tanagers. You drifted through the days and the nights and you forgot about the European Union and the council tax and the first grey hairs in your brows and the emerging sadness in the eyes. Or rather than forget them you failed to remember them any more. Here it was a leaping from one hour to the next, and inside those hours were all the pleasures you needed and which elsewhere were so much harder to obtain.

When the day died away he dried off and roamed the streets as he usually did, stopping on corners in the dusk to gobble down *prahok* and cold beers and, on Street 130, the same fresh oysters he had enjoyed on the terrace of the Dutch painter. He went to the cinema and watched a ghost epic with screaming teenagers and old women who covered their eyes when the phantoms burst onto the screen. Afterwards, he was less spooked and unsettled. The rain, the gutters racing. He went back to the Viet cafes and took a sweet Vietnamese coffee with condensed milk and smoked until his eyes watered and he felt the supreme, stationary happiness of which the many bodhisattvas have spoken.

Twenty-Four

He didn't see anyone on his way back to his apartment and that night he slept with a generic Ambien and a bottle of gin by the bed. In the end, he didn't touch the bottle and his dreams were logical and free of menace. It was always England in his Eastern dreams and by now he had come to accept that if he did not go back they would be of England for the rest of his life. And so: he came up to a farm called Eddington on the crest of the hill above his grandmother's house — it was said to be named after Alfred the Great's stirring victory over the Danes — and looked down at the Brighton racetrack in the distance, the place that Graham Greene had immortalised, and the Bevendean council houses with their sloping gardens of rhubarbs and runner beans and the cornflowers and poppies that had frothed up around the fields of wheat. He always came here in moments of crisis. He looked out and saw chalk paths — brilliantly white — cut into the grass and the stiles dividing the fields. And there was a man striding along the hill, his black coat flapping about his legs and some kind of crazy tam-o'-shanter on his head. The man came to a stop and then looked at him and Robert shaded his eyes and, for no reason, the light outside was inside his head and he heard larks high above the fields, that thin, warbling, continuous sound that he knew from childhood and that was, in a sense, always inside him as well. He looked up, at the broken and gaping roof, and as he did so a cloud moved across it and the sun dimmed —

In reality, his eyes opened and he heard something beating against the shutters — little wings — and he thought, Eddington, isn't that where the king fought the Vikings? So it's the Vikings!'

He packed for a four-day trip, for who knew how long it would really last. In a sense the longer it lasted the better. He took his new shirts and a pair of swimming trunks he had bought for a dollar in the Psar and a banded straw hat from the same. It only made him realise how tremendously little he owned in this world. He glanced up at a clock. It was five thirty and he had time for a coffee in the lobby and even a swim if he wanted, and yet in the end he had just the coffee and took it out onto the front steps to wait for Davuth and Sophal. The weather had changed for the better, just as the guide had said it would. He sat and sipped his coffee and laid his bag next to him. A blue sky emerged. Construction workers filed through the clear, dustless alleys and their feet were almost soundless. Fifteen minutes later Sophal arrived in a tuk-tuk with a small travelling bag and a large hat and when their eyes met it was a moment of peacefulness and reassurance. She asked one of the Colonial Mansions boys to bring her out a coffee and she sat down next to him and they soaked up the cool while the street came into definition. There was an apprehension just before the expected appearance of their curiously domineering guide, and within it they were thrown closer, like children about to be reprimanded.

'You seem nervous,' she said. 'Are you anxious to leave?'

'I am. I don't know why.'

'You shouldn't be so anxious. It's just an escape.'

'Yes, and it was my idea —'

She nudged him and said, 'Yes it was, and now we're stuck with it!'

But somehow it wasn't entirely his idea. He began to feel foreboding and doubt; when the redoubtable guide appeared at long last, Robert felt an immense relief but also an even greater uncertainty. They got up and they shook his hand and Davuth looked them both rather searchingly in the eye and asked if they had slept well.

Davuth himself had risen early and prepared himself meticulously. He had put his rooms in order and left everything spare and neat. He had crammed the bag with the money he had taken from the barang's car that night into the apartment safe, and when he recounted it now he was surprised to find that he had spent so little of it. He had made himself a coffee in the unit's kitchen then gone outside to sip it, looking down at Robert's door. It gave him a feeling of delicate power.

He had become, over the years, remarkably attuned to the fear in others. As he opened the back doors for them now and they got into the car he could smell it on them — and yet it was not a conscious fear, it was more an anxiety that they were being taken somewhere they didn't know. It was strange, indeed, how human beings liked to be taken places they didn't know. It was the impulse that lay behind a lot of otherwise inexplicable events. He thought this, at least, as he drove smoothly and quite slowly through the still-sleeping city. The air was like spring in a northern country. As they passed the lovely train station he saw birds rising and then falling from the roofs in wave-like formations. In the public gardens the frangipanis stood stock-still and cool like giant storks, exuding an atmosphere of composure and haughtiness. Further out, the traffic was beginning and he went more quickly; the dust was quiescent. His two young passengers lay back on the seat and watched the grinding suburbs roll by. It was the same road they had taken to Phnom Chisor that day, the same factories and dusty verges and the fields opening up to vistas of sugar palms. Yet it looked completely different. Great pools in the paddies reflected a cloudless sky.

They passed Ta Phrom and pressed on until they were at the great roadside brick structures known as Prasat Neang Khmau, 'Black Lady' in Khmer. Davuth parked under some trees and they got out in the delicious sparkling air and walked over to the two towers. He told them, with an air of confidence, that the name referred to the goddess Kali.

'Tenth century,' he said, smiling and leading them right up to the brick, upon which he laid a hand. 'Splendid!'

They walked around the towers while Davuth smoked and watched them with a jovial expression. Like them, he felt the clear and dry air as something fresh and new, perhaps a harbinger of the rainy season's imminent end. In the secrecy of his own thoughts he had not yet decided anything. He had no plan whatsoever, he had resolved merely to see what happened moment by moment, but this very plan – or non-plan – felt so right, and so inevitable, that he went along with it happily. So he smoked and sat by the dry road and watched the longhorn cattle in the fields glowing cream in the sun and he felt at peace with himself and with everything that was going to happen from now on.

Sophal took some pictures of Robert standing by the towers and they then wandered around the bright modern temple next to them.

'It's better now,' she murmured. 'I feel better. It's so dry in the sun. I'm glad I came.'

'See?'

'I should have trusted you – Mr Tourist.'

'You should have. I know best.'

'No, but it's OK. Sometimes you do.'

It was strange, to her, that the early hours of a day could bring a new magnetic charge. As if a magnet had swept across the earth rearranging secret filings inside all living things. You had to be out in the countryside to feel it. Your senses were aware of it; you felt an almost appalling calm. The moments were pure pleasure, ticking away like the drops of a water clock. It was then that the boy to whom you were drawn came closer, suddenly filling all of your consciousness.

She was swept by a wave of accepting love, though she was not sure if that was what it was. Her father always said that in this traumatised country no one ever loved. He said it was a sentimental country with no love. No empathy, no trust. But she was beginning to disbelieve it. The generations change, she thought as she tasted slightly bitter iron dust on her lips and smelled woody incinerators from distant and invisible fields. The sun-glare made her quiver and blink and feel wonderfully alive. The generations change and love comes back into a people, even into a people that has been raped. Suddenly, one morning, it happens – the atoms shift, the animal life reasserts itself quietly and by some miracle life goes back to what it was meant to be. It happens inside the heart where no one can see it. The crucible comes alive again and there is a stirring inside the once-cold ashes. It is lovelessness that is short-term and narrow and destined not to endure because it has nowhere to go. If life is a stream, it is the dam made of rubbish and twigs. It cannot last. It breaks, twig by twig, and the movement begins again because it has to. There is nowhere else for it to go. Life *moves*.

She glanced over at Davuth sitting with his smoke and she saw the tension in his shoulders, the brooding droop of the head. There it was, the old world, the lovelessness. It was pathetic and dry and static and out of that immobility came a quiet hatred that was mysterious even to itself. Was that evil, then, in the Buddhist sense? She had exchanged barely a word with him in their shared language. It was as if he was forcing her to speak English with him. He's not a real guide, she thought.

They drove on and by midday they were in Takeo. At this time of year it was a riverine town with a quay and boats coming and going across the vast Mekong flood plain. By this seasonal waterfront a row of stalls had been set up alongside the jetties and here the pilots of the longtails sat in the shade waiting for infrequent customers. Behind them spread a desultory, ramshackle town with rows of shophouses and first-floor balconies with plastic columns. There was a messy, chaotic market where the butchers were in full swing. Traffic circles with sad lawns baked in the sun.

They stopped at the quay. They got out and Davuth sauntered down to the pilots. He bargained with them with surly charm. A boat until dusk. So he did not, after all, know a man here with a boat. Unconcerned, Sophal and Robert lay on the wall and sunbathed in the glare of the dirty water that lapped below them. The flood plain looked like a limitless lake, an island sea with no visible further shore. Its water was smooth and flat, rippled by slow, gentle swells. Here and there the tops of submerged trees popped up, crowned by feathery swarms of white birds. The upper branches were clotted with nests.

This great body of surly, placid liquid created its own dark light, within which the floating beds of water plants and their flowers shone with a muted malevolence. The men who piloted the longtails looked over at the young couple on the wall with a soulful cynicism. City kids, easy money. On the far side of the waters lay the mysterious ancient town of Angkor Borei and the flooded temple mountain of Phnom Da which, as Davuth had said, could only be reached by boat during the rains. These were the points of interest which the occasional barang visitors invariably wished to see, and once or twice a week each one of them made the eerie trip across the flood plain with a group in straw hats. Robert now gazed out at this featureless prospect and his heart sank a little. It looked like it would be a long and uncomfortable ride, to say the least. He stroked her warm shins and caressed the backs of her ankles and he could see that she was thinking the same thing.

'It won't be so bad,' he muttered, forcing himself to smile.

But he didn't know. He didn't even know what they were going to see over there. Davuth, as far as he could see, was haggling with the boatmen.

In fact, they were telling him that they were ready to embark immediately and he was trying to put them off.

He glanced at his watch and said, 'No, we'll leave at three.'

'Why so late? It'll be dark when you come back.'

'It doesn't matter. We need to have lunch. The young lady insisted on it.'

They looked up at the upper-class girl on the wall and grumbled.

'All the same, sir, it'll be dark and it's not good to be out there in the dark.'

'Maybe, but there we are. I can pay a little extra.'

But Davuth was thinking fast.

'We might even stay out there tonight. In which case, it doesn't matter. You can come back at once.'

This sweetened the deal.

'All right, at three,' they cried.

He shook a few hands and it was a deal.

He went off to the wall and told Robert and Sophal that under no circumstances would the stubborn vermin agree to leave before three o'clock. There was nothing he could so. He threw up his hands and laughed.

'I suggest we go and have lunch near the market. We can pass three hours easily enough.'

'But it'll be dark when we come back,' Sophal said at once.

'They said it wasn't a problem. We also get to see the sunset. There's nothing better than the sunset from Phnom Da. In fact, it's the whole point of going to Phnom Da in the first place.'

'Then I suppose we could,' Robert sighed.

'Or we could leave tomorrow.'

Sophal's voice was hopeful, but Davuth waved the suggestion down.

'No, that would be a waste of time. What is there to do in Takeo? Nothing! There isn't even a single decent three-star hotel here. Not even a two-star.'

They looked around for a moment and concluded that this was likely the case.

'Then let's get lunch,' Robert said brightly.

They left the car there and walked in towards the market. They soon found a run-down place to eat some soup and satay and as they did so they looked up at the clock on the cafe wall and internally counted down the minutes. It seemed interminable, this unnecessary wait. But for Davuth it served a purpose. He needed to collect his wits and think a little more. He let them buy him lunch and during it he said very little, chewing his food methodically and listening to the radio behind the woks. It would be an hour to cross the waters and maybe more, maybe two hours. The return would indeed be tricky, and in darkness. But it could be done.

The boy's eyes had flared up a beautiful dark blue. Did he really like this little Khmer girl? It was hard to say. Davuth bantered with them.

'So you like our country and want to stay?'

'I like it,' Robert said.

The Vikings — they had eyes like that.

When they had finished their Vietnamese coffees they walked back down to the quay in the sticky afternoon heat. As they approached the water's shimmer, clouds gathered far off over its horizon. Davuth went down and got hold of the boat and paid the man upfront for a one-way trip. 'What about the return?' the pilot asked hopefully. Davuth shook his head impatiently and said, 'We'll talk about it later.' They went down into the longtail one by one and Davuth sat next to the pilot and the other two seated themselves behind the prow. It had not been that difficult to arrange, Davuth reflected as they set off across the harbour filled with water plants and oil, and headed out into the flood plain with the sun on their right.

*

Halfway across they lost sight of land altogether. Here the trees sticking out of the surface were white as bone and draped with creepers. Driftwood floated idly past them, a few household items, broken birds' nests and strands of dark yellow flowers like garlands tossed from an abandoned wedding feast. The pilot asked no questions above the roar of his engine. Shaded by his jungle hat, Davuth watched everything pass by: the dead fish lying on their sides in the sun, the crowns of interlaced branches. As they approached Angkor Borei he saw the red roofs of distant houses on dry land and now they seemed improbable and exotic. The land there was under shadow. The rains were coming back, but they were doing so incrementally. They swept into a wide, obviously ancient canal that curved around. On the banks lay upturned little boats, knee-high shrines and men fishing with poles at the edge of pale and impenetrable mangroves.

Twenty-Five

Angkor Borei was little more than a municipal museum with stone replicas of Vishnu statues standing in a shabby garden. While Davuth remained with the pilot at the jetty, Sophal and Robert walked around it wondering why they had been taken there. From the back wall they looked down, however, at an idyllic river scene which might not have changed much in centuries. Children swimming naked in the shallows, boats tethered within the reeds; the sun blazing on the water. They went into the dark and stuffy museum and peered at a few exhibits of prehistoric artefacts. There were aerial photographs made by a French archaeologist called Pierre Paris in the 1930s showing the canals of the ancient city which had been called Vidhapurya. A guide appeared out of nowhere and began to beguile them. He told them about the mysteries of the lost kingdom of Funan, whose capital they were now standing in. 'One dollar,' he asked politely in the middle of this discourse, holding out an even politer hand. Robert paid him and the young man shadowed them as they went from case to case. He seemed to understand that they didn't really want to be there.

There were exhibits of piled human bones from

funerary sites, beautiful pottery and stone friezes depicting Vishnu.

'I feel a little claustrophobic,' Sophal said at last, and Robert thanked the guide to dismiss him and took her back outside. The sun had ripened and the skies were half clouded. Next to the museum stood a decomposing French colonial mansion of moss-thickened vaults and balconies, not dissimilar to some antebellum plantation house of the American South. They walked around it and mosquitoes came and nipped their necks and they found themselves wanting to go back to Takeo.

'But the temple will be special,' Robert said at last. 'Let's just go there now.'

'Let's. I'm being bitten alive.'

The mosquitoes, in fact, launched a major assault as they clambered back into the longtail and the pilot uttered a ritual cure aimed at these well-known belligerents.

'The mosquitoes of Angkor Borei – they are the worst!'

They crossed the flood plain in about half an hour.

Before they arrived at Phnom Da, however, the conical hill appeared with the dark ruined prasat at its summit. At the bottom was a dark mud beach with a few shacks scattered in the jungle behind it. There was a small bridge over an estuary, a few fires in the clearings, woodcutters or fishermen squatting under thatch. It looked like a dozen people and no more. The pilot left them there and Davuth made an abrupt sign for him to leave, but the man simply hung back near the bridge and waited. Davuth knew he would not depart without a return fare. He turned back to his charges and cheerfully pointed to the path that led up from the beach through the woods towards the stone steps of the temple. He said it would be a long, sweaty hike up to the top, and it looked likely that it would be. They saw that the hill was now an island entirely surrounded by water. The dry-season roads that connected it to land had disappeared and there was just the little bridge.

It was Sophal who led the way. By the time they were at the foot of the steps the forest had closed in all around them and the heat, though now decreasing, made the prospective climb forbidding. Bringing up the rear, Davuth encouraged them. It was not, he said, as bad as it looked. They climbed for half an hour and then rested.

Davuth told them a few stories he had cribbed from a guidebook and they listened as if he knew what he was talking about. He sat with his hands hanging between his knees. Already the hamlet by the water seemed a long way off. The sun began to dip towards the horizon as they soldiered on towards the summit. When they got there it was shining almost horizontally through the jungle into the prasat and its tumbledown shrine.

Two human figures were there. A young cowherd stood in the long grass at the edge of the clearing with four or five animals grazing. At the door to the temple an old man with disfigured ears sat begging in a monk's robe. They walked around the prasat. Its bricks were dark as brewed tea. The interior shrine made of concentric rectangles of cracked stone rising to an open skylight. Wild flowers washed against the outer walls, dark gold and blue.

They sat on pieces of stone and waited for the dusk to come down. But the sea could only be seen through gaps in the dense jungle. Soon, the old man and the cowherd moved off, lethargic as the longhorn cows. They could hear the bells of the latter tinkling as they receded down the hill. When they were alone, Davuth offered them a sip from his whisky flask and they watched the sun decline into a rising bank of rain cloud. Further down the hill, Davuth said, stood a small seventh-century temple known as Ashram Maha Rosei, or the 'sanctuary of the great ascetic'. Built of laterite, it was considered architecturally unique in Cambodia because of its remarkable Javan and Indian style — it was thought that parts of the Mekong were once ruled by Java. He seemed to know all about it. And indeed, Davuth had sat up half the night reading up on the matter.

'Let's go and see it,' he said, standing and brushing off the dust from his seat. 'Then we'll go down and find the boat.'

Robert, however, was feeling tired of the place already and refused to move.

'It's all right,' he said. 'Sophal, you go and look.'

Reluctantly, she agreed. 'I'll just be ten minutes. I'll take some photos for you.'

'I'll be here.'

'All right,' she said. 'We'll be back in a minute.'

She felt awkward leaving him, and she didn't want to be alone with Davuth, but it was only a few hundred metres down the hill and there was no one else there.

Davuth led the way and he plucked out a switch from the undergrowth and playfully flicked it left and right as they made their way down a forest path. 'Over there,' he said vaguely, pointing towards the east, 'is Vietnam.' She wondered why guides always felt the need to point out the most mundanely obvious things, as if they were in danger of being left out of consciousness. When the path dipped more steeply on its way to the forgotten temple she looked up through the gaps in the trees and saw a soaring dusk cloud rising into the indigo sky. Its edges were brilliantly lit as if electrified from within, its apex snow-white and supremely elegant as it evolved ever upwards. How far did such formidable clouds reach in their ceaseless straining for height and power? They seemed to be driven by awareness and desire for dominance. At its core, the cloud was almost black and one could taste the imminent rain on the lips. Davuth, too, stopped for a moment and looked up at it and his eyes went pale and empty and languid. For him, everything in the sky was an omen. Signs became material in the heavens and they were fashioned by multitudes of gods.

Robert also watched it, lying on his back on a carved plinth that must have been well over a thousand years old. He shaded his eye to look at it directly. One last sloweddown flash of light before dusk. A flicker of lightning from somewhere else. The forest quivered. He was glad to be alone for a while, to be cut off from living things. From a fair distance he could still hear the tinkle of the cowbells, the animals lumbering downwards.

The recent days had been the loveliest so far and now he could see a little more clearly the uphill and pleasant path that might lie before him. His prospects, it was true, had no solid footing, but did they need to have one in this place? He could stay here until the ground solidified under his feet a bit. Sooner or later other doors would open to a charming and undesperate young man. The doctor was right: it was a country fast becoming rich and corrupt in novel ways. There would be unexpected openings in the years to come and those who stuck around and were patient would be able to profit from them almost unnoticed.

Gradually, he had lost his bearings in the face of these

temptations. He had come to appreciate the power of secrecies and dissimulations practised on a daily basis. Below him, vast as a labyrinth in a nightmarish myth, an ancient and subtle culture that the whites had settled on like flies on the surface of oily water, trembling and nervous and falsely righteous. The con men and the opportunists were little different from the pasty evangelicals and NGOs and savers of souls who you saw next to them huddled around tables in expensive restaurants every night. Indistinguishable to the Khmers. He was one of them and he no longer minded; con man or Baptist hustler saving children, it was not a chasm separating the two. The motives behind the two were not as dissimilar as either assumed. They both wanted a better life in a country where they could do what they wanted, where they remained unexamined. They were both frauds in their way, interlopers exploiting their whiteness. It was disgusting and comic, but in the end no one was going to punish either of these eternal types. The Samaritan and the criminal.

He himself could spend a lifetime here living off other people's money. It could be done. He could be Simon for the rest of his life, living off that man's unstable identity, and eventually he would actually *become* Simon. Unless, one fine day, Simon actually showed up. But he had an intuition about that. He sensed that it would never happen. Once a man cons you, he avoids you.

Then what if he was safe from now on?

When the first stars appeared he shook himself out of his reverie and sat up and saw behind him the moon which had risen over the Mekong. Shadowy longtails skimmed silently across the waters. He had forgotten the time a little and he realised now that almost an hour had passed. So they had not returned from Ashram Maha Rosei.

He went to the edge of the clearing and called out. Then he thought about the boat waiting for them on the mud beach far below. Would the man really wait for them so long and in the dark? He noticed how quickly the light was draining out of things and he wondered to himself if a certain urgency might be called for. Nevertheless, he ventured down onto the path with an annoyed reluctance, not wanting to climb down merely to have to climb back up. And the mosquitoes were now out in force. He clucked and called out again and then cursed quietly and resolved to go find them. He swept down the overgrown path occasionally calling her name and feeling an increasing surprise that nothing came back at him. They must be inside the shrine, then, buried in masonry and out of earshot.

At the temple there was no one there. He peered inside the unlit core and caught a whiff of stale incense and ash. He looked quickly around it. It was a nuisance that they had gone off without telling him, leaving him alone in the jungle. But perhaps the best thing was to wait there.

He sat on the threshold of the shrine and soon he heard a clicking sound from a little further down the hill. He got up and went back to the path and looked down into the gloom. Almost at once he saw a flicker of light, like a lighter being flicked on, and when it repeated he called out. It was now too dark to see anything but the vague shimmer of the Mekong below and the spark of light going on and off. A wave of fear came over him and he plunged down towards it with a hoarse yell, which to his surprise was simply her name. He came down into the thick undergrowth and when he came close enough to see that it was indeed a lighter he saw that they were sitting together under a tree, and that Sophal had her back to him and that she was sobbing.

Davuth sat facing the other way, towards Robert, and his thumb flicked the lighter on and off. When it was on his face was lit from below, calm and smiling. He seemed to have been sitting like this for some time, waiting for the Englishman to show up. In his lap lay a regulation police pistol with the barrel paid against his knee but not pointing at anything. It looked like something carved from soapstone. Davuth left the lighter on now and then he invited Robert to sit down as well. The latter understood everything within a few seconds and his mind went wild with rage. He looked around for a heavy stone to use, to launch himself into an attack and smash the policeman's head. But in that flicker of instant calculations he realised how lost the cause was. Even if he managed the move in a second he would be too late. He was snared, and Sophal had been snared already. They had walked into it blind. They had walked off a cliff and it was too late. The policeman, then, knew that Robert understood and he smiled peaceably. Let's be reasonable, Davuth seemed to be saying, and after a few moments Robert did sit down and Davuth talked for a while.

'I know who you are,' Davuth began. 'The easiest thing is you just give me your apartment key. I am going back to the city. By the time you get there yourselves I will be —' he made a strange gesture with his fingers, like falling snow — 'long gone.'

It was said very gently. Nobody would come to any harm and since he, Davuth, had his passport it would be a foolish thing to pursue him or go on his own account to the police. Nobody would listen to him anyway.

'Also, what is the code to the safety box in your apartment?'

Robert gave it, and he handed over his phone at the same time.

'This is absurd,' he said, and took out the key and threw it over to Davuth. 'You didn't have to do all this just to get a key.'

'No, I thought it through very carefully. I want to be invisible – and you want to be invisible as well. This way you can carry on being invisible. I don't care what you do. You are nothing to me.'

'There's nothing in my room.'

'You've been throwing your money around. There's enough to keep me happy.'

'There's nothing there at all.'

'Well, I am not going to believe that now. You can say what you want. I know you went to the Diamond and won a lot of money.'

'All right, whatever you say.'

'You barangs. You think you can get away with it.'

Robert talked to Sophal but she said nothing back. Her shirt was ripped and her hair was tangled. There had been a struggle. The policeman offered him a cigarette and he declined. Davuth got up and dusted off his trousers and walked off nonchalantly until he was at the path and the forlorn couple were plunged in darkness. He felt it was appropriate to say a few more words but he could not think what they should be. People talked far too much anyway. He felt the key in his pocket and memorised the code and was happy that it had all gone so smoothly for him. He had enjoyed the girl as well, she had not put up much resistance in the end. Those types were always soft at their core. They had not had to struggle to survive. He looked down at them from the slight advantage of the path and he felt a twisting, momentary pity. But at least they were alive and, in his case, unharmed. They had got off lightly.

'You can get a boat at daybreak,' he said, in a more conciliatory tone. 'There'll be one at the beach.'

'There's nothing in the room,' Robert called back mockingly.

'I'll see about that. So long, bye-bye then.'

Robert stood as well, then sat down and put his arm around Sophal. There was no reason to delay this fortunate departure.

Davuth thought for a moment before striding way, and tossed the lighter in their direction as a small mercy. A few minutes later he was at the top of the hill in the menacing shadow of the prasat where bats now wheeled in the humidity. The steps on the way down were covered with leaves and at the bottom the jungle seethed with fireflies. He composed himself, dried his forehead with his handkerchief and walked down to the shacks where a couple of kerosene lamps burned from the rafters. There was no one out and about, just the cows tethered to a few trees and their eyes shining at a measured distance. He stood at the edge of the water and raised his arm.

Hunters in the Dark

Twenty-Six

A few moments later the longtail which had taken them over appeared, paddled in silence by the pilot who had been waiting by the closed-off bridge. The boat nosed up to the beach and Davuth stepped into it without a word. The boat rocked and he steadied himself; there was a stifling moment of awkwardness between them. The man was not afraid. He was merely unsure what to do.

By the same token he knew better than to ask any inconsequential questions and without explicit instruction he turned the vessel around and started up the motor. The sound shocked them both. Davuth took one last look back at the beach, where the clotted nets lay in wet piles on a mud dark as cocoa. The Englishman had not followed him. They sped out onto the flood plain as the first drops of rain began to fall and the moon disappeared. He lay back in the boat with his hands behind his head and the spray washed over him. In a mere twenty-four hours, the long years of drudgery at his humble station had been left behind and he thought of his daughter asleep in her bed, unaware that he was at that very moment slaving on her behalf and safeguarding her future. She would discover it all later. Either way, it was fated and the fate that had chosen him had made no errors. He had done everything perfectly and the laws of the universe remained undisturbed and serene. At the quay of Takeo the lights were off and he took a roll of dollars and gave them to the pilot.

'If you talk to anyone, you'll see me again. You don't want to see me again.' He was sure that he had made his point because the man turned away and said nothing back.

Davuth then walked to the car still parked under the trees and drove through the deserted town. There were no karaokes here, no late-night bars, no nocturnal flimflam. The air was still. Just the needling, unrefreshing rain. It was as boring a town as a man could wish for. It would be fine in the early morning and never afterwards.

Within minutes he was back on Route 2 and he was alone on the white-edged road with the gardens and orchards and paddies flowing by. He drove for two hours without thinking about anything. Finally he stopped in a lonely stretch and went into the fields to take a pee. He wanted to be back in the city before first light but he had a few hours to spare. As he stood there surrounded by the whispers of the crickets, however, he felt a strange desire to return to the island in the Mekong and take back everything he had done and said. It couldn't be done, of course, but still he wanted to go back and make amends and let things take a different course. It was always the fields at this hour that took him back to the old days and the nights of executions which had gone virtually unrecorded. It was quite a thing to consider that he was the only man alive who remembered the last moments of many dozens of people. They lived within him still, he liked to think. But to whom had he ever made amends?

To whom had he prayed for forgiveness? He had got away with it, and who was he to get away with it? Many of his comrades had also got away with it and when they were awake in their beds they reasoned to themselves that they had been young, far too young to be held responsible for anything. It was their extreme youth that explained their ecstatic sadism and skill at killing. It was a skill which only came from a knowing enjoyment, and therefore it was a youthful knowledge, a dementia of immaturity. But in the end he didn't really believe it.

While he was there he went through their bags, finding nothing but clothes and toiletries and a hundred dollars in cash, and then he took the mobile phones and threw them into a canal running alongside one of the paddies.

He drove into Monivong and stopped at one of the late-night Viet places for some *pho* and *nem*. He was starving. At the family tables it was only young clubbers still high and wide-eyed. They gave him a curious jolt of energy. Restored in spirit, he drove back to Street 102 and parked the car a fair distance from Colonial Mansions near the top of the alley by the boulevard. Then he walked calmly down to the property and passed unnoticed into the lobby where everyone, as usual, was asleep at their post. He went up to his apartment, let himself in and turned on one light. His own orderliness reassured him and reminded him of a superiority which he had always known was his. An organised man, they used to call him.

He opened the safe and took out the bag with the banknotes and laid it on the bed with the passports and a few other things he had kept there. He was now ready to disappear forever from this oppressive residence. He assembled everything on the bed then turned off the light, closed the door quietly behind him and walked down to Robert's apartment. It was now past three in the morning and the bureaucrats and corporate officers were asleep in their chilled rooms. He effortlessly opened the door and passed inside and then walked into the rear bedroom and turned on the light there. The curtains to the main room were already closed fast. He locked the door from the inside and then began his patient combing of the rooms, beginning with the safe which he opened easily.

There was nothing inside. It was the first blow. He felt his face flushing with blood and fury, and he then ransacked the bedroom. He upended the bed, tore up pieces of carpet and emptied out all the cupboards. There was nothing even in the bathroom. The boy had taken everything with him and it now dawned on him – it had been inconceivable only a few hours before – that he had been telling the truth. The little bourgeois parasite had not been lying after all. It was a surprising thing. He gave up after half an hour and sat forlornly on the Englishman's bed and let his hands dry slowly. It was now possible that it had all been for nothing. All he had was the money taken from the roadside in Battambang.

It was a fair sum but far short of the sums he had been hoping for. He had even hoped to be able to blackmail the Englishman, but he was sure now that it would yield nothing.

Well, he thought, it was worth the try. It's always worth the try.

He cleaned up the unit and went back out into the corridor after locking the door behind him and keeping the key. There remained two hours of darkness and he considered simply walking out of the Mansions and driving home in defeat. He had, after all, lost nothing in the end, and for that matter he was still many hundreds of dollars in the black. Better to leave, then, and go back to his daughter. There would be more barangs floating in the river at a later time – they were inexhaustible bounty.

So he went back up to his room, locked the door and took a shower. The night was cool, he left the windows open. The water cold and reviving, the moths becalmed on the bathroom walls.

He had been a bit of a fool, and he didn't relish the failure.

When he came out into the bedroom he felt tired and yet restless. His anger had risen and would not subside. He lay on the bed in his towel and thought and thought until his mind had exhausted itself and finally come to a standstill. He opened the bag and counted out the money and looked over the passports and resolved to throw them out on his way home. Two invisible men who didn't matter to the world. Two crooks who didn't even know they were crooks.

He dressed and combed his hair in the mirror. As he was patting the last jet-black strands there was a knock on his door. Carelessly, he had left the main room's light on. Perhaps it was reception nagging him about his tab. But at four in the morning?

Going to the door he waited for a moment then sensed that the person on the other side of it had not gone away. He opened it then and saw Sothea standing by the rail of the corridor. She reclined casually against the rail and her eyes were cool and unhurried. Surprised, he opened the door wider and asked her bluntly what she was doing there. But then he reconsidered. Why not?

She came in.

'It's a bit late,' he said, closing the door behind her.

'It's never too late for this.'

'True.'

He calculated the time. What difference did thirty minutes make?

'I wasn't expecting this,' he said all the same.

'All the better.'

She walked into the bedroom and sat on the bed. By now she knew the room quite well and she spotted at once the small signs of his imminent departure. His affairs were all packed, it would seem.

'You're going away?'

'Yes, back to my job. I shouldn't have stayed away so long as it is.'

'I see. In the middle of the night?'

'Why not in the middle of the night?'

'No reason. Still . . .'

'Still what?'

He came and sat next to her and his breath was cold and scented with a touch of whisky.

'The roads are empty,' he smiled. 'I'll need to leave within an hour.'

'Then there's no point talking.'

There's rarely any point talking anyway, he thought.

She took off her shirt and shoes and went into the bathroom. The mirror was misted and the tiled floor damp. She was wearing jeans and in her front pocket was a small screwdriver. She gripped it for a moment as she inspected her mouth in the mirror, then she washed her hands and let the hot water run a while. She was composing herself. Then she turned and went back into the room where the policeman was already naked and lying on the bed. How quickly he always dressed and undressed. There was an uncanny efficiency about him, even when it concerned nothing more consequential than his animal needs.

Sothea turned off the main light and they lay together for a while, saying nothing, until he said, 'Why are your jeans still on?'

'I was just thinking.'

'Don't.'

'All right, I'll take them off.'

She put them on the floor beside the bed but kept the screwdriver in her hand. He had turned over on his front as if waiting for a back massage and his head was laid on his arm, his eyes closed. In reality, he was suddenly exhausted after the long drive. The futility of the whole thing had been sinking in moment by moment. He was disgusted and discouraged. The moths fluttered around the main room and he heard them knocking softly against the plastic shutters and the walls. Slowly, he fell into a semi-doze. It was an unexpected gift to her. It was now, indeed, that she wanted most to talk to him. She wanted, in the first place, to tell him everything she had seen and everything she had lost because of him and the filthy driver he was in cahoots with. But there was no time for that. She thought of Simon lying by the side of a sugar-cane field on a nameless road. Was that really necessary? A policeman was supposed to report such things and then investigate them. It was only amazing that he had failed to recognise her after they had met that day on the way up to the Scot's sinister hotel. He had desired her then – for a moment – and he desired her now. But he had failed to connect the two moments in time. Did he think she was two different women? It was a blind spot that was all the more surprising in a man like Davuth. She would make him pay for that oversight. She and Simon could have had a decent enough life together; it was one version of the future she had never given up on. It had been taken away from her by a disaster not of her own making.

She raised herself up and realised that now he was asleep and noticed nothing. She whipped the screwdriver up high and then plunged it straight down into the back of his neck. She put so much force into the blow that there was no struggle. He hasped and stirred and before he could wake she had struck a second time and with even greater ferocity. His blood rushed up out of the two wounds and she straddled him and raised the screwdriver once more. This time with both hands, driving it into his neck as far as she could. His whole body shook like a pig impaled.

The moths in the next room still beat against the shutters. When she was exhausted in her own right she rolled off the squalid body and sank onto the floor for a while. She had already decided that it was all the result of Simon's karma and of her own, and it was all foreordained. Against the unleashed consequences of karma one had no defence. The circle of samsara was mostly fixed; there was no liberation. Events piled up against each other like logs being thrown onto a pile. She would meet Davuth in a future life and with luck he would be a fly and she would be a gecko chasing him down and eating him. If, that is, she was lucky. She might not be lucky. The seeds laid by any given karma were not entirely known, the outcomes could not be foretold with any accuracy and it was likely, in any event, that one would remain floating and turning within the circle of eternal suffering.

Twenty-Seven

She left the screwdriver on the bed after wiping down the handle and took – with a slow deliberateness – a cold shower to wash herself down. She felt nothing at all. She washed her hair and her fingernails scrupulously. She felt she was honouring her dead lover.

In the main room she re-dressed without a spot of blood on her. Now the moths had stilled and there was a taste of dawn in the air. The Mansions were about to stir with weary life. She saw at once the bag that he had packed, stowed next to the bed. Inside it was her and Simon's money, and the two passports. For a moment she was blindly elated and triumphant, and spotted too the amulet which Davuth always wore to protect himself and which, crucially, he had neglected to wear as he went to bed for his pleasures. It was the one thing she would leave untouched and it was surely fate that had made him forget it. If he had been wearing it the screwdriver would never have pierced, he would have sensed her intentions. The thought made her shudder finally. He had hunted her, and them, and now she had hunted him. Yet neither had really been hunting the other. There was another key on the table in the main room, with an apartment number tag attached, and she took it.

When she was finished she took hold of the bag, went over the room again carefully and then slipped out into the corridor, locking the door with the push button in the handle. The cleaners were scraping the surface of the pool below with nets. They did not look up. She went down to the apartment number on the key and opened the door and went in. This unit was plunged in darkness and she had to reluctantly turn on one of the lights. The place had obviously been ransacked, the floors strewn with damaged toiletries, and the violence of the pillage appalled her. She began to understand how the English boy had been wronged. First by them and then by Davuth. And how, in the end, had he harmed to deserve such a thing?

On the way down to the room she had still been sure of her intention, to run with the money after leaving the passports in Robert's room as a small atonement. But when she opened the bag now and looked at the notes she felt that this was the wrong plan and had been all along. The disaster had happened because they had taken something that was not theirs. Recall, then, the first night after she and Simon had fled. They had stopped in a village by the river and the ever-superstitious Simon, who believed in Khmer folk magic far more than she did, insisted that they visit a fortune-teller together, a *haor teay*. He took with him one of the dollar bills from the stash and asked the man to look at it and 'read' its future.

The *haor teay* lived alone in a hovel by the water. They sat together at dusk among the rubbish and reeds. Simon was slightly delirious and obsessed. He kept telling her that the money might be jinxed, it might

320

be cursed by spirits and he wanted to find out if it was. He considered going to a *rup arak* to see if it could be connected to someone who was already dead. All money once belonged to people now dead. It was not just paper; it transmitted things from the past and contained within itself an unknown future. It connected people but not in ways that they could understand. He had a feeling – he said he could feel that it was 'bad karma' money because it came from a casino, from the world of criminals. It had a supernatural smell to it and he thought about having it exorcised. It was crazy of him, and yet now she remembered the visit to the *haor teay* and she was not so sure. The old man had fingered the bill and pressed it against his mouth. Simon became more excited and asked her to translate in case he had misunderstood anything. It was then that the first fear had gripped her. The man said, 'Leave the money where it is and run as fast as you can. It is not yours and it will bring in spirits.'

'What spirits?' Simon burst out, gripping her hand.

'I can't say what spirits.'

'Leave him alone,' she whispered into Simon's ear.

But Simon was in a lather.

'Get him to tell me – we need to know! What spirits? What the fuck does he mean, bring in spirits?'

But the *haor teay* wouldn't say. They left in a mood of high hysteria. Simon wouldn't calm down and he paced about for hours gibbering to himself about spirits and exorcism. But how could money be exorcised?

It was she who needed to be exorcised now. She changed her mind then and decided to leave the bag on the bed with everything inside it. That was the best karma she could obtain. The spirits would then leave her alone and move on to someone else, if spirits there were.

Either way, she was superstitious about the money. She left it there and everything with it, along with the keys to Davuth's car which she had found as well, and let herself out of the apartment, taking the key with her, however, and leaving it by the desk of the receptionist. The boy was fast asleep with his head laid upon his folded arms and as she dropped the keys quietly on the floor next to him he did not wake up. Robert would be handed it when he returned and his surprise would turn everything upside down. She walked down the steps, then, and into the street where it was raining and nothing could be heard but the pools and the trees bending slowly under the onslaught. She was one of those people – and they are rare, even in that fluid and shifting place – who know how to disappear within a few moments, within a few paces. She passed Davuth's car on the way, and on the seats she saw old newspapers, a hat and a sprinkling of glittering small change. Above her, at the same time, the massive clouds had begun to form towering pillars which had suddenly become faintly visible: their rise had about it an irresistible determination and slowness, a fantastical inevitability and negative brilliance.

Twenty-Eight

They were mirrored in the flood plain and formed there dark, unmoving reflections. From across the water came the silent flickers of lightning and the sweet morning thunder. By seven that morning Robert and Sophal were back in Takeo, having persuaded one of the men in the village to take them over. She had convinced the boatman to call her father and, without explaining anything to him, had got the doctor to send a car down to pick them up with some money for the boatman. When they got to Takeo, therefore, they only had to wait an hour before the driver appeared. They had not spoken for some time and it was better to be isolate and silent as they sat in a cafe and watched the rain. She went into the establishment's bare toilet and washed her face and hands, damping paper towels onto the little cuts on her knuckles. Vast areas of her being had been snuffed out in a few moments of time, but she was still solid in the mirror. Her scabs still tasted saline and she still flickered in and out of life – just like that silent lightning. It's the ghost side of oneself that carries on.

During the night, huddled inside the prasat as the rain pounded down, she had poured out all her rage in a brief explosion. He had told her everything finally and when it was done there was no point talking any further and she went over the sudden catastrophe in her mind as they skimmed over the half-lit Mekong in the longtail until the lights of Takeo came into view. What was surprising was that she was not truly surprised: something had been wrong all along. When the family driver appeared she walked silently to the car and got in and waited for something to happen between them as they drove back to Phnom Pehn. His apologies, however, were pointless; it's in the nature of lies to catch up with the perpetrator and strangle him. But her? So, she kept thinking, I have to be destroyed for the sake of his lies. In the end they slept and it was past nine when they arrived back at Colonial Mansions. It began to feel like a small, nasty dream. She woke and told the driver that she didn't need to go back home. He was to tell her father that she was fine. They had simply forgotten the time at Phnom Da and they had forgotten their money, too, at a cafe in Takeo. All he had to do was cancel her credit cards and she would come home later.

The driver seemed to hesitate, as if he had received very different instructions from her father. But in the end he relented and let the young mistress do what she wanted. He gave her the envelope of cash her father had entrusted to him and was glad to let the master and mistress do what they wanted and go their merry ways.

In the lobby there was a paradoxically dreamlike normality to everything. The boys in their laundered white shirts, the Chinese women doing their dutiful laps in the pool and the maids patiently spraying the ornamental palms. The rain pattered on the windows and two American Embassy officials took their morning coffees under the photographs of colonial Phnom Penh and Hmong tribesmen. The man on duty smiled when he saw Robert and his silent noting of the dishevelled clothes and hair was kept under perfect control as he searched for the key that had been left there earlier and finally handed it over.

'One of our staff,' he said politely, 'found it in the lobby earlier this morning. You must have dropped it on your way out.'

'Of course. Thank you.'

A stroke of luck, then, as the world sometimes throws your way when things have reached their end. He felt a sullen wonderment.

'You might consider,' the man went on, 'leaving it at the desk from now on. People lose their keys all the time.'

'Yes, it's a good idea. Who found it?'

'One of the boys. It was lying on the floor.'

'On the floor?'

'Yes, sir.'

'I must have dropped it then.'

'Yes, sir.'

On their way up to the apartment he glanced up at the third floor. There was something there, some riddle. He could feel it in his nerves. And yet he had come through the riddle unharmed. They went into the disordered room and he saw the bag on the bed at once and he opened it while she stumbled into the bathroom to have a shower and there was everything that he had lost a few weeks earlier. The first image that came into his mind was a boomerang whipping through the air: the useful cliché. Then he saw, too, the car keys laid next to the bag and looking inside the bag itself he found the two passports.

She was under the shower now, sobbing and wailing, and he tried to think how the boomerang had found its way back to him; but that was impossible. He gathered up all his scattered and despoiled belongings and made them orderly and then he sat on the bed and waited for the rain to stop. When Sophal came out of the bathroom she had calmed down and what was left of the bitterness was a coldness that would last until something healed it. Time, he thought banally, and left it at that. His own actions had ceased to mean anything.

They went down together as the sun broke out and, as previously suggested, he left the key with reception but with no intention of ever recuperating it. In the room, they had merely decided to leave.

'I have the keys to his car,' he had said.

'How do you know it's his car?'

'I just do.'

'Where is he then?'

'I don't know.'

They had stared at each other for some time.

'How do you have the keys?' she had spat at him.

'I don't know, but I have them.'

'They were just in your room?'

'Yes.'

It was so inexplicable she had given up.

'I don't want to go home,' she had said. 'I want to go away somewhere.'

'All right, we'll go away.'

'Where?'

'I don't know. Back the way I came.'

She had looked at the bag.

'What's that?'

'The money. It's all there.'

326

'Throw it away.'

He had nodded.

'All right. I'll throw it away.'

'I mean it.'

'I said I would, didn't I?'

Down in the street they saw the car parked under mango trees, the windscreen covered with drops of dried mud and crushed flies. The merriness of a Sunday morning flooded the streets around the day markets, the dogs running in packs, the drivers squatting in the shade of the magnificent trees. The sun brought a bright lucidity. They stood in it for a moment basking and warming themselves, and without knowing why they sensed that Davuth was not around and that someone had made them a mysterious gift. They climbed into the car and their mood lifted. A great zone of porcelain-blue sky had opened up at the apex. As they drove slowly out of the city the river was lit up by the sun and the frangipanis seemed to turn into foam. Soon, the city had thinned and they moved along tattered roads among the trucks and the bikes with their angry dust. The rain had soaked everything but the man-made things had dried in an hour. 'We'll go back to Battambang,' he said quietly. 'We can stay there a few days. Is that all right?' She said nothing, and it was her assent.

Through the whole afternoon they drove without speaking, until the river flashed in the distance and the billboards rose up by the road and showered them with images of a France that no longer existed. They came into Battambang as the dust dried and they stopped and went for a walk along the stagnant, softly luminous green river.

*

Here once again was the building of Electricité de Battambang and the old French mansions ranged along the road. The same boys lounged on the step banks, lulled by the chugging generators. They too lay down in the grass and they slept a little with their bodies close together. Small white clouds sailed across an open sky and he stared up at them and felt the crickets in the grass whispering as if from afar. Vaguely, he was considering crossing the border again if she would agree. They could spend a few days together in Bangkok perhaps. They could go to an island somewhere and her father could wire them some money when they ran out. Or he could keep the money he already had. He looked over and saw that she was lying serenely with her face upturned as if still deep in sleep. The sound of a fairground of some kind came wafting across the little bridge nearby. The faint call of a mosque, the mosque he remembered standing over the river upstream. He raised himself on his elbows and squinted at the sun. How long had it been since he had last been in this very spot? A few weeks, a few months – he couldn't really say any more. He had long ago stopped counting his days and the longer he stopped counting them, the faster they passed. He was not even sure why he had returned there. He didn't know why he had the car and the money he had won long ago at the Diamond Crown in Pailin. It had been taken away from him and then returned to him, but by whom and why? It was like a wheel that had shifted in the dark, but so slowly that one didn't notice it turning. He saw little spiders scattering through the grass as if alarmed by his shadow. We'll go over the border, he thought. He roused Sophal and she opened her eyes and there was no emotion in them whatsoever. Down in the river the boys had jumped into the water with nets and fishing rods and some of them were swimming under the bridge, engulfed in its shadow. The sight of them made him think of his parents, far off in their wintery realm. In their heart of hearts they knew that he was alive.

They went to a place called Pomme d'Amour and had a quick dinner washed down with Chilean wine. Still they didn't speak. The streets became ominous and still. There was a small meeting of the Cambodian People's Party at a street corner near the restaurant, the voices amplified through the cheap megaphones somehow dulcet and detached from the usual menu of political angers. They sat outside, close to the bustle of passers-by. The warmth of bodies unconcerned by the secret dramas of others. The delivery girls from the restaurant itself came out with enormous plastic bags which they balanced on the handlebars of their bikes before riding off. Along the top of a roof the silhouette of a cat appeared; Sophal pronounced it bad luck. 'Rubbish,' he snorted.

'Let's go into Thailand and find a place in Bangkok. No?'

'Do you mind?' she asked, as if she had been wanting this all along, but without mentioning it to him.

'Of course I don't mind. I wouldn't suggest it if I minded. I'm glad you want to as well.'

'I just need to get out of this country for a while.'

'I know what you mean. Then we'll get out.'

'Can we take a car over the border?'

He laughed grimly. 'Of course we can't take a car over the border. Why would we want to anyway? The car is evidence – we'll dump it.'

'Really?'

'Obviously. We'll take a taxi on the other side.'

So that's how it's done, she thought.

'Then what?'

'Then nothing. We'll let everything calm down.'

'But the very fact that we're not there —'

He rolled his shoulders and looked away.

'What does it matter? We haven't done anything wrong. We don't know where that bastard is. I don't care where he is.'

'Who is he?'

'How do I know? I'd never seen him before I met him in the lobby. Anyway . . .'

Robert turned it over in his mind but there was no way of accounting for it. It felt, to him, like a coincidence that he would just have to leave by the side of the road.

She sipped at her wine and soon she began to feel more resolved.

'All right,' she said, 'we'll go to Bangkok and then the sea. Maybe we can come back through Trat. One can cross the border there.'

'It's a plan.'

He tried to telegraph an encouragement through a better smile than the last one.

'The situation's not as bad as all that,' he went on. 'It's just confusing more than anything.'

'And what about your American friend?'

'No idea. He's not my friend though. He's probably selling dope to some hippies somewhere.'

But he didn't know, he couldn't imagine.

After dinner she got a new $7 mobile phone with SIM card and called her father. There was a small uproar. Her mother came on the line.

'I'm perfectly fine,' she hissed. 'Simon and I are going to Bangkok — oh, for God's sake stop worrying. We'll call tomorrow night.'

Her mother spoke.

'No, no, leave us be, we're fine. I'll call tomorrow.'

They went for Vietnamese coffee at the White Rose and suddenly they didn't care as much. The border closed at eight and they just had to be there by seven thirty. There was a little time. They wandered down to the fairground which they had heard from the river. It was rustic and loud and they went on one of the machines as the light dimmed and the ancient bulbs large as grenades came on and began to steam. The whole town stirred into nocturnal illumination, or so it seemed to them. The villas, the utility buildings, the rows of shophouses by the river, the cement French buildings which looked, for once, like the monuments of tenuous conquerors. Bats swirled around the riverbanks and the hospital, too, was lit up. Was it a celebration neither of them had heard of? He had the feeling – it could not be verified – that the population was turning through the grid of streets in a wheel-like formation. Cabarets on the pavements, the old ladies with their tea and shots laughing uproariously and holding up their hands to their faces where the make-up had streaked. The cats sat still and watched. Girls in bridal dresses came down the street they were navigating, their heads covered with plastic flowers. And, a few streets away, moving within that same crowd, Ouksa was walking with an ice cream, morosely picking his way from street to street looking for openings.

His wife was now in the hospital and he had been to see her an hour earlier. Finally, exasperated and drawn outdoors by the sound of music in the streets, he had gone wandering along the lit-up river and turned into the maze of streets. It was here that he came upon Davuth's car parked next to a barber's shop. He recognised it at once and yet continued walking as if nothing had happened, then stood at the corner looking back down the street and licking his ice cream. He was not sure, in fact, if running into that demonic personality was such a good idea. But at the same time, he had a secret he could maybe cash in and now that he was more desperate than he had been, he was more prepared to risk it. So he waited until the night was almost upon them and he was sure that eventually Davuth would appear and this time the odds would not be stacked against Ouksa. They would just be two men in the street, almost equals. In that context he would no longer be afraid of the policeman. He would act friendly and surprised and Davuth would find it awkward to get away easily. He would ask him for money, and if he refused he would suggest a bribe, a threat.

Wild, and on the spur of the moment! But the man who came down the street to reclaim the car was not Davuth.

Ouksa dropped the ice cream at his feet and rushed down to greet Robert and a nice-looking girl he had with him. They met right at the car itself, in a whirl of teenage boys in party hats.

'You!' Ouksa shouted, and his mood had to change into a different gear. Robert, stunned, simply shook his head.

'It's Ouksa,' he said to the girl. 'My driver from the first day.'

They shook hands and the driver began to think as fast as he could. In the first place, he said nothing about recognising the car.

'I was just walking down the street,' he said, smiling his smile.

'My friend and I are just leaving.'

'Leaving? Leaving where?'

'Back to the border.'

'In that Khmer car?'

'It's what we have.'

'But why didn't you call me? I could have driven you!'

'I didn't have a number.'

Ouksa felt a keen anxiety now.

'Shall we have a drink?'

Robert tried to remember the hour.

'We haven't got time. The border closes in two hours.'

'You'll never make it.'

'Of course we'll make it. It's not that far.'

'A quick drink —'

'Sorry, it's impossible.' Robert turned to Sophal. 'Isn't
it?'

'Totally,' she said.

'No, no, you can't leave like this. Not after such a
coincidence!'

Robert opened the car and the driver became a little
frantic.

'Just one drink —'

'I'll tell you what. Why don't you drive us to the border
then? We don't need the car anyway. You can keep it.'

'What?'

'You can keep the car.'

'Keep the car?'

'Yeah, you can keep it. I want you to keep it.'

It was a huge windfall and Ouksa blinked and picked
at his mouth.

'Then I'll drive you!' he cried.

They all laughed and Sophal got into the back seat.

'I can't believe I ran into you,' Ouksa rambled on in
Khmer. 'It's because I prayed to Buddha last night. I was

in the hospital and I prayed. Buddha listened this time. He didn't ignore me.'

He went into the driver's seat and Robert sat next to him. As he turned to speak to Sophal he noticed the bag sitting next to her and he recognised that as well. So it was a bonanza, and the Lord Buddha had laid it at his door. He felt suddenly elated and hopeful about his wife. Such a large bounty and in the space of a few minutes – he was re-entering the loop of luck. Soon, moreover, they were out of the town and on the road to Pailin, where the monkeypods were now red from the dried dust again. It was a ninety-minute drive.

It was a road he travelled daily in his taxi searching for fares at the border and he knew every inch of it. He knew all the villages and bars on the way and he knew how long it took to get to the border from any given point. As he drove it now he kept an eye on the position of the sun and he wondered where he could force a stop en route. In fact, he knew just the place. A village to one side of the road where drivers often stopped for a drink. They made such good speed that when they came to it, he told them out of the blue that they could easily stop for fifteen minutes and go to the toilets. The Khmer girl was unwilling but Robert relented. He was sure the Englishman wanted to stop.

They went into a shack bar a few metres from the road and Sophal stayed outside to look at the dusk. Behind the bar was a field, and around it tall sugar palms and ponds. There was no one there and the great music of the dusk-lit fields overwhelmed them. Ouksa offered Robert a cigarette and they stood at the bar for a while smoking and Ouksa thought of a sudden act of violence. Something there and then. The idea for it had come suddenly. He tensed and it was as if he was falling through empty space, his senses scattering and his temples beginning to sweat. Across the fields swallows dipped and whirled and he felt his hands clenching around a long-bladed penknife he always had in his pocket for self-defence. He thought of the sordid injustice he had suffered at the hands of Davuth, the humiliation and the abjection. He had not killed anyone for the pleasure of it, it was fate and nothing but. Not a moment of hatred or spite. A man killed to feed his wife and buy her antibiotics. But now he would do it again just to seize his moment – and why should a man not seize his moment? If he didn't he was just a dog.

He said, 'Shall we walk out a bit into the field? I like this time of day.'

'It's the best time,' Robert agreed.

They began to walk out along the bank between two paddies.

The buffaloes knee-deep in water looked up and their expression was mild and murderous at the same time, their horns as if pricked like ears.

'I hope you are coming back soon,' Ouksa said when they were halfway to the far side and they were outside the zone of light cast by the cafe. It was surprising how quickly darkness moved in, snuffing out the usual securities. As it grew darker, Ouksa became mentally bolder. His mind went wild and reckless and he felt invincible.

'I hope so too,' Robert said.

He was enjoying the fresh onset of dusk and the wind coming in from the higher ground nearby. For the first time in weeks he felt that nothing could happen to him now.

'When you do, you call me, OK?'

'Sure, I'll call you.'

They came to the sugar cane at the far side and from there, surprisingly, the cafe looked quite tiny and remote. Had they really come that far?

Ouksa gripped the handle of the knife and silently opened the blade inside his front pocket. The cafe's jukebox started up and a thin Khmer pop song came floating across the emptiness. They were surrounded by darkly reflective water touched by orange sun. It was the only moment Ouksa would have to recuperate all his losses and make good. He stepped closer to Robert and pretended to gaze back at the cafe. One movement and it would all change and he would be the victor.

But then, out of the blue, Robert began to talk. Ouksa could not be sure, in fact, that the barang had not been reading his mind all along. Was there not an air of sorcery about these people?

Robert was talking very calmly.

'Ouksa, listen to what I have to say. You remember the money I won at the casino that day? I still have it, it's in the car. But I'm not going to take it into Thailand. I'm going to leave it here. I want you to have it. All of it. It's in the bag on the back seat of the car. I'll leave it there and you can have it. Do you understand what I'm saying? Just take all of it for yourself.'

'Why?'

'Because the girl says it's haunted.'

'She does?' Ouksa guffawed and rocked back on his heels. 'That's the stupidest thing I ever heard.'

'But you told me about the Ap. You believe in that, don't you?'

'I don't know.'

336

'Well, she doesn't want it and neither do I. If you believe in the Ap you can believe anything.'

'Why does she say it's haunted?'

Robert shrugged and turned to him and smiled. He didn't know himself. But in fact he was now speaking as much for himself as for Sophal. In the dark of his own mind he had come to believe it. Karma swirled around all things, lending them destinies over which mere desire had no control. It made one's little calculations irrelevant. If they took the money and went to Bangkok something inherent in those soiled notes would follow them there and an unpredictable outcome would play out. He was now so sure of it that he was anxious to get rid of the money.

'It's your country,' he wanted to say.

'Then maybe it is haunted,' Ouksa muttered. 'Maybe I am entering a magic place.'

He thought it over. Yes, maybe — he would have to spend it as quickly as he could. It was possible that it was evil money. He threw his cigarette far out into the ponds and watch it go out with a hiss. All one could do was hunt in the dark, there was no other course of action.

They walked back to the car and the first stars had come out. The girl was sitting on the bonnet of the car and looking upwards at the luminosity. She was thinking, for some reason, of the man who hanged himself in Paris long ago. They drove in silence to Pailin. They passed the Hang Meas with the life-sized deer shining on its roof. The red lanterns were still out and the girls in long dresses walked across its car park. Dead leaves swirled through the air, lit rose by the lanterns. At the border the crowds had thinned out and the drivers on the Cambodian side, who waited there all day for fares, were beginning to walk reluctantly back to their idle cars. The lamps that exposed the no-man's-land between the two sides were still lit, however, and the last departures for Bangkok, in their crocodile shoes and plastic umbrellas, ambled over it with an air of exultant financial defeat. There was a gambling bus waiting for them on the far side and it seemed to Robert and Sophal that they might as well join it if they could. Ouksa parked the car and Robert reached back into the bag on the back seat and took out his British passport, leaving Simon's behind. He met Ouksa's cool eye and the two men were curious about each other.

'Whatever happened to Simon?' Robert asked as he got out of the car. 'Did you ever see him again?'

'Never. I wondered about him too.'

'What do you think?'

All three walked slowly towards the visa line, where the gamblers were laughing in a vodka-fuelled way.

'Can never say with barang like that. They come and go. You know what I mean? They come and go like clouds.'

'Maybe the Ap got him.'

But Ouksa didn't laugh as Robert had expected.

'Perhaps she did, yes. It's possible.'

'You think so?'

'Yes, I think.'

'Well, if you see him, please give his passport back to him. I don't feel any ill will towards him. He was just being who he is.'

'OK, I will do that. If I see him.'

'Do you think you will?'

'It's possible. But maybe not.'

They shook hands in the half-light and Ouksa

remained with the car as they walked over towards the uniformed men with pitted faces who would see them off. He leaned back against the side of the car and wondered how a man could remain so beautifully ignorant and innocent. It defied belief. He thought, too, of the days that would come now. The amazement and gratitude of his wife when he showed her the money, the medical treatments for her that he would now be able to afford. Life would be good again for a few weeks or even a few months. And if one night the ghost of Simon appeared at their door demanding atonement, he would apologise and explain everything to him. And then, most probably, life would return to its normal darkness. The rains and dry seasons, the silent lightning and the clouds which rose every night at certain times of the year — as they were doing now in the night sky above the border — into towering shapes that suggested demons and spirits.

Acknowledgements

A few years ago I spent some evenings in the rooftop studio of the painter Vann Nath, long famous around the world for his eye-witness images of the Tuol Sleng extermination camp, S-21. Although this novel is not about the Khmer Rouge period, the germ of it nevertheless lay in our long conversations in the hammocks of the studio upstairs from his restaurant in Phnom Penh. The space was filled with canvases which perhaps have not yet seen the light of day; images of sadism that didn't seem to have come from such a gentle and forbearing man. He was one of only seven men who had survived S-21, largely because he displayed an enviable talent for rendering the cherubic face of Pol Pot himself. There was something in his fatalistic sense of humour and unrelenting memory that seemed to open a door into a hidden world – and so, in a far humbler capacity, I dedicate this novel to his memory.

Lawrence Osborne
12 November 2014
Bangkok

Born in England, Lawrence Osborne is the author of *Bangkok Days*, *The Forgiven* and, most recently, *The Ballad of a Small Player*. He has led a nomadic life, living in Paris, New York, Mexico, Istanbul and Bangkok, where he currently resides. *Hunters in the Dark* is his fourth novel.

www.lawrenceosborne.net
@lawrenceosborne

www.vintage-books.co.uk